CONTENTS

ACKNOWLEDGMENTS   4

WELCOME TO THE EDGEWORLDS   5

Mutant Audit   6

1.   7

2.   14

3.   18

4.   24

5.   30

6.   36

7.   46

8.   53

9.   62

DR. BG's Saturday Night Fever   65

1. EDGY   66

2. TODD   70

3. JEFF   78

4. EDGY   84

5. TODD   91

6. EDGY   101

7. EDGY   113

8. TODD   125

The Callisto Incident   128

1. EDGY   129

2. TODD   134

3. EDGY   138

4. EDGY   143

5. TODD   151

6. EDGY   155

7. JEFF   159

8. TODD   163

9. EDGY   167

10. JEFF   170

11. TODD   173

12. JEFF   178

13. EDGY   184

14. TODD   187

15. EDGY   190

16. HYLUS   193

Miner Rescue On Verdi IX   198

1.   199

2.   205

3.   214

4.   220

5.   227

6.   235

7.   239

8.   245

9.   251

THE STORY TIMELINE   259

ABOUT   260

COPYRIGHT   261

Books By This Author   262

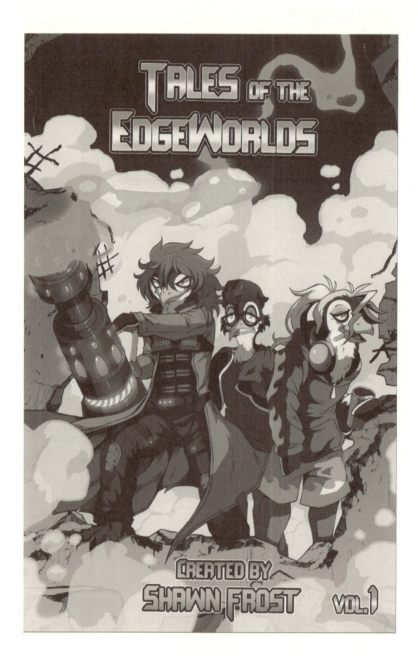

BY SHAWN FROST

ACKNOWLEDGMENTS

I want to thank Bezel Leblanc for the amazing covers for this. The results were amazing, especially for our first time working together. Her social media is below and I highly recommend checking her stuff out:

Her main social media account: https://www.minds.com/bezelleblanc/

She also has a web comic on Tapas called Soul Ascendance that is full of amazing artwork.

Soul Ascendance: https://tapas.io/series/Soul-Ascendance/info

I also want to thank everyone who read a couple of these stories for free where I posted them online. It means the world.

WELCOME TO THE EDGEWORLDS

TALES OF THE EDGEWORLDS is a series of short stories, all set in the chaotic edge of a multiverse called the EdgeWorlds. These stories are comedic, wild, and unpredictable. I initially intended to just focus on Edgy, Jeff, Todd, and Hylus, but when I sat down and started fleshing out stuff and organizing the chaotic notes in my head, I realized there was a lot of potential out there to expand. I made a list of humorous ideas for the first volume of stories. The stories were to be self-contained, so that they could be released and understood without needing to read the others. For some of them, I posted them online to test the waters. I had one rule when writing these: make them fun, and go nuts. This first volume is an introduction to the madness of the jumbled up dimensional dumping ground the protagonists call home. I arranged the stories by when I wrote them, not necessarily when they take place. For those that want to know the chronological order, the collection concludes with a timeline that I'm sure will grow longer as I release more of these. With all that being said, welcome to TALES OF THE EDGEWORLDS. Please enjoy.

MUTANT AUDIT

1.

Sitting upright brought the world back into focus. I couldn't quite feel my beak or the left side of my face as I looked down the rusted, crumbling hallway as a bug-like creature tried to flee. As everything came back into focus, I crawled to my feet and chased after him. This little shit got lucky with that sucker punch. The emerald bug man spun around. His four eyes widened in shock as he saw just how well I could keep up with him despite his much longer legs. He whipped out a small black handgun as he made it towards the window. Dumb ass should've led with that. I jumped and tackled him.

I should've thought this through.

We both tumbled out of the window and into the unpaved streets below.

I felt that, everywhere. The mantoid shrieked in its native language. To me, it sounded like garbled gibberish with a few grating clicks. As I rolled over on my back, he hopped up on his long, stilt-like legs and raised his scythe-like claws. I rolled and felt his blades chop a bit of my dark red hair. Despite my bruised ribs, I was on my feet and drew my sidearm.

Fucking mantoids.

He knocked my gun away, and before I knew it, I was taking a kick to the chest that knocked me into a pile of muddy water. I couldn't breathe.

I am a penguin, and if you expect me to start tap-dancing on ice, well, sorry to disappoint, not sorry. My dark red hair covered the right side of my face and eye, as usual. Just as well. It was bruised up, but not as bad as this fucking guy was going to be once I got my flippers on him. I glared at him with my crimson eyes as my lungs remembered how to function. The cold mud soaked into my black shirt and caked my long red jacket. I shook it off and stood up.

The mantoid was already down the street and knocking random aliens out the way. I hauled ass after him, but the moronic bystanders, who always seem to get in the damn way whenever I'm trying to chase someone or something, slowed me down. One of them dared to get pissed because I knocked over his shitty caffeinated drink with a name I will not attempt to pronounce.

"Asshole!" He shouted.

I came around the corner; I was closing in on the bug. He turned around and screeched at me. Maybe I should've updated the translator implant for this one. Whatever, my job was to capture him and drag his ass to the spot, not interrogate. He crossed the street between hovering cars but had to stop halfway through as a car came past. That gave me the time I needed to football tackle him. We hit the ground hard, and I chopped at his face.

Fun fact about my kind: we have bones in our flippers, and getting struck by them hurts like hell. Soon, I saw purple blood, and the broken shards of his green exoskeleton. As I kept striking him, he brought two of his legs up, and I took another kick to the chest. I crashed in the middle of the street and everything spun.

I'm just glad there wasn't traffic. Think I pissed him off now. He was on me before I could get up and swung his blades like an angry, living weed whacker. I scurried out of his reach as he kept advancing towards me. His attacks pushed us towards the bar's entrance. I wished I had my sidearm. Instead, I did something stupid and risky. I rolled through his slashes: he sliced the tails of my coat, better that than my actual short tail. After rolling, I kicked off the ground and aimed for his face.

Once again, fucking mantoids.

His arm caught me in the gut, sending me through the glass

window and into a bar. Pain exploded through the back of my skull as I struck the edge of the bar back, and someone's goddamn beer spilled on me. If I wasn't mad before, I was now. The mantoid jumped into the room and barreled towards me on his four legs. I looked up at the unopened liquor bottle on the wooden bar and grabbed it. The little three claws on the inside of the flipper gripped the wide neck. I struck the green bug with the heavy box-shaped part of the bottle as he tried to behead me.

I heard something crack as I struck him. He almost fell flat on his face. He attempted to sit up, disoriented by that. I swung the bottle like a baseball bat against his head, knocking out a few needle-like teeth. Now he hit the ground. I doubt he knew where he was anymore, could've stopped at this point.

But he made a fatal mistake.

He pissed me off.

I tested how sturdy that handle of booze was by using his body. The bar patrons glared at the two of us. They were taken aback. Others seemed curious. I pummeled him until he was barely conscious and couldn't move. He was lucky I needed his ass alive.

I unscrewed the cap to the booze, threw my head back, and opened my beak. If they considered this shit good, I'd hate to see what's bad. It tasted like a mixture of unpleasant medicines, but it dulled the pain. After a large swallow, my raptor-like toes stopped aching. However, my face and everything beneath it still stung. The mantoid groaned and tried to crawl away.

"Oh shut up," I muttered before taking another large sip.

The bartender and the guy whose drink I just used as a mace stared at me.

"Fuck you looking at?"

The short, lanky blue alien with four eyes shrank back as I scowled at him and chugged more alcohol. The bar matched the shabbiness of Javin. Broken floorboards, missing wall panels, and flickering light bulbs littered the place. Just like the city, everything was falling apart. I reached into my pocket, pulled out the small little black cube, and pressed the button in the center, placing the call. To prevent escape, I used my foot to hold down the mantoid.

A tall humanoid in black body armor answered. His red helmet, like other Shard members, mixed medieval and sci-fi aesthetics. The helmet covered most of his face.

"I got the bug. I'm at a rundown bar."

"Um...which one?" He asked while looking at nearby bars.

I looked over my shoulder. "What's this place called?" The bartender's answer was some weird language that I did not understand. "Please tell me you got that."

"We have it, but we're across town. So we'll meet you halfway at the inn."

I wanted to tell them to fuck off, but the boss man would withhold my pay. Using one hand to hold the half-finished handle, I grabbed the bug boy's head and pulled him out of the crumbling bar. Dense clouds made it difficult to see the setting sun. Creatures of all shapes and sizes were in the streets, all of them glaring at the short penguin dragging the bleeding insect behind him.

While I'm dragging this sack of shit, I might as well explain what's going on.

My name is Edgy. Some people call me The Edgy Penguin. I live in a region of the multiverse called the EdgeWorlds. Picture a stack of glass sheets, more than you can count. Each sheet is a universe housing millions of worlds and millions more creatures and its own rules. Now imagine if something dropped a weight at the very edge of the glass stack and all the pieces fell towards the bottom in a jumbled-up mess. Well, now you've got my home. Fragmented worlds in the same place. Some call it reality's dumping ground. It fits.

We got our name because we are at the edge of the multiverse. You cannot go beyond that edge; if you try, you'll just be moving in place like you're on a treadmill. The distance won't change. The collision of different universes was chaotic. Thousands of worlds got annihilated, and some only exist as fragments. Some are livable, others are not.

What caused these chunks to break off and crash together? No one knows. It happened billions of years ago. Because of that, this place is lawless. No governing body regulates the EdgeWorlds and its sectors. You got bandits, space pirates, crime rings, space monsters, and more. All efforts to unite the worlds here have been unsuccessful.

Where do I stand in this situation? Am I some hero on a noble crusade to unite this dumpster fire and bring order? Nope. I hate rules. I'm just great at killing things and blowing shit up. So why am I dragging this giant bug? Well, because right now it's my job. I work with an organization called Shard; they serve a group called the Edge Lords. There are five of them. I work for one named Hylus. They want to get rid of the groups trying to control everything. I don't care; they pay me, and I get to go around space doing what I do best. Right now, I'm supposed to hand over this insect to Shard for questioning.

The two Shard agents with energy rifles met me halfway. By the time I reached them, I had finished the handle and dropped it in the mud amongst the other junk. Both of them looked surprised as I tossed the target at them.

"Good *lord* man!" One of them shouted.

"What?" I asked.

"Uh..." the one I was talking with on the communicator tapped his ear. "I-I need the medical team prepped."

I rolled my eyes. "Tell Hylus to get my pay ready," I told them as I turned away and made a call.

A scrawnier penguin with green eyes and a longer beak appeared on display. A purple beanie covered his hairless head. He also wore black-framed glasses and focused on reading a Japanese comic book with some busty witch on the cover.

"Todd!" I shouted, startling him.

Todd yelped and tossed his comic into the air.

"Y-yes!?" He asked in his usual soft voice.

"Get the ship ready. I'm coming back."

Todd adjusted his glasses and his anime T-shirt. "Um...okay."

"Thanks, and quit looking at that trash."

"Leave me alone!" He whimpered.

I laughed and ended the call. Todd was always a gigantic nerd, but he took a liking to Japanese entertainment after Hylus sent us to Earth for a bit. He pirated so much anime and manga that it hogged all the bandwidth during our stay. Then again, I can't talk. You guys have some good ass alcohol, and the video games are pretty good. After we left, Todd bought more anime, and we discovered other means of getting Earth goods in the EdgeWorlds at a premium.

It didn't take me long to reach the *Vermillion*. It was a red ship, with the occasional black panels here and there. The body's center was broad and tapered to a sword-like point. The front had a long neck ending in an angular V-shaped visor-like window. Its "chin" ended in a sharp horn, as did the top of the "head". Two yellow-orange patches illuminated the lower sides of the ship's neck, mirroring its face.

Long arms branched out from the sides of the ship's main body, and they split into two smaller arms ending in long, pointed structures. These were the thruster units. Without them, we couldn't fly or hover. Although they were a clear red now, when the ship was in the air, they glowed a deep red and emitted matching particles. On the underside of the main body were two laser cannons; they kind of look like bird talons to me. People have told me the entire ship looks very bird-like. The back held two ovals for missile pods and two triangles concealing the heavy cannon. Working with Hylus had its perks.

Jeff, the second freeloader on my ship, greeted me as the back ramp came down. Jeff was a penguin too. His eyes were blue but glazed over from all the weed he smoked. He tied back his long blond hair, but he left some of it loose in the front. As usual, he wore his blue hoodie with white wave patterns on the sleeves and shorts with the same pattern at the bottom.

"Yo, you look like shit," he said in his usual slow, sleepy voice.

"You should see the other guy."

He raised his flipper, and I slapped it with mine as I entered the ship. I passed through the black and red airlock. Since we weren't in space, it was just a door. The cargo area was overflowing with dehydrated food and other necessary supplies for space travel. I climbed the steps to the living quarters. To my right, a kitchen area in red and black had a stove, microwave, and small oven. Ahead of me was the couch and a large black wall where videos would play in full 3D. Someone had connected one of our game consoles to it. With chips in hand, Todd stepped down.

"H-hey Edgy."

"Hey, time to go."

"Where we going now?" Jeff asked, while heading for the fridge.

"Away from here."

2.

We left Javin behind in no time. I set the ship towards an asteroid dive bar, glancing at the dull planet behind us. The autopilot kicked in after pressing a button. I had the urge for a stiff drink and a nice bucket of something fried to help me forget this crummy job. I double-checked our sub fuel and saw we had enough to get there without refilling. Pushing the last button, I kicked us into subspace. Seeing the endless sea of lights was a sight that never got old, despite traveling through space since I was a teenager. Todd could tell you all the science details about subspace.

It's a forbidden sub-reality where things move much faster than usual. Think of normal space like the surface and subspace as pathways through the underground. In subspace, any object moving through it can move faster than light itself, but there's a catch. That fuel isn't to keep your ship going in subspace; it gets you in and out and powers the shield, keeping this place from affecting you. If that barrier falls, you are vulnerable to what we call sub blight. Remember when I said we weren't supposed to be here? Nasty things can occur, like fusing with your ship's hull or worse.

If that wasn't bad enough, you better hope you plotted the fastest route to where you're going, as you're not alone out here, and I'm not talking about other ships. Sub beasts exist. They're said to be planet-sized and terrifying; few have survived encounters. They seem drawn to us when we cross over into their turf like they can sense it, and it's not a matter of if they find you. It's when. I had caught a brief glimpse of one, nothing more than a limb, and our ship would have been too small to be its dental floss.

Despite the danger, it can be very colorful and trippy until they find you. It's like a psychedelic trip in a movie, as many pretty colors and shapes form around you. Right now, it looked like we were flying down an endless spiraling rainbow that would burst into countless random patterns. Beneath the ship was the path, a glowing beam of white and blue light. I watched it for any flickers. A flicker meant a sub beast was nearby.

As I sat back in the chair, I heard Jeff climbing up the steps and smelled the burning weed.

"Hey bro, you figure out where we going?"

"Yeah, Starkey's, I need a good drink."

Jeff's grin widened. "Hell yeah! Bucket of jumbo celphos rings here I come!"

Celphos consist of tendrils and a large central mouth. Jumbos get as big as basketballs, while most are the size of tennis balls. They chopped the tentacles into rings because the central body is toxic and cooking the toxins out leaves a burnt tire for a body. They are an invasive species on most ocean planets and considered pests, but man, are they tasty when fried, and the best place to get them fried is Starkey's. My stomach growled at the thought of that, but I'd have to wait an hour before our ship reached the bar. Jeff inhaled from his blunt and sucked the smoke into his lungs before coughing it up all over the co-pilot controls.

"Man, this place is always vibing!"

"Of course you'd say that," I grumbled, looking at the ever-changing patterns. "You wouldn't be saying that if you saw a sub beast."

Jeff's eyes widened. "They're real?"

"I saw one back during a drug haul with Gary. Damn thing started eating the track behind us. If we weren't close to our exit, we would've been chow."

Jeff took another hit of his weed. "How big was it?"

"Planet eating big."

Despite the weed in his system, Jeff looked worried and made his way down the steps. I followed and found Todd watching something on the screen. It looked like a news report. One he must've downloaded before we went into subspace. A news anchor with red skin and four arms from another world appeared.

"In local news, Union and their daring, heroic commander, Cissus Gnar, thwarted a pirate takeover on the colony vessel Spirit IV."

I swear she was drooling as she said his name. Union was the group I hated the most. They operated in the Alpha Sector, the smallest and most controlled region of the EdgeWorlds, and served as a military and police force. Bunch of worthless boy scouts trying to force their will on everyone else. They've been struggling to control other sectors.

Cissus Gnar was one of their commanders and the face of Union, and I despised him. Gnar, as usual, had to pose for the cameras. He's an ulteon, a race of ten-foot-tall humanoids, all of them with metallic, glistening skin and hair. Gnar was no different. He had the physique of a Greek god, silver skin, bright glowing blue eyes, and locks of golden hair that looked like metal. He had the typical comic book superhero thick square jaw as well. At the top of his forehead was a short shark-like fin. Cissus Gnar wore his Union uniform of white and blue that I assume they made as tight as possible, so he always looked like he was flexing, which he almost always was. There was always wind, so his hair billowed behind him like a shampoo commercial. Gnar stood atop a pile of imprisoned pirates with hands on his hips and chest puffed out. He had his head to the side and tilted upwards while flexing his arms.

"What can you tell us about these pirates?"

"They're clearly from captain Death Head's fleet." He said in a theatrical campy superhero voice. "But fear not citizens of the EdgeWorlds, I, commander Cissus Gnar, and Union, will bring Death Head to justice." As he spoke, he made a habit of showing his blinding white teeth.

"God, I hate that dude," I growled.

"Yeah. He looks like an asshole," Jeff remarked.

"Do you think he'll catch Death Head?" Todd asked.

"He caught Rex Villan a few months ago. Man's been out there since we were kids at the orphanage," Jeff answered.

"True," Todd replied. "At least he's going after someone other than us."

I suppose that was the silver lining. Todd switched to some anime he bought during our last purchase of interdimensional goods, and it kept his eyes glued to the screen.

I crashed on the couch next to him and shut my eyes. It wouldn't be long till we got some food.

3.

We emerged from subspace near the asteroid belt. A blue gas giant lay beyond. Todd and Jeff climbed into the seats behind me as I grabbed the controls and prepared to take us in.

I never got my drink or those celphos rings.

Instead, I got a priority message that flashed on the screen displaying a name I didn't want to see: Hylus. I tapped the button; his face didn't appear. Instead, it was merely an audio spectrum.

"Edgy!" He growled in a deep booming voice.

Hylus sounded like a chain smoker with a deep voice, and he always sounded overdramatic and pissed, like he was growling at you. I swear he has a voice changer in that armor he wears.

"What do you want?"

"I need you to report to planet Moxia."

"Moxia? What for?"

"There's a ship there. You're going to dock on it and await further instructions."

"Hylus, I'm right outside Starkey's and trying to get some food. Can this wait?"

"No, report to Moxia immediately!"

"Alright, geez."

Hylus ended the call. Without needing me to say anything, Todd fetched the quarax whiskey and a glass full of ice. Exhaling, I punched in the coordinates and made sure we had enough fuel. Then I had to check if there was a fuel station at our destination. So back to subspace. I took a sip of my drink and spun around in my chair.

"Guess I'm not off the clock yet," I grumbled as Todd gave Jeff some but didn't pour any for himself.

Quarax whiskey is some powerful stuff, as if it's dark red, almost black, color didn't give it away. Humans can't handle more than one perfectly portioned drink without needing a trip to a hospital, and it's just what I needed before the shit storm I was about to walk into. I don't remember the trip to Moxia and couldn't feel my body for almost all of it until the end. Swiveling in the chair, I faced the ending psychedelic trip around us. Jeff was in a stupor behind me and groaning to himself as we came to a large green gas giant with hundreds of white rings around it.

"So, this is Moxia?" Todd asked.

"Yup," I said as I sat up. "The ship. Where is it?" I asked, my limbs and face still feeling odd.

Another incoming message flashed on the screen. "What?"

"Unidentified ship, transmit your code."

"The code is fuck off," I muttered as I transmitted the code before he could get mad.

As they verified it, the ship popped up on sensors just outside the large rings. Theirs was a war machine, easily eight times the size of ours. It was longer than most skyscrapers. The ship was too large for on-planet hangars.

"That's a large carrier class," Todd said as he leaned over my chair. "I wonder what weapons it has?"

"I'm not in a hurry to find out," I muttered.

"Vermillion, bring your ship down to hangar ten and remain inside."

"Alright."

Luckily for me, docking while intoxicated wasn't an issue. The auto dock took over as soon as I got close. Our ship glided into the rectangular opening, with the number ten displayed in front of it as a hologram. Docking clamps secured the ship. Then a tube connected to our ship via the airlock. They wanted to send us something. Before I could ask about it, Hylus called.

"Hey, Hylus."

"Report to your holodeck. We have much to discuss."

I muted and looked over my shoulder, "I'm in trouble, aren't I?"

"Knowing you, probably," Todd replied.

Both Todd and Jeff knew me better than anyone. We'd been friends since we were kids. I nodded and crawled out of my chair.

"Fuck this day," I muttered while entering the holodeck.

The holodeck was a small, black chamber with rising chairs. I didn't bother with them and saw that Hylus was calling from there. I tapped the button, and the room changed. Now I was standing in a giant, darkened stone temple with a large rock desk. The throne chair was designed for a giant and swiveled. A lit fireplace sat behind the chair. The temple windows lowered so I could hear the pattering of rain against the stone walls. This was Exaal, Hylus' domain, an old planet destroyed thousands of years ago.

Speaking of Hylus, he sat behind the desk with his back to the massive fireplace. No one knows what he looks like beneath his black, orange, and red armor. Spikes covered many parts of the armor. The helmet had a mane of razor-sharp glowing red crystals coming out of it. A purple diamond-shaped crystal with golden ornaments around it rested at the center of his helmet. Larger, spikier crystals of the same type covered his shoulders. On his hips, he had smaller crystal spikes too. He wore a black and red cape with his insignia: a sword and shield featuring a monstrous face. I couldn't see his face behind that armor, only his glowing yellow eyes. The suit also had several glowing orange lights on it. The largest one sat on his chest and looked like an upside-down triangle with two smaller triangles branching off it at the sides. His armor resembled a cross between an ancient knight and some high-tech armor. A large goblet, likely filled with wine, lay on his desk. No idea how he drank it when his helmet obscured almost all of his face.

"What are we doing here?"

"The mantoid, I instructed you to apprehend him, unharmed!"

"You said to bring him in alive. So, I brought him in alive."

Hylus' gargantuan fist struck the table, and he leaned in a bit. "He is in a *coma*, thanks to you!"

I shrugged. "So? Quiz him when he wakes up."

Hylus leaned back in his chair. "I am growing tired of your rogue behavior! For example, last month, you caused millions in collateral damage during a rescue mission by setting the pirate ship on a crash course with the planet below!"

"Hey, I had to take out the ship somehow."

"You leveled *half* a city doing so, Edgy! Not to mention your previous job, you were supposed to secure the package and keep a low profile. Instead, you led a bloated chase across half the planet against Union, and you landed yourself on Commander Cissus Gnar's radar!"

He went down the list, including some missions I had forgotten about. I couldn't contain my smile when he mentioned what happened on Katon VII. I baited a great ice worm into crashing through the Union base by getting it to chase me on a jet bike. It displaced small towns on the way. But, in my defense, it was the most direct route.

"You need to follow orders!"

"You know how I feel about rules," I grumbled.

"I know! But when the situation requires you to follow our rules, you must comply! You are a loose cannon, and you must have *some* sense of control! Unfortunately, because of your antics today, we have to wait for him to awaken before we can interrogate him!" He stood up, towering over me even more.

"What's the big deal anyway?"

Hylus pressed a button on his console, displaying a chemical equation via hologram.

"A new drug is flooding the populations in my territory. It's turning people into violent mutants. We've had mutants attacking my forts and structures across sixteen worlds now. The man you abducted is a supplier of one of the key ingredients needed to synthesize it."

"Mutants huh? Sounds fun."

"They mutants are dangerous. I'm sending you to planet

Karr. We've located another criminal that supplies one of the rarer components. You're in charge of interrogating him."

I smiled a bit. It's been a while since I had the chance to interrogate someone, and I wanted to beat my record.

"Cool. Send me the info."

"That's not all. To make sure you fall in line, I am sending one of mine to observe you."

I froze. "Am I being *audited*?"

"Yes, you are. He will monitor and notate everything you do."

"Seriously?"

"The situation is dire; I need you to handle this properly."

"Fucking hell, *fine*. Send in the snitch!"

"One last thing. I suspect Dr. Woo is behind this."

That got me to pause. I hadn't heard that name since the time Jeff stupidly bought one of his products. The packaging claimed it would remove all traces of drug use from your system so you could pass a drug test. It may shock you to hear that it didn't do that. Instead, Jeff spent the entire day in a hospital, getting his stomach pumped. Not pleasant. Woo was a deranged scientist that concocted highly dangerous and addictive drugs. The guy made his own criminal empire and found himself on Union's shit list and then Shard's.

"You told me he was dead."

"We never found the body," Hylus answered. "It seems like something he would do, cause discord in our territories for trying to kill him. He did the same thing to Union when they locked him up."

"You're paying me double for this," I told Hylus.

Hylus' fist balled. "We've refueled your ship. We will discuss payment when the job is done."

"Fine!" I groaned as he ended the conversation.

When I got there, the auditor was in the living room. He was a celium, a living mushroom. His head resembled a straw hat with a single eye at the center of the mushroom stalk. Coiling, vine-like structures made up his arms and legs. Like other members of Shard, he wore black and red armor that hid most of his body.

In addition, he had a red split cape with Hylus' emblem on it. His body was largely tan with specks of green, and the mushroom cap was a deep red. Two flaps that moved like sideways lips rested beneath his single yellow eye.

"Hello," he said. "I'm Zoltar."

"Yeah, whatever, Todd, help the shroom into the guest room, and make sure Jeff doesn't eat him to get high."

"Did you say *shroom*?" Todd asked as he poked his head down the steps.

Snitch did not like me calling him a shroom and glared up at me with his eye. I didn't care. He couldn't reach my lower chest and was here to annoy the hell out of me.

"I'll have you know I am here to survey you, and as the auditor, I outrank you, and I must see everything!"

"You're welcome to watch us jump through subspace, Snitch."

"My *name* is Zoltar."

"Your *name* is Snitch."

We disconnected from the ship, leaving Moxia.

4.

To reach planet Karr, we had to travel through half of the Epsilon Sector and pass over a thousand worlds, which was a long journey. Because of the high risk, we had to exit subspace multiple times for safety reasons. Zoltar made the trip even more agonizing. He walked around with his tablet, noting everything and asking me questions I didn't know how I was supposed to answer.

He disliked Jeff's constant weed smoking and his questions about celiums. I was just grateful Jeff kept his attention by annoying him. When we finally came out of subspace, we saw Karr. The main landmass was split into four colors, representing the planet's massive rainforests. Emerald Forest in the west, Crimson Forest in the east, Platinum Forest in the north, and Golden Forest in the south.

"Wow... is the whole planet forests?" Jeff asked.

"Almost," Todd said. "Except for some coastal towns and research camps." Todd then presented a 3D planet readout.

"Hylus said our target is a hydrix named Skaltak. He's in a town on the east coast near the Crimson Forest." I told them.

"I must mention that the town is full of botanists and scientists belonging to the Hermes Medical Federation. Therefore, we should avoid causing unnecessary damage," Zoltar spoke.

"Buzzkill!" I complained as I brought the ship down towards the planet's surface.

When we passed through the atmosphere, we saw deep blue waters and a large earthen cliff. Dozens of white and red tents dotted the cliff and people wearing shorts and T-shirts moved between them. Beyond the camps was the Crimson Forest. As the name suggested, all the plants and trees in the area had bright red leaves.

Several large circular disks that served as landing pads rested on the edge of the cliff, with an open spot close by. Since we were in a more regulated part of the Delta Sector, I expected a message about our arrival, but no one called. So instead, we got pinged by the AI managing the landing pad. It functioned like a posh parking meter, soliciting payment for the length of my stay. Being on the safe side and cheap, I told it two hours and landed.

"Fucking Delta Sector," I remarked as I watched the two hundred credits transfer on the screen.

Cargo ships dropped off supplies or loaded local plant medicines. As I docked, I hopped out of my chair and headed for the armory. On the wall, I had a few of my favorite guns. As I decided which one to pick, I heard footsteps behind me and turned; the Snitch was there.

"What do you think you're doing?"

"I beg your pardon?" The talking shroom answered. "I am an auditor. I cannot audit you if I cannot observe you."

I face palmed as he spoke. "Goddammit Hylus." I turned back to my choice of weapons and settled on one.

"A Zeus cannon? Is *that* level of lethal force necessary?"

I ignored him as I grabbed the gun. It seemed like an exaggeration to call it a cannon based on its appearance. The device had a cylindrical body that ended in a small box shape. I paid good money for the portable mode feature. With it already collapsed, I could attach it to the slot on my lower back and hide it in my coat. Then I grabbed a shield generator, snapped it to my hip, and set it to active.

"Trust me, when it's a snatch and grab, it almost always gets lethal." I muttered, grabbing four small orbs with a blue light on the side, shock grenades, perfect for stunning. "You better not slow me down." It was hard to read the snitch's face, but I could tell that offended him. I didn't care. "You armed?"

The fibers making up his left arm split apart, twisted, and changed into a disgusting-looking barrel, with small mushrooms pulsating on the side.

"One benefit of being a celium," he replied. "It's a paralyzing agent, non-lethal, but I can only make a certain number at a time."

I shrugged. "Good to know."

His arm returned to normal, and I opened the door and extended the bridge to climb out. I regretted wearing a long orange-red coat. The humidity on this bitch was ridiculous. Despite the ocean breeze, it felt like a cranked-up sauna.

"Rather sweltering, isn't it?" Snitch complained.

"No shit. Alright, he's supposed to be in that lab up there," I pointed.

A large green tent loomed on the edge of the red forest. As if the heat wasn't bad enough, the bugs wouldn't leave me alone. Snitch expelled spores that reeked, but it drew the bugs away at least. I just buried my beak in my shirt. Researchers of a bunch of different species looked at us.

Penguins were super rare. Outside of Jeff and Todd, I had only ever seen one other penguin, a famous pilot named Ace Starborne. He used to be one of the most feared starship pilots in the EdgeWorlds. No one could rival his ship, the *Azure Flash*. They considered him a hero in many systems and a celebrity. Honestly; as a kid, I'd watch anything and everything involving him. After one last battle against Death Head's fleet, when they tried to attack a medical station, he vanished. No one knows where he is.

The penguin homeworld, Aves, disappeared and nobody knows why. Penguins stayed isolated, so when the planet vanished, most of us did too. Guess I'm an endangered species now.

Entering the tent, some researchers questioned my choice of wearing a jacket in this weather. Zoltar told them he was here to study the local fauna and mentioned something called Mother taking an interest in this planet and that I was his ride. I did my best to play along and looked around. Eventually, I found our target sitting at the far end and bent over a microscope.

Hydrix were easy to spot with their multiple heads and tails. This one had blue and white scales and two heads sprouting from the top of the serpentine body. Six eyes, three on each side of their head. Left head had blue eyes, right head had green eyes. If memory serves, a hydrix gained more heads the longer they lived. Every century, they grew a new head and tail. One head jotted notes, the other examined a microscope. I didn't think he saw us.

I walked towards him and reached into my pocket for the stun grenade. He sat back in his chair, and I saw him rise. He spun around and fired a pistol. His aim was way off and meant for someone much taller than me. He climbed out of his chair and hissed. I tossed the stun grenade.

I forgot one nasty detail about the hydrix.

Energy breath.

I got hit by two streams of arcing energy, striking me dead in my chest and knocking me down. The shield bore most of the impact, but the dome turned orange upon my landing. The grenade went wide, and Skaltak bolted out of the tent. I coughed and crawled to my feet.

"*Edgy!*" Zoltar shouted.

I looked over my shoulder and realized why he had missed. A researcher, a large cat-like alien with a scorpion tail, pulled a needle from his neck. I watched as his body balloon. His claws grew more prominent, and so did his teeth. Green veins exploded across his body. Rather than waiting for him to finish mutating, I reached for the Zeus cannon and flicked the switch. The cylinder part extended out, and the box shape at the front unfolded into four rectangular barrels.

I squeezed the trigger, and four blasts of lightning fired from the gun. Then, with a loud bang, the lightning slammed into the ballooning cat's chest and sent him flying through the side of the tent.

"Don't kill him!" Zoltar exclaimed.

"You *can't* be serious!" I complained as I ejected the spent thunder shells by pulling the charging handle in front of the trigger.

The cat growled, viciously scraped the ground with its claws, and arose despite consuming enough electricity to deep fry a pig. I brought the gun up as it charged. Firing again, I watched it jump over the wall of lightning and slashed with its claws. I ducked, but I didn't dodge its giant body as it pinned me to the ground. I planted the gun in its chest to keep it back. The tail lashed at me, going for my eyes. I dodged to the left as it got stuck in the soil. Zoltar ran up and swung with a blade arm and sliced off the tail.

The shrieking mutant slashed him. It tore through his armor and sent him flying across the dirt. That gave me the time to pull the lever and load the new cells. I targeted the cat and fired; the blast sent it high into the air. I rolled to my feet, pulled out fresh cells, and plugged them into the empty mag.

"Shroom? You alright?"

"Ow," Zoltar grunted as he sat up.

White fluid trickled from the cuts to his chest. The angry kitty rolled to its feet and roared. Damn thing almost made me deaf. Zoltar transformed his arm again and fired a pod. A cloud of spores slammed into its face. The beast snarled, and I hoped that would slow it down, but no. It just charged me. I fired another shot, and it dodged. I used the cannon to deflect the claw that came for me. Unfortunately, this knocked me on my ass, and my back hit a rock.

"*Fuck!*" I screamed as a sharp pain surged through my spine.

Before I could recover, it snatched me in its claws and tossed me into the tent. I hit a desk full of glass beakers and vials and fell over the other side. Many researchers hid under the desks, others fled. I spat out blood and crawled to my feet. The world spun, and I couldn't feel my ribs.

"Somebody's been pumping them Arnolds," I groaned.

Buff kitty tore open the tent and roared. I shot him again and sent him back outside. Zoltar had already fired three spore pods when I arrived. I watched the juiced-up mutant stagger around, and then it keeled over on its side. It snarled and tried to bite me; I aimed the gun at its face.

"*No!*" Snitch pleaded.

I pulled the trigger and watched its charbroiled brains hit the ground. I looked around and spotted Skaltak. He was running for a ship. Not on my watch. I retracted the gun and threw myself into a full sprint. I shouted at the panicked researchers to clear the way. The left head spun around and snarled at me before firing another energy blast. I dodged it, but the researcher behind me wasn't so lucky and exploded into a pile of ash.

He stopped to load the gun again—big mistake. I tossed the shock grenade, and it went off right above his heads. He did the electric boogie in place while I caught up. He tried to say something, but his tongues weren't working. I crowned him with the cannon and knocked him down. One of his heads was asleep, but the second wasn't. I knocked it out with two hits. I wanted to hit him again, but Snitch had caught up.

I pulled out two sets of cuffs—one for his hands, the other to keep his necks together.

"Why did you kill him?"

"I read what Hylus sent. They don't turn back."

"They're innocent people. We could have restrained him and delivered him to Hylus for a cure."

I shook my head. "Does my ship look like it can contain *that* shit? It'll take Shard a while to collect him, and he might rampage again. You shot him four times, and he was still going."

"There must be a better way," Zoltar sighed.

"I wasn't hired to be a mutant wrangler. Let's go."

5.

"Is he waking up?" Todd asked.

"Looks like it, bro," Jeff answered.

Adjusting the ice pack on my face and ribs, I leaned forward to see the slight twitch in his arms. I wasn't taking any chances. I had his tails cuffed, his legs cuffed, his arms cuffed, and I chained those necks up so he couldn't lunge and bite me. In several spots in his necks, there were nails I "carefully" hammered in. Todd used his computer to display where I needed to apply them so he couldn't use his energy breath. Snitch came downstairs as Skaltak's heads moved.

"Took your sweet time," I grumbled.

"I had a lot to report to Hylus," he answered. "Is he awake?"

"Yeah."

I slurped up the last of my noodles and stood. Now came one of the fun parts of my job.

"So, uh, what's the plan?" Jeff asked.

I had many ideas to get this guy to talk, but I started with a polite ask. I headed into the cell and pulled out the chair. Skaltak's twelve eyes rolled and focused on me as he tried to sit up all the way. It took him a minute to realize how fucked he was. Then he hissed and tried to snap at me like an angry snake. The chains pulled him back. I couldn't help but smirk. He balled his fists and inhaled to blast me. Instead of two beams of white energy, all he got was a hoarse cough.

"What did you do to me!?" He hissed.

"Little magic trick." He saw the nails in his necks. His confusion was amusing, but I needed to get answers. "Who are you sending the drugs to?"

"Piss off. I ain't telling you shit!"

I smiled. "Oh, you said the magic words."

"Edgy, is it interrogation time?" Todd asked through the intercom.

"Yeah, get the timer!"

Skaltak's two heads exchanged confused glances. I exited his cell and walked into the armory and strode past the huge stockpile of weapons that could obliterate entire cities and then some. As I kept walking, I came to the super dangerous shit. I pulled out the large containment box and a backpack full of torture devices. Hadn't needed them in a while. I walked back to the gray interrogation room where our confused guest waited and dropped the bag and black box on the table. I looked out at Todd, Jeff, and Zoltar.

"Todd, display the current best time!"

Todd pushed the button and a three-minute timer displayed on the left wall. Skaltak's heads snapped towards it. He realized just how in the shit he was.

"Place your bets, how long till he talks!? Can I break my record!?" I called.

Jeff took a sip of his soda. "Man, twenty bucks says you get it in three."

"Twenty, you'll beat your record," Todd said, showing the purple physical chip.

"Got twenty on breaking my record," I said with a smile. "Shroom, what about you?"

Zoltar did not seem amused. "I will not gamble. I will observe."

I shrugged and cracked my neck. Skaltak laughed and threw both heads back.

"You don't scare me, *chicken*!"

Skaltak's statement aged like mayonnaise left in the desert sun. I opened the bag and debated what I should use. I could've tried the nanobot injector, make him feel like he's got tiny insects chewing him out on the inside. That was a slow one. I could've done laser clippers and lopped off his fingers, but that one was kind of boring. My eyes drifted back to the containment box. It was probably ready for use by now, and I couldn't imagine someone resisting it for long.

A smirk came across my face as I tapped the console on the box. "Todd, start the clock."

"Alright, starting in three...two...one!"

The buzzer went off. I put in the code, and the box opened. Cold fog exploded out of the container. A claw-like device emerged from one side. I grabbed that and activated it. The claw was easy to control with the joystick and trigger, and I would need it. What I was about to handle, I couldn't touch with my bare flippers without losing them if I was lucky.

"What are you doing?" Zoltar asked.

I ignored him and activated the switch on the side of the claw. The screen told me the inner containment glass had opened. I snatched the arm to grab it and held it as tight as possible without killing it. A screech emerged from the fog as I brought it out so Skaltak could see. The worm was as long as an adult human arm, with praying mantis claws along its body and a mouth of tendrils that ended in sharp points.

"Are you *insane*!?" Zoltar screamed. "That's a *neurex* worm!"

"Yeah, it is."

Skaltak's eyes widened, and he reeled back in terror as the defrosted form lunged and tried to whip at him with the tentacles.

"Aw, she likes you already," I smiled. "Feel like talking?"

Skaltak didn't answer and flinched every time the parasite tried to go for him.

"You put us all at risk!" Zoltar shouted through the mic.

"Oh, you ain't seen nothing yet, bro," Jeff told him.

I was running out of time. I extended the arm, and the neurex worm went to work. We consider neurex worms some of the deadliest parasites in the EdgeWorlds. One of them could easily infect and kill everyone on a star cruiser in just a few hours. Tendrils and claws dug into his right neck. That wasn't the worst part. The twitch gave away what was happening. It was embedded in his nervous system.

Skaltak screamed in pain as it pushed further. I looked at the clock. We were almost two minutes in. I'd be in trouble if I left it connected to him for more than that. Todd explained to me what was happening; when it began fusing with the host, it overloaded all the pain receptors in the body. It would start converting his insides and body into incubator pods for its offspring, and they would explode out of his body. And if we were lucky, I'd be parasite chow. If we were unlucky, everyone was going to be parasite chow. His screams made me want to grab a headset to drown him out.

"You feel like talking!?" I shouted.

"Make it stop!" He howled.

"Pause the clock!"

Todd pressed the button. Two-minutes-forty seconds: a new record. The arm grabbed the worm, and the syringe plunged into the parasite's side. The worm stopped and retracted its tendrils, but it clung to his neck.

"That'll only stop it for two minutes. Better talk fast."

Oh, did he talk.

I'll summarize. The bat shit crazy Dr. Woo made the drug, and he was on an icy planet called Maegar in the Gamma Sector. Woo was close to finishing an airborne version of the drug. I used the arm to pull the neurex worm free from his neck and then injected him with a chemical that would destroy any embryos that it may have deposited in his body. After icing the neurex, I turned on the drone on the box's side. It coated the entire room in a unique light that fried any embryos or tissue from the worm. Remaining tissue could turn into a new worm, but the light prevented that. After a confirmation beep and a flash of green, we were in the clear.

"Alright, Jeff, pay up!"

"Goddammit!"

I packed up all my stuff and exited the room. Zoltar was shaking and couldn't hold his tablet straight.

"What's your problem?"

"You're *absolutely* insane."

"Whatever gave you that idea?"

"That was chill for him," Jeff told him.

"*Chill*?!"

Jeff smiled. "Remember Big Hoss?"

I smirked at Jeff.

"What *happened* to Big Hoss?"

I looked at Snitch. "Do you have a weak stomach?"

"I do not require food."

I told him everything. As a teen, I was in a gang that was at war with Big Hoss' gang. When I left the gang after doing one last job for the boss, I had stashed away some cash in case I ever lost the gang income. Only one other person knew about it, and they got caught by Hoss. Hoss got them to talk and tell every secret about the gang, including my stash. Hoss took my shit, so I found him, killed all his guards, and captured him.

"Well, capture is a bit of a stretch," Todd said as I explained.

"Without the batteries for his pimped-out scooter, he wasn't going anywhere," Jeff spoke, making me laugh.

"Getting his fat ass on board wasn't easy."

"Why?" Zoltar asked.

"One kinesis unit wasn't strong enough to lift him. We needed *three*, and they broke when we finished!" Todd told him. "And the smell, he should've come with a warning label!"

A kinesis unit could levitate objects up to half a ton. Calling Big Hoss "big" is a bit of an understatement.

Jeff cackled. "That's right, you threw up!"

After getting him on the ship, I had to get tubby to speak. It took me over twelve hours of careful fat trimming before he felt like talking. He spent all of it on a fucking buffet. Zoltar just stared at me and shook as I described all of this. His gang called and wanted him back, and I agreed to give Hoss back to them. I dropped him off at the location they wanted, well, a couple of thousand feet above. Then I came in and finished the survivors. I doubted they would've given me the cash they promised, but I checked anyway, and it wasn't there.

"Why in *heavens* is Lord Hylus paying you?"

I shrugged. "Before you get your boxers in a twist, he ate people and children on the regular, not someone to feel sorry for."

His anger lingered as he glanced at Skaltak. "Is he safe?"

"Yeah."

"Contact Hylus and tell him *everything* right now."

6.

"So, Woo is on Maegar?" Hylus asked.

"Yup. It's close to me. I can go in and blow it up real quick."

Hylus leaned forward in his chair like I was standing in front of him, and then he climbed out of it and adjusted his cape. I was eager. I could cut loose, and best of all, I'd get paid for it. In my head, I was trying to figure out which weapons I'd use. Several weapons in the armory had gone unused for some time. Leveling a building would almost make up for not getting my deep-fried celphos, plus it would mean the job's over, and I could get Snitch off my back.

"No," Hylus spoke.

"*What*!?"

"No, Stand down. I'll handle it."

"Oh, come on, Hylus! You haven't let me destroy something in *months*!" I growled.

This looked like a job for me! I needed something fun to do aside from video games.

"No," Hylus muttered. "We will come up with a plan of attack and strike."

"Why? A few hours is all I need to handle this."

"Edgy, you are *not* concerned with stopping Dr. Woo. You only want to go so you can cause more wanton destruction."

"You're goddamn right! With all the *boring* shit you've had me do, let me do something fun!"

Hylus leaned forward. "You will stand down and drop Skaltak off at the coordinates I'm sending you, and he needs to be delivered alive, understood?"

I understood. I just didn't give a fuck. "Fine. We done here?"

"That will be all."

When I killed the connection and left the deck, I found Todd playing a video game in the living area, some action game with a busty chick swinging a big ass sword. I wasn't paying too much attention as I headed for the bridge. This whole thing was pissing me off. I typed in the coordinates Hylus sent and booted up a playlist of metal music. I pulled up a feed of Skaltak in his cell. He was still feeling the effects of the neurex worm. Hylus was sending us back to Moxia to drop him off. I turned to see Todd after hearing the door open.

"So, what are we doing now?"

"Dropping Skaltak off."

"We're not going after Woo?" He asked as he climbed into a chair.

"Hylus said no."

"You're not happy about that, are you?"

"*Fuck* no. I wanted to blow some shit up!"

Todd fidgeted with his glasses. "Well, what are we doing after this?"

"No clue. We might get celphos and drinks if I'm off the clock. Hope we can get rid of Shroom, too."

"He seems okay, but the Big Hoss story messed him up."

I smiled at that. It was an excellent example of why you do not fuck with me or my money. It didn't take us long to return to Moxia. Similar to before, we docked at the warship and I allowed Shard's men to take Skaltak off the ship. I was expecting payment, but they told me I would get paid once they resolved the situation on Maegar, which I couldn't end myself. Despite being there, Zoltar said nothing.

"Are you leaving?"

"No. Lord Hylus gave me instructions to continue auditing you until this ends."

"*Goddammit!*"

At least they supplied the ship with fuel for us, but evidently I wasn't free yet, which was terrible. I sat on the bridge, trying to figure out what the hell to do. After a few moments of staring at Moxia and its rings, I pulled up the coordinates for Maegar. The long trip would be worth it for a round of carnage.

"Lord Hylus *ordered* you to stand down," Zoltar said, announcing himself. I set the destination and turned around. "You *will* do as ordered."

I couldn't help but smirk as I pushed the button. "You don't know me very well, do you?"

The ship was gone with a slight shake. We had about four hours before we reached Maegar from here. I went down to the armory, ignoring the protesting mushroom. He got even more annoyed when he saw the weapons in my possession. My eyes went to the giant black and red laser cannon on the wall. It was heavy as hell, but it packed a punch. I pulled it down and sat it on the table. I saw Snitch staring at another weapon, the black hole gun. Yes, it does exactly what you think it does.

"Is *that* what I think it is!?"

"Yup."

"That's a WMD!"

"You're right. It is."

"*Where* did you get this!?"

"Oh, it wasn't easy, and a lot of assembly required."

"Does Hylus know about this!?"

"Nope."

"We're turning this ship around!"

"If you touch my ship, I will shoot you." I threatened. He jotted that down and knew I was dead serious.

I plugged in the large battery the size of a college binder into the bottom of the gun and watched it hum to life. I hadn't touched it for a year.

"A *mini-nuke* launcher!" Zoltar exclaimed, looking at the large dark gray gun with a long barrel ending in petal shapes that closed around and sealed it up when not in use.

"Yeah, that's custom. Added an autoloader so I can fire four without needing to load it."

His mushroom cap twitched as I told him this. "*Why* would

you need *four* of them?"

I shrugged. You never know when four soccer ball size city-destroying bombs could come in handy, especially out here in the EdgeWorlds. Zoltar looked at the black case next to the gun and yanked it down. He sat it on the table and opened it. When he saw what was inside, he was shaking with anger.

"You have *four* miniature thermonuclear bombs!? *Why*!?"

"So I can use the launcher with a full mag," I smirked. Zoltar was about to have a stroke. "Relax, I haven't used that on anyone yet."

"*Yet*?"

"Do you have any idea how goddamn expensive those four bombs are? Few places sell them."

"For good reason!" Zoltar growled.

Was it overkill, probably, but that's the best part. Besides, it's fun to have something you shouldn't. Someday I'd like to think I'll need that thing to level something. I wish I had it the last time Hylus asked me to destroy something for him. It would've made it much easier. Zoltar seemed more shocked and horrified as he kept looking at stuff. It irritated me.

"There's a dimensional ripper over there if you want to keep getting your panties in a bunch."

I think I pissed him off. He dropped his tablet and stormed out. This would bite me in the ass later, but I didn't care. It was time to blow shit up and have a blast. Well, in four hours at least. I grabbed a large handgun with giant rounds and loaded four mags for it, just in case I needed to do some cleanup that the laser would miss. The next four hours dragged on forever. I found Todd sitting and playing a video game while Jeff rolled up another blunt on the table. Jeff looked up first as he grabbed the plastic bag full of herbs.

"So bruh, we're heading to Maegar, right?"

"Damn right."

Jeff smirked. "Sweet. what's the plan?"

"*Plan*? I'm just gonna shoot my way in and out. I just need you two to keep the ship ready for pickup."

Todd paused his game. "I know you don't like to plan, but you'll want to grab a mask and filter in case it's airborne."

This is why I keep Todd around. Every once in a while, he does something useful.

"This is a bad idea," Zoltar spoke. I looked at him as he came up from below deck. "The minute we exit subspace, I'm contacting Hylus. Doing this is reckless and endangers *thousands* of lives. Hylus has a plan. Just let them handle it and stand down!" Zoltar shrieked and shook.

I smirked and looked at Jeff and Todd. "Okay, make sure this guy doesn't get in the way."

Todd jumped like someone just told him he would walk into a firefight butt ass naked. His glasses fell off his beak and into his lap.

"*W-what*? How am I *supposed* to do that!?"

I reached behind the couch and fished out one of the many tranquilizer guns stashed around the ship. You may wonder about my possession of a tranquilizer gun, let alone several. Well, they're not for me to use. You know the saying "BLANK has an explosive temper"? Well, that's me, but literally. Not gonna lie; Todd has had to use an entire magazine on me a few times because of what happens when I'm beyond furious. It ain't pretty, at least when you're on the receiving end.

"Hit 'em with this," I told Todd.

Zoltar was already jotting down something and was fuming. Todd took the gun and then looked at Zoltar.

"I'm not sure this will work on him since he's a living plant."

"Dude, pistol whip him or something."

I thought Todd was gonna piss his pants again. "Um...what about Hylus? He's going to be mad if I—"

"Todd, don't be a bitch."

"You are out of control." Zoltar remarked.

"Control is boring," I replied, walking past him. "And I'm only going to tell you this once. Don't get in my way."

"Are you threatening me!?"

"Nah, that's a promise. He will fuck you up," Jeff replied.

I said nothing else to Zoltar, and I didn't need to. Instead, I cranked up the music and gazed out at the psychedelic light show around us.

When we came out of subspace, a small blue and white planet greeted us. The center continent was icy, except for a circular gray and rust area. That was the city we were heading to. As I locked in on the city, Todd and Jeff came in. Jeff's eyes were bloodshot, and the smell of burnt grass was everywhere.

"Wow, it's bigger than I imagined," Todd said while leaning over my chair. He sat down at the station on my left and typed something. "Oh, you're going to n-need a t-thicker coat."

I turned around in my chair as the ship dipped into the atmosphere. "Why?"

Todd stammered. "The temperature in the city is negative one-hundred-and-fifty degrees now. So you'll need some thermal gear."

"Are those the winter temperatures?" I asked.

Todd shook his head and pulled off his glasses so he could clean them with his shirt. "It's *summer* right now."

"Oh goddamn!"

"You're a penguin. So the cold shouldn't be a problem," Zoltar remarked.

"That's cold, even by penguin standards."

Todd looked at me. He had the tranquilizer gun at his side, but he didn't look eager to use it.

We breached the atmosphere and pierced a sea of thick gray clouds. The winds were strong and affected the ship despite the auto stabilizers. The city was hard to see at first, but became visible after a few minutes. All the buildings were large and bulky. They didn't design them to be neat and pleasant from the exterior. Appearance was not a concern, warmth was. As we got closer, I saw they designed it so no one had to go outside. Metal tubes connected the buildings with giant, orb-shaped areas in the center of several halls. They must've been parks or something. The places for landing looked like giant skyscraper-sized cubes. Each panel served as an opening for ships. I found one that was open and flew inside. We had to fly down a long shaft of orange lights before reaching a landing pad.

As soon as we docked, I noticed a meter I needed to pay. I considered ignoring it, but the last thing I needed was my ship being impounded. However, five-hundred credits for what likely would be an hour was absurd. I winced, then entered my payment information before grabbing an environmental suit and heavier jacket downstairs.

I fucking hate environmental suits. They're heavy and are not ideal for a shootout, but it beat freezing to death. It felt like I was stuck in a giant marshmallow from the neck down. I grabbed a thicker gray jacket with a fur collar and picked up the laser cannon and my sidearm. When I looked over my shoulder, I saw Zoltar standing there with his arms folded.

"It is not too late to stand down," Zoltar said. "I'm sure since you're here now, Hylus might fold you into the operation he has p—"

I powered up the laser gun, and it hummed and hissed. I couldn't contain my smile as I shouldered it and headed for the exit. Zoltar followed.

"Edgy! *Think* about this for a moment. We don't know what forces Woo has! This is *suicide!*"

"Great, don't want this to be boring."

Todd met me at the entrance with the mask, and I put it on my face. The air-tight seal was immediate, and now I looked like I had a metal beak.

"You cannot do this!"

"T-that will not work on him. He'll just do it more," Todd whispered.

I flipped the switch, and the airlock opened. "Alright, keep your communicator on and get ready to power up the ship as soon as I tell you." The mask deepened my voice, like I was trying to sound like a supervillain. "This gonna be hot."

"O-okay."

Even with the heated building interior, it was still cold as hell. Felt like I had gone skinny dipping in liquid nitrogen. Todd's beak chattered as I hopped off, and he closed the door. Pulling up a holographic map, I began the long trek to where I needed to go. I despised the environmental suit, especially while shouldering a bulky gun during my run. I saw some people waiting for the elevator. By the time I reached them, they knew I was packing a giant laser, and a few of them were freaking out.

"Dibs on the elevator," I announced.

Some larger aliens, who looked like engineers, did not feel intimidated. Revving the cannon made them move out of the way. The people in the large elevator were in for a surprise when it arrived. Seeing a short penguin in combat gear and coat threatening people with a laser cannon almost as tall as he was made everyone take notice. One of them reached for the door controls. The sight of a charged laser cannon got him to stop.

"Hold that elevator!"

I muttered under my breath as I stepped into the elevator and pressed the button for the ground floor. Some old lady with four eyes eyeballed me as we went down. One of the taller aliens moved towards me with his claws out. I pulled out the pistol.

"Back off," I growled.

The alien scowled at me and took a step forward. Guess he thought I was bluffing. I wasn't. I made him take a knee and take a trip to a hospital. He grabbed his bleeding knee. Thankfully for them, the suppressor was on and dulled the sound of the gunshot. Almost everyone inside flinched, but the elderly in the elevator didn't. Everyone looked at me without speaking.

"I'm not here to hurt you people. Just stay out of my fucking way." I put the gun back in my jacket and watched the elevator.

I underestimated the number of floors in this place. We had just emerged from the upper nine-hundreds of the thousand floors. The jingle in the elevator became more obnoxious and repetitive with each passing second. When we passed floor eight-hundred-and-fifty, the damn song looped again.

I shook. "Is there a way to shut that *fucking* song off!?"

My voice shocked some of them. I checked the console and saw no options to turn off that jingle. I could no longer ignore it. After another dozen floors of hell, I found the speaker and emptied my pistol into it, scaring the others in the elevator. With a loud bang and a crash, it stopped. When I examined the speaker's corpse, I observed far more bullet holes than bullets fired. Now it was just silence and occasional whispers from the other aliens.

When the elevator approached the bottom, I readied the cannon, expecting security. Seeing the cannon, the guard at the desk froze and stared at me. Bet he shat his pants. I exited the trapezoid-shaped entry hall, and I was out in the freezing cold.

Freezing is an understatement. I appreciated the giant laser gun; the winds nearly knocked me over. The walk to the next building wasn't far, but felt like an eternity with the subzero temperatures and strong winds. My suit's inner layers activated the heated gel inside, helping fight it off a bit. I kicked the door in, and I realized I was in the slummier part of Maegar City. They covered every surface with graffiti in various languages, and druggies clustered around bonfires in trash cans. Thankfully, most of them didn't react to me as I headed down the hall.

Shattered windows and vandalized shops littered the area, my kind of place. I entered the central court. Dr. Woo and his people were on floor seven-hundred-and-twenty. Skaltak had said Woo controlled the three floors below, and the elevator wouldn't let you up without a key. I'd have to fight my way up.

Perfect.

I found the shot-up elevator. There was a mound of ash from cigarettes and a pile of bloodstained clothes and some dirty needles. I was glad the suit insulated my flippers. Who knows what sort of infections I'd get from touching the buttons or anything in there?

"H-h-hey Edgy," Todd whispered.

"What?"

"Um...well..."

"Spit it out Todd, I haven't got all day," that was not true, given the speeds of these elevators.

"Zoltar...he left the ship...h-he's trying to s-stop you."

"*Seriously*! Why didn't you stop him!?"

"I shot him with the tranquilizer, but he's a plant! It didn't work!"

"You should've used the weed killer!" I growled.

Todd yelped. "I'm sorry, Edgy. I don't know if he knows your route or not. Where are you now?"

"In the elevator, I'm heading towards Woo's turf."

"Oh, and Shard agents are calling. What should I tell them?"

"Tell them I've got this shit and don't need their help."

Todd answered the call but muted me. It was what I expected. They told me to stand down, and they were already mobilizing a strike team to handle Woo. However, they said one thing at the end that made me want to use this cannon on them: they threatened to impound my ship.

"Todd. You tell those mother fuckers if they touch my ship, I'll come over there and break *every* bone in their bodies then disembowel them and *feed* them their entrails!"

Todd was silent for a while. "You want me to say it *just* like that, or do you want me to leave some stuff out?"

"Todd. You tell those mother fuckers if they touch my ship, I'll come over there and break *every* bone in their bodies then disembowel them and *feed* them their entrails!"

"Y-you sure you want me to say that? They pay us and u—"

"Todd, if I have to repeat myself again, I'm beating the shit out of you."

"Okay! Okay, I got it!"

"You sure?"

"Yes!"

He relayed my message to them, but with more fear than anger. The guy on the line didn't buy it. So, I told Todd to take me off mute. I don't remember what I said to them, but it involved shoving a chainsaw down their throats, gutting them like pigs, and making them eat shit. All I heard was silence, then the call disconnected.

"W-was that necessary?"

"Todd, grow a pair."

7.

The elevator was almost on floor seven-hundred-seventeen. I couldn't contain my excitement as the doors opened in front of the central area where the railing was. Two aliens stood there, both in hoodies. The moment they saw me, they reached into their coats clearly drawing weapons. I used the cannon on them in low-power mode. The beam only vaporized the first guy's chest and diced the second guy in half like a knife through melting butter. A fiery orange streak and trail of smoke adorned the wall. I readied my pistol and continued down the metal corridor.

A homeless person sat by the wall. He panicked and fumbled for his gun. Two rounds hit his skull before he could draw. The speakers abruptly came on, and a corny psycho laugh blared over them.

"Attention all employees of Woo pharmaceuticals. There is an undesirable among us." Dr. Woo's unhinged voice spoke. "Find him! Kill him! Burn him with acid!" He shouted in a somehow even crazier voice. "Oh no, don't burn him with acids. Penguins are rare; he'll make a nice test subject, yes! Yes!" There was a delay. "Woo, buddy, it's not always about the science. It's about sending a message!"

The fucker's talking to himself, I thought. Before I knew it, the entire floor had turned into a warzone. People erupted out of doors with beam weapons and regular guns, and some nutjobs brought knives to this fight. I switched the laser to medium power and fired. The laser pointer of death demolished an entire row of apartments, leaving a giant trail of melting metal, fire, and a few vaporized bodies.

Bullets and beams rushed past me as I tried to aim and fire the laser with one hand and shoot the handgun with the other. I moved as fast as I could down the hall, leveling apartments full of Woo's goons as I made my way to the steps. As I neared the staircase, a group of aliens with four arms and pistols approached. I raised the cannon, but it beeped, indicating it was empty.

The gunfire started. I had to duck behind a column as their shots ripped through it. I pulled the side handle back. The large battery pack dropped on the floor with a loud thud. Multitasking between reloading, dodging, and counterattacking proved challenging. The body shield absorbed some of their shots, but I kept to cover. The handgun clicked empty after I finished killing three of them. I dropped into a crouch, yanked out the second battery, and shoved it in. I pulled the charging handle forward; the gun accepted the new battery and the laser's lights returned.

Just in time. More thugs approached from behind. I liquidated the entire corridor behind me with a single shot, leaving an even bigger trail of super-heated melting metal and fire. I brought the cannon forward and trained it on the mooks in front of me.

"Oh, *fuck* this!" One of them screamed before dropping their weapons and running for it.

"Are you *serious*!?" Another shouted after their friend.

"We don't get *paid* enough for this shit!"

"You can either run like a bitch or turn into a pile of goop on the floor." I told the remaining two gangsters as I had my flipper on the laser's trigger. "I'm down with either."

One of them wanted to be vaporized. I obliged. The other one ran for the hills. I headed up the steps to the next floor.

Woo's laughter came through the speakers. "Whoever kills the bird will get a pay raise. Do *not* disappoint me! My work is more important than all of you combined! That wasn't very nice. Woo, we should be more encouraging and less threatening. Fear keeps these animals in line. Now be quiet and focus on the research! Fine."

I kept moving and ran into a fresh problem. A giant plasma turret blocked the hallway leading to the next floor. I had to duck as a perpetual torrent of blue-white death came flying at me.

I tried to get a good look at the turret and what I could hit in between volleys. The turret had six rotating barrels, each capable of energizing and firing plasma at a ridiculous rate per second. That wasn't the major problem. The problem was they had installed an energy shield projector that protected all but the tips of the barrels from weapons fire. I tried shooting with the laser, but the shield absorbed it. My cover was melting as the plasma streams continued.

I needed a way past it before I'd ended up as a cloud of vapor. I remembered that the plasma they used was heat sensitive. So I set the laser cannon close to max and waited for them to stop shooting. Then I leaned out of cover and fired the cannon.

The beam at seventy-five percent power was bright enough to blind someone if they looked at it directly. Several guys near the turret covered their eyes and shrieked as the beam slammed into the shield. The shield held, but that wasn't the point. After a few seconds, I already heard the hissing and knew their ammo supply was getting excited.

A dome of pale blue light went off, followed by a loud bang that shook the entire building. When the light died down, I was staring at a burning, collapsing corridor. Flames engulfed the room, dense smoke filled the air, walls and floors lay in ruins, and an enormous hole gaped in the ceiling.

It was awesome.

I smiled as I checked the laser cannon. It had enough for another medium powered shot or two if set to low. Then I checked the battery pack on my right hip. It was my last one.

I heard gunshots and looked down over the floor's edge. I saw muzzle flashes from at least twenty floors down.

"Hey Todd, what's going on?"

"Um, city security has arrived. Woo's guys are fighting with them. Shard's moving in. They're a floor above you, but on the opposite end, they're getting hammered by corrosive gas grenades."

"Todd, is there a way around them?"

"Um... l-let me see," there was a delay, but I could hear Todd's flippers hitting the keys. "Okay, I got it. When you get up the steps, there's a path leading to the indoor park. Use the other end's elevator to reach the next floor and avoid the crossfire."

"Sweet. I'll let them handle Woo's goons."

"So, you will not help Shard, despite *jeopardizing* this operation?" A voice spoke from behind me.

I turned around with the pistol ready, but I saw Zoltar in his usual uniform and no other protective gear. His right arm was a sharp wooden blade, and the other arm resembled a launcher with spore pods loaded into it.

"How did you get in here without turning into an ice sculpture?" I asked, lowering the gun and not happy to see the Shroom.

"We celium are adaptable. I kept generating a hardened shell to protect me."

"Lucky you."

"You've caused quite a lot of collateral damage, I see. We could've avoided this had you stayed out of it. We need to help our men and regain control over the situation."

I ignored him and started up the steps. "Whatever, I'm going after Woo. You can do whatever you want."

I felt one of the spore clouds hit me in the back. The mask blocked them out. I snapped towards him with the pistol. He had his blade arm aimed at my throat.

"Apologies. Maybe I wasn't clear. That was *not* a suggestion."

My arm shook as I pressed the gun against the top of his mushroom cap. "You've read my file, right?"

"I have, several times, and it does not do your impulsive, volatile nature justice."

"Did the file mention what happens when I'm *livid*?"

Zoltar's eye blinked rapidly, and he pulled back the blade. "I read what happened on Callisto."

Zoltar was an annoyance before, and now he was pissing me off. I grabbed his blade arm, letting the rage take over for a second. The temperature rose in the room, unrelated to the fire. As my flipper touched the blade, it started to blacken and burn, and embers formed on it. Zoltar pulled away and jumped back. He raised his gun arm.

"Go ahead, piss me off further, and *see* what happens!" I growled.

The inside of the suit felt like a pressure cooker. The ground smoked as I stood there and scowled. It would be so easy to kill him. I'd barely have to use it on him.

Zoltar took another step back. "You'd bring this *whole* building down on us all!"

"We both know I've survived worse. If you think *this* is collateral damage, you haven't seen shit!"

Zoltar didn't lower the gun. He had to know it wouldn't do him any good, especially since he read about Callisto. If he attacked again, he'd be a deep-fried shiitake. Zoltar lowered his arm, realizing he had nothing to threaten me with.

"Hylus will know of this."

"Do I look like I give a damn?"

I took a deep breath. Letting it take over was much easier than forcing it down. I used my communicator to play metal music and took a moment to close my eyes. The sudden temperature rise stopped, and my heartbeat slowed. I turned my back to Zoltar and headed up the steps. He followed behind me.

"You looking to get scorched?" I asked.

"No, I am still auditing you."

I ignored him. "Just don't slow me down."

I followed Todd's instructions, ignored the gunfire from the corridor ahead, and took a right. The interior park was much nicer than everything else I had seen up to this point. The room, still in its box-like shape, was adorned with neat plants and trees. Sprinklers misted the room with fresh water, and heating units kept the area humid. The pond in the middle teemed with fish of many vibrant hues. There were benches and a holographic sky that looked like what I'd expected to see on a planet with normal weather. They even had UV lights to mimic the sun. It wasn't all perfect; there were piles of trash, and the cleaning bots covered in graffiti and bullet holes.

"What a shame," Zoltar remarked.

I kept going. However, those pretty fish looked tasty. I'd have to see if I could find somewhere that served them. We were nearing the edge of the pool.

Gunfire slammed into me. My shields stopped the first three hits, but not the fourth. I felt the bullet hit my stomach, and I fell over and hit the grass and dirt below. The internal plates stopped the bullet from going further. I heard Zoltar attacking them with his spores.

Now I was angry. The surrounding grass caught fire. Zoltar jumped back as it threatened to swallow him up. I undid the strap of the laser cannon and let it fall to my side as I stood up. Woo's goons kept shooting. The wave of heat intensified. Their bullets melted before they touched me. I aimed the pistol at the center of their group. I focused all of my anger on the barrel of the pistol. The gun glowed a fiery orange.

I pulled the trigger.

A gush of fire erupted from the barrel, and it plunged into the ground directly in the center of them. The explosive energy I had infused into it went off. A sea of orange and red devoured them. The sound was louder than the meanest thunderstorms. A wall of superheated air slammed into Zoltar and me. I didn't flinch; I was used to it.

Only a smoldering crater of warped metal remained. Embers filled the air and set parts of the park ablaze. The fire suppression systems kicked in and filled the room with a gray cloud.

I'm not sure how I can do this. Maybe I was born like this. It first occurred at the orphanage, where I met Jeff and Todd. Someone was bullying Todd, and I snapped and ended up giving him some severe burns. This is a mystery to everyone, including Hylus. I only know two things, one, it triggers when I'm pissed, and two, it knocks the wind out of me when I use it. Even though that wasn't much, it made me lean against a tree and take a minute to catch my breath, like I had done laps around the track.

"The file was referring to *this*?" Zoltar said, stepping out from behind the bullet-ridden tree.

Too exhausted to talk, I nodded to him. I heard a groan and investigated. One of Woo's men was still alive and crawling across the burnt ground. The fire burned his body in half, leaving one side overcooked and the other side undercooked. I staggered over to him.

"P-please."

He was begging for his life. It didn't matter. I ended him.

"Was that necessary?"

"Mercy will get you killed."

"He wasn't a threat anymore."

"He signed his life away when he shot at me."

I grabbed the laser gun and checked the pistol. Funneling that red power into firearms seemed to always break them. I reinforced this one, and it paid off because the gun still worked. Two goons blocked the way to the nearby elevator. I took them out with the pistol and set it to the next floor. Zoltar hesitated at the door.

"You can either go back and help them or come and help kill Woo. I don't give a shit which."

He climbed into the elevator. I was hoping he'd help Shard instead. While in the elevator, I loaded my last mag into the pistol.

8.

"Todd, anything I should know?"

"I don't know what's on Woo's floor, but city security is also dropping in from the roof. It looks like Woo has guys on the floors above seven-hundred-twenty."

"How's Shard doing?" Zoltar asked.

"From what I can gather, they're at a flight of stairs, but Woo's goons have a turret blocking them from getting past it. A backup team is approaching using the elevator." Todd told him.

The floor was empty. I readied the cannon. "Smells like a trap."

"It most certainly does."

Following Todd's route, we reached the building's central part with a view of upper and lower floors. We could see the roof, twenty stories above us. That wasn't what caught my attention.

A lineup of armed goons and turrets stood on the other side of the gap.

"Shit."

Woo's cackle came from the speakers and his face projected as a giant hologram in front of us. Calling him ugly as fuck would be a compliment. His eyes had no pupils. They were just a solid piss shade of yellow. He was beyond skinny. He looked like a skeleton in a skin-tight bodysuit. You wouldn't need an X-ray machine to check his bones. His skin was pale as a corpse and covered in chemical equations. Some painted on with marker, and others cut into his skin. He wore a black gas mask with green tubes sticking out of it, and his four bony arms were doing something just out of frame. The two antennae on his head twitched as he watched us. His long head had a sharp spike at the back and gray hair patches sticking out. He was an aflatox. That mask he wore wasn't because he had a bad pair of lungs. Their home planet, Aflatoxus, has an atmosphere so poisonous they evolved to breathe it instead of oxygen.

"I'm impressed you made it this far," he began. "You know Woo Pharmaceuticals is always hiring. We could always use some more muscle around here." His brows furrowed. "Especially since these worthless chumps are too inept at protecting me from door-to-door salesmen!"

They pointed a shitload of guns at us. Even if I had reinforced my shields, the guns would have shredded me in seconds. Zoltar seemed to realize they had outgunned us here. I doubted I could let that power out again or create a large enough blast. Then I remembered I had some grenades, but the problem was, could I get them out fast enough before they tore us to pieces?

"Ah, I can't stay mad at you guys. Some of you are my best customers too," Woo said, being friendly and polite. "So, penguin, what do you say? There are plenty of medical benefits and free checkups. After all, I am a doctor."

I felt something tapping my leg. I looked at Zoltar to see what he was doing. He was growing something from his legs. It snaked across the wall and took shape: cover. His eye gestured to the nearby apartment a few feet away with a window.

I turned back to Woo. "No thanks, I'm good."

"No one says no to me!" He shouted. "Kill em boys!"

The wall came up. A storm of bullets, lasers, and plasma slammed into it. It wasn't holding up at all. Bullets brushed me, and bolts of plasma closely missed me as we sprinted. Grateful for the suit, I jumped through the window without getting a face full of glass. The second I hit the floor, the barrage resumed. Bullets ripped through the walls and hit everything, lasers melted through the walls, and globs of plasma followed. I was prone and trying to ready the laser cannon.

Zoltar followed me, cobbling together a dome of plant matter on his back. The incoming torrent shredded it. He climbed into the window and killed the dome. He looked exhausted too.

"Well, now what?"

I ejected the low battery and shoved in a new one. I cranked the laser to maximum. The screen on the gun told me the battery didn't charge properly, meaning I'd only get one full-power shot.

"Can you cover me from the other window!?" I shouted.

Zoltar nodded as plasma rounds knocked the door off the hinges. It hit the damaged table and collided with the bullet-riddled fridge. Zoltar made a break for it. He grunted and grew arms on his back. They ended in spore launchers. He began shooting. I doubted he was doing much to them, but he got their attention.

Propping the gun on the shattered window, I fired it. The light was too bright; precise aiming wasn't possible, even with the mask filtering out the glow. I didn't need to aim. From secure cover, I raked the death ray across the line of apartments.

Similar to the other turret, the plasma cells ignited, but the explosion was much stronger. After the initial eruption, I couldn't hear anything. A pressure wave slammed into us, and any windows that hadn't already shattered were now in millions of pieces. I fell on my ass and so did Zoltar as the entire structure bucked like a pissed off bull. When the wave subsided, I assumed it was over.

It wasn't.

I felt secondary explosions throughout the building. Then it all went quiet. I pulled the laser off the window, swapped out the empty battery for the almost empty one, and stood up. The explosions caused half of Woo's building to be annihilated while the other half melted and caught fire. The blaze reduced around twenty apartments near it to rubble. Deadly explosions occurred in the same location on the floors above and below. Even with the mask's filters I could smell all the smoke.

"What did we just do?" Zoltar asked.

"I think the laser fried the heating units. Must've blown them all up."

Zoltar shook in anger and shock. "So much damage in a

densely populated area, Hylus will not be happy about this."

"Who cares? Right now, let's make sure Woo is d—"

A roar sounded. From the balcony, I looked down at the floor below. A security guard with a pistol tried fending off a mutated person. The mutant pounced him and tore him apart like pulling drumsticks off a chicken. That's when I noticed the white mist spreading throughout the building.

More screams sounded from all around us. The building was getting high on Woo's supply and was about to have one hell of a roid rage. Zoltar's face changed, and he grew something there that I guess would help filter out poisons.

"Todd, what's going on?"

"Woo must've been prepping the airborne strain! It's spreading throughout the building! Shard and security are getting torn apart!"

I winced at that. "Alright, what about Woo?"

"You fools!" Woo snarled from the smoldering path ahead of us.

He stepped out, blood trickling from his face. He did not look happy to see us.

"Months of research just gone like that! All because of you trigger happy morons! You ruined *everything*! Now I'll have to go back to formula!"

I noticed his lower body was robotic. His waist was a giant metal saucer-looking thing with six thin mechanical legs beneath it. He stood up and calmed somewhat.

"Oh, come now, there's one bright side to all of this. What's that!? What could *possibly* be the bright side to this!? Think of it as an unscheduled field test for the aerosol version. Plus, there's one thing we can use them to test."

While he was having a riveting conversation with himself, I raised the laser gun. He didn't seem that concerned with a laser aimed at his face. When I fired it, I saw why. His shield stopped the beam cold. He reached into a compartment on the saucer and pressed a button.

There was a roar, followed by something approaching.

The giant creature knocked me down before I could get a clear look. Woo's trademark cackle sounded again; this time even more unhinged.

"Meet the super mutant I've been working on! His name is Bubba! Bubba, can you kill them for me!?"

Bubba's response was a roar. Woo turned and fled. Zoltar tried hitting him with spores, but they had no effect. He fired a blade, but Woo was already down the hall. Bubba raised his arms and tried to turn me into tomato paste. I rolled back and grabbed a beat-up shotgun on the ground. Fortunately for me, the mag tube had ammo. I pumped two rounds into Bubba.

My shots bounced off his body. He stood on two legs, with crab-like claws and a tough shell. On his back were a pair of long arms ending in sharped blades. Bubba shrieked and stabbed with those. Shooting again, I aimed for the armored face. It didn't break through, but stunned Bubba for a second. I ran for it, trying to get some distance.

Bubba was fast.

Real fast.

He caught up to me and knocked me into an apartment. I crashed into the mostly intact stove, and I felt my helmet dent. I saw stars as I sat up. Bubba stepped inside and began flattening the kitchen island between him and me. I looked at the stove and realized that it and the oven were gas. I turned them both on and cranked the burners to the maximum. Bubba stepped over the shattered island and roared.

I got up and tossed a frying pan at him. While he recovered, I reached the doorway. I fired the shotgun, aiming for the stove. The explosion engulfed the entire apartment. Compared to what was happening earlier, it was nothing.

"Edgy!" Zoltar called. "Woo made it to the elevator."

I ejected the used shotgun shell, and I realized that was the last one. I could barely walk properly as I limped towards Zoltar and the direction Woo went.

"Alright, let's go after him," I said between breaths.

I discovered a fucked up rifle on the ground, similar to my

current state. I found a somehow intact magazine and grabbed that as well.

"Todd! Get the ship over here now! Be ready to pick us up!"

"I'm almost there already."

Then I heard something behind me. Out of the burning apartment came Bubba, and he was angry. Parts of his shell had turned from blue to red, but the explosion hadn't bothered him.

"Are you *fucking* kidding me!?" I growled, firing the rifle at him.

That did nothing but make him madder. He came running after us, using his giant claws to knock all the debris and rubble out of the way.

"Todd! I need your help!"

I tried to run, but my bruises were slowing me down. The elevator was right there. Zoltar tried hitting Bubba with spores and blades. Both were useless. Without losing speed, he snatched Zoltar with his claw and slammed him onto the ground. Then he caught up to me. I spun around and emptied the mag into his face. Bubba snarled and moved to avoid the gun. Then I felt his claw collide with my stomach.

It felt like a freight train and then some. He knocked me into the air, and then I hit the ground hard. Bubba stomped and roared. I couldn't move; I was too busy coughing up lunch. He raised the back limbs to stab me. Then Bubba stopped and turned.

Two sapphire lasers slammed into Bubba. The mutant stumbled back and hit the railing. Another blast followed this one and sent Bubba off the edge and down all seven-hundred-and-twenty floors below.

I grabbed the railing and pulled myself up, then I glanced at the hole in the wall. My ship was there.

"Thanks Todd."

"Don't mention it."

"Woo's probably escaping on the roof," I said.

"Okay, I'll try to take h—"

A rocket slammed into my ship. Security was trying to take

on my ship with one of theirs. Todd broke off and tried to give them the slip. I limped to the elevator. Zoltar employed vines to drag his damaged body into the elevator with me while he quickly fixed himself up and reattached his limbs. I noticed the missing chunks from his mushroom cap, and a green fluid dripped from it. I guess that's his equivalent to blood. While we sprinted up the steps, I hastily loaded the rifle.

"Security is trying to take us down! I'm trying to give them the slip!" Todd told me.

"Shoot them down. Don't let them damage my ship!"

"But they're just doing their j—"

"I don't give a damn. Hurry up and get rid of them. We need to go."

I looked at Zoltar. "You aren't going to say anything?"

"You wouldn't listen to me."

I smirked; he wasn't wrong. When we made it outside, we found Woo surrounded by dead security. Their bodies were a dead gray and looked like grapes left in the sun for way too long. Woo turned to us, surprised to see us there.

"You escaped Bubba!?"

"He's probably paste on the ground floor by now."

Woo checked something on his wrist and laughed.

"What's funny?" I asked, raising the rifle.

I got that answer real fast. Something broke through the roof. When I saw the claws, I knew what it was: Bubba. Only now he had four legs, and the back arms mutated into wings. He had also grown a lobster-like tail covered in little legs and an extra pair of claws from his abdomen.

"Oh, just *fucking* great!"

Woo threw his head back and laughed. "You nearly had me! But you should know better than to cross someone like me!"

Woo jumped off the building. A ship rose from below. He stood on it and climbed down the side.

"I'll leave you to my creation. I'm eager to see the results of this clinical trial!"

When he made it inside, the small ship rocketed skyward and

swiftly left the planet's atmosphere. Only Bubba, Zoltar, and I remained. He rushed us. The *Vermillion* loomed nearby and Todd intercepted with a barrage of cannon fire from smaller rapid-fire guns in compartments on the thruster arms. The volley of energy rounds created clouds of blue smoke and dust.

Something happened when the smoke cleared. Bubba's claws crackled with lightning, and they opened. Two beams of energy shot from them and almost hit the ship.

"You have *got* to be shitting me!"

Not only could he shoot energy from his claws now, but he had also grown a second layer of armor and looked completely fine! He turned to us and snarled as he stood up on his four main legs. Just one way to end this now.

"Todd! Toss me the black hole gun!"

"The *what*!?"

"You heard me!" I shouted.

Todd hit it again with the cannons, but they had even less effect. He steered the ship over us and kept firing.

"Jeff, take control and keep shooting!" Todd ordered.

"Alright bro."

Bubba started firing back again. Jeff's dodge was slow, but the armor held and Bubba only grazed the ship. I wasted the rifle on it, and when it ran out, I seized one off a dead guard and used the attached grenade launcher.

"I-incoming!" Todd shouted.

I looked up as Jeff brought the ship closer, and Todd tossed me the long white and black gun with a big ass battery in the back. Several panels covered the barrel area and got thinner the closer they were to the front of the gun. Behind the barrel rested two cylinders, one black and one white, containing the black hole materials. When I caught the gun, I forgot just how heavy that bitch was, and I nearly fell over. My other hand went to the forward grip as I rested it on my shoulder. I adjusted the black hole's duration and diameter using the golden-framed screen on the gun's side. The gun was halfway charged as the ship's cannons fell silent; they were out of ammo.

Bubba stood up and aimed his claws at us.

Gunfire slammed into it from the opposite rooftop. Security deployed snipers on the roof. Their rounds only staggered it for a moment and drew its attention. It quickly annihilated them with a blast from its claws, engulfing the rooftop in fire. The gun finished charging. I squeezed the trigger. A ball of black and purple light shot from the gun and floated out towards Bubba.

"Go! Now!" I shouted.

Jeff brought the ship to the edge of the roof. We jumped for it just as the orb changed. It became a giant black orb with a glowing purple rim. The world distorted around the black hole. The edges of objects appeared to stretch, and any light around it vanished. Bubba screamed as his body stretched, as the black hole's pull was inescapable. The shell instantly started to crack and break apart. Then the hole swallowed him. Bubba had vanished without a trace.

The building soon followed. It peeled apart layer by layer like an onion. We were out of harm's way, but we still felt the hole's draw on the ship. The buildings around it warped, and their windows cracked and exploded. The glass floated into the vortex as it descended deeper into the building, swallowing it whole.

Then it stopped as it reached the entryway. The orb of destruction collapsed in on itself, and with a blinding flash, it vanished. Only the building's foundation remained. I took a deep breath and put down the black hole gun.

"Hey Edgy, Hylus sent a message. He wants you on Moxia," Jeff spoke.

"Jeff, plot the *longest* route you can to Moxia. I'm getting out of this shit and getting a stiff drink." I shut the door behind me as Todd stared with his mouth open.

9.

I was standing in a dome-shaped room overlooking the massive green gas giant. Hylus was on the other end, and Zoltar stood next to me. Zoltar's report on Karr and Maegar left Hylus fuming.

"Let me get this straight. Not *only* do you own a black hole launcher, you fired it in a *densely* populated area and leveled an entire city tower!"

"Actually, the lobby is still standing."

"That does little to remedy the damage you have done! How many people died *because* of you!?" Hylus growled.

I shrugged. "Hey, the building was full of mutants anyway."

"A problem *you* caused by blindly rushing in there instead of trusting me and my plan! Woo has escaped and will go further underground now thanks to you!" He shook his giant fist at me. "I've read Zoltar's report, all of it. Somehow, you are even worse than I imagined. You abandoned my team, you have several WMDs on board your ship, and you do not understand the concept of restraint!"

He wasn't lying. "Are we done here? I need a replacement laser cannon and more graviton materials for the black hole gun."

"You did approximately six million credits' worth of damages to Maegar City!"

"Only six million? I thought it would be higher than that."

"This is a disaster! I will withhold your pay for the rest of the universal standard year!"

"What the fuck am I supposed to do to keep the ship running,

Hylus!?"

"Perhaps you should've thought of that *before* you defied my orders!"

I crossed my arms. "Fine."

"You may go."

"*Wait!* My lord, are you not going to request he *surrender* the weapons I included in my report!?" Zoltar spoke up.

That got me to stop in my tracks and look at him. "Zoltar, try that shit and I'll incinerate you right here, right now."

He recoiled back in surprise.

"Enough!" Hylus boomed. "I will not attempt to take his weapons."

"But Lord Hylus! He is a loose cannon, you said so yourself! Are you certain it is safe to allow him to carry such destructive power!?"

"Even if I were to have him surrender your comprehensive list of destructive armaments, there is nothing stopping him from acquiring more."

He left out an important part. If he tried to take them, I'd fight back. I would cause so much destruction and wouldn't need a gun to do it. I'm already a walking WMD.

"But—!"

"You should listen to your boss," I muttered without looking at him.

I felt Zoltar's eye on me, as if he still wanted to protest. "Yes, my lord."

With that, I left. Members of Shard, in black and red armor, eyeballed me. Their whispers stopped after I gave them a stern look. I'm sure they knew what happened the last time Shard ended up on my shit list. When I got back to the ship, Jeff and Todd were there.

"How bad was it?"

When the doors closed, I laughed. "He's cut my pay for the rest of the year!"

Jeff's and Todd's eyes widened in shock.

"But *how* are we going to pay for things!?" Todd asked, after hyperventilating into his shirt.

I put my flipper on his shoulder and smirked. "Guess we're back in the bounty hunting and raiding business for a while," Todd shivered at that. "Relax, Todd. What could go wrong?"

"*Everything!*"

He wasn't wrong. "It'll be fine. Let's go hit up a bar." I set a course for a local dive bar.

"Then what?" Jeff asked.

"We'll stay in the Epsilon Sector, find some gangsters to raid for all their cash."

Jeff stood up and fished out another joint. "So our usual?"

As we disconnected from the Shard vessel, I smirked and flew away. "The usual."

There was an entire jumbled-up multiverse to explore, and if there was one thing I knew, there were plenty of ways to make money and plenty of chances to blow some shit up.

DR. BG'S SATURDAY NIGHT FEVER

1. EDGY

"What do you want?" The fat slug with big-ass glasses and messy white hair asked in a nasally voice.

I moved up to the scratched and rusted desk.

"Claiming the bounty on Grel Edora."

She scoffed, like she didn't believe me. "You got any proof?"

I placed the silver hexagonal cryo box on the table and pushed the switch. The panels unfolded and revealed Grel's preserved head. The part that survived after he tried to run from me and got melted by plasma. He looked like he was going to have a heart attack when I stormed his ship and disintegrated his crew.

The giant slug apathetically leaned forward and then sighed. "Wait here. I'll be back shortly."

We must have very different interpretations of the word "shortly" because I had to sit there and wait for over twenty minutes. I sat down on the fucked up benches that looked like a pack of pit bulls had mauled them. As I did, I shook my red hair out of my right eye. Between losing my pay and other unplanned expenses, I was broke. It was either sit here and wait or go back to raiding, hoping someone carried valuable goods in this goddamn sector. Was not having the best luck with that. Closing my eyes, I turned up the black metal song I was playing on my way to this sad excuse for a bounty office. I adjusted my long, red leather jacket and eyed the handgun on my hip. It tempted me to make more holes in this place, but judging from the look of things, they had nothing valuable. The gun had a logo on its side featuring a winged woman's silhouette and the name HH CUSTOMS around her in a ring. Money was tight, so I couldn't buy new guns from there.

As the eight-minute song finished, I saw her slinking from a room behind the desk. The giant slug stabbed a needle into the half-melted face. She looked down at me as it began processing. I guess she didn't think a short penguin in a long red coat with red hair and eyes could kill a ruthless warlord like Grel. That meant she didn't know who I was.

The device beeped. The slug's brow raised, and then she huffed and started typing on her bulky keyboard. She stared at her 90s-style off-white computer. Don't know what this lady's problem was, but she seemed annoyed about doing some work for a change.

"Enter your account information. We'll wire you three hundred credits within twenty-four standard hours."

Following her instructions, I left the head there. I wouldn't have taken such a dog-shit bounty if I wasn't hurting for cash. Annoyed with the whole thing, I searched for a liquor store and some food. All the people on planet Noron lived in underground cities. The surface was too hot because of the dual suns, one blue and one orange. I looked at the artificial sky that mimicked the surface. It was all assembled with panels. The smell of broth and fried seafood drew me to a shop selling noodle bowls for cheap. Then I found a liquor store, got the strongest of the cheapest shit they had, and headed back to my red and black ship. The central body's back ended at a point like a sword tip.

The front had a narrow neck, an angular visor in orange-yellow, a jaw horn, and a head horn. Its main body had two bulkier arms with orange and red lights on top and bottom, branching out into two thrusters. The thrusters were smooth pointed blades that glowed red and emitted glowing red particles when engaged. My ship had a raptor-like appearance, according to people. I could see it, especially with the two laser cannons on the underside. On the back were two oval-shaped pods, housing six missiles each. The two angled triangular panels in between them hid the heavy cannon. The *Vermillion* was a ship designed for high-mobility combat. It had seen a ton of that over the last Universal Standard month. When I entered the ship, I spotted the two freeloaders: Jeff and Todd. Jeff was pressuring Todd to do something.

"Yo, how'd it go?" Jeff asked as I walked in. Jeff and I were both penguins, but he was shorter, fatter, and had a wider beak and blue eyes.

"They talking about twenty-four standard hours."

Jeff took a sip of his beer. "Damn, that's slow."

"No shit," I grumbled as I worked on my noodles.

Jeff adjusted his long blond hair. He had tied back most of it, but he styled the front with gel into jagged strips. Not sure why he does that.

Jeff smiled and turned to Todd. "Well, now we have lots of time to go to the Cadence Nightclub."

You'd think Jeff said he was taking Todd to the gallows with how horrified he looked.

"Absolutely not!" Todd shouted as his large glasses almost fell off his face.

He was also a penguin, but scrawnier than both of us, had no hair, a longer beak, and green eyes. He fidgeted with the purple beanie on his head and his T-shirt with some anime chick on it with a spear.

"Aw, come on, man. What are you gonna do, stay cooped up in your room?" Jeff insisted while grinning. Even though I couldn't smell it, I knew he was high.

"Yes!"

"Boring!"

I didn't have a dog in this fight, but seeing Todd looking like he was shitting bricks made me smile. Todd looked at me, hoping I'd bail him out. Although I thought it would make for a funny story or silence on the ship, I now wish I had done it with hindsight being 20/20. Either way seemed like a win-win for me.

"Go with Jeff and get some drinks. What's the worst that can happen?"

Famous. Last. Words. Realizing he wasn't getting my help,

Todd's head drooped in defeat, and he meekly nodded, saying he would go with Jeff to the club.

"Sweet! Trust me, man. Once you get a good buzz and you check out some of the honeys there, you'll be fine."

Before Todd could object, Jeff snatched him and dragged him to his room, saying he would get Todd club-ready. I devoured the noodles and broth, turned on the holographic display, and began watching something, unaware of the nightmare to come.

2. TODD

I wanted to turn back and run, but Jeff wasn't giving me a chance. I will say, City 15, or C15 as the locals called it, is pretty looking for an underground city, especially the holographic night sky above us. Ads and holograms surrounded us, but that wasn't the issue. An ear-splitting boom emanated from the nightclub. Even before we were close to it, I felt the bass. The number of people increased as we got closer to the club. It made me want to return to the ship and binge another season of anime I bought from inter-dimensional traders. My flippers shook, and I found it hard to breathe as Jeff weaved between people. I kept my eyes down to the floor and whispered, "excuse me," to anyone I bumped into.

"Come on, Todd, we're almost there!" Jeff shouted.

"W-wait up!"

A tall alien bumped into me with their knee, and I almost fell onto the rocky soil. I didn't want to dirty up the oversized black and blue shirt Jeff insisted I wear. He strived to get me to ditch my glasses, but I can hardly make things out without them, and I had to remind him by demonstrating it. He forced me to leave my beanie at home. Jeff traded his hoodie for a blue T-shirt with white sleeves, while mine had black sleeves. We saw the club in the distance. The structure resembled a dome with a protruding tower. Animated holograms with silhouettes of dancing women surrounded it. The dome kept shifting from white to purple, in sync with the high BPM electronic music they blasted us with. When we rounded the corner, we saw how bad the line was. My jaw hit the floor.

Jeff recoiled and turned to me. "I guess they weren't kidding about this place always being packed. We might be here a while."

"A *while*!? The line's going halfway around the block! We'll be *stuck* out here for hours!" I snapped.

I tried to turn around, but three aliens about seven feet tall each got in line behind us.

Jeff shrugged. "Relax, man. We'll be in there before you know it."

Now would be a terrible time to mention I'm profoundly agoraphobic, wouldn't it? I'd rather be on the ship than in this queue. Jeff just stood there listening to the music and then pulled out a joint.

"*What* are you doing!?"

"Pre-gaming." He reached into his other pocket and pulled out a silver flask. "Want some? It's cheap, but it'll get you buzzed."

I don't drink, and whenever I do, it's because either Jeff or Edgy pressured me into it, kind of like right now. I shook my head. Jeff insisted I take some to calm down, but I refused. He shrugged and threw his head back and took a heavy sip, then he grimaced, closed it, put it away, and went to his joint. We lingered for an unknown amount of time, but my feathers felt itchy and breathing became difficult.

"Bruh, you sure you don't want some?" Jeff asked, looking back at me. "Man, you gotta ease up sometimes."

"E-e-ease up!? I'm stuck in this giant line with you h-h-how am I supposed to ease up!?"

Jeff inhaled from his joint and then blew the smoke out. "I mean, you got two options, and you might wanna hurry and pick because both of 'em going fast."

Against my better judgment, I took the flask of alcohol. It tasted and burned like mouthwash as the booze went down. It somehow got worse when it hit my chest, and I found myself hunched over and coughing for several seconds.

"Yeah...when our money problems are fixed, I can get better stuff."

It took me a while to stop coughing as I gave Jeff the flask.

I saw the club gates as the line picked up speed. Gray, petite androids in tuxedo vests and short shorts acted as bouncers. I wondered about the small robots at the entrance until someone in line answered. He stepped out of line and started brawling with a smaller bug-looking alien, and one android zeroed in on him like a rabid cheetah. It took me a minute to realize what happened as the little android girl's arm became a cannon. She zapped both potential customers after diving into a combat roll and landing in a crouch like an 80s action movie star.

They twitched like a fish out of water on the floor. The robot stood up, and her cannon transformed back into an arm. The line cheered and shouted at the android, instead of being scared.

I understood why as I watched her turn around and strut back to the entrance. Jeff elbowed me and smirked. He made fun of me for staring at the android, but others were also ogling as she passed by. They charged three-hundred credits per person at the entrance. Jeff winced and looked back at me.

"Goddamn, this place ain't cheap."

"*P-please* tell me you got this?" I whispered. I only had a hundred credits. I didn't think to ask Edgy for more.

Jeff pulled out his credit chip, checked, and sighed. "Yeah, fam, we good."

The android, which previously expelled two people from the line, required payment for tickets. Jeff paid, and the robot welcomed us inside. As we walked in, I took one last look at her back.

The interior was massive. A DJ booth and music equipment rested in the center, floating high above. The walls pulsed and flashed with trippy audio visualizers that matched the music and displayed info on what drinks they had and any specials. They packed the purple dance floor with people, hindering visibility. Androids danced on elevated platforms and metal poles. These androids wore less than the bouncers and had lights on their thighs and abdomens, but most of their bodies hid in the dark lighting.

The purple colors hid a lot of the club's details. As they shoved us deeper into the nightclub, I saw multiple levels above, with dozens of people partying, drinking, and having fun.

"Oh, this is wild man!" Jeff proclaimed.

"W-what do we do now?"

"Get drinks, food and hit on girls."

Three bars flanked the dance floor. Jeff headed over to one of them, and I followed his lead as two seats were open. The bartender was a tall alien with tentacles sprouting from her head. Three eyes, with one in the middle of her forehead, were present on her face. A holographic menu came up the minute we sat down, showing all the drinks. The menu displayed some drinks with confusing and complicated terminology. The bartender tried to smile despite her scary mouth full of dagger-like teeth while she created and served multiple drinks with her tendrils. Jeff ordered some fancy drink that came in a tall glass and was a mix of black and purple liquid. I got a simpler red drink. We delighted in watching the bartender make both of our drinks. She must've known we were new because she showed off and tossed the mixers into the air and caught them a second before they hit the glasses she had set up.

The other patrons cheered as she poured both drinks. Although I had little, I tipped her. Jeff knocked his glass into mine and told me to drink up. The carbonated drink I ordered tasted sweet, but then the bitter taste of the booze kicked in.

"Damn, this is good. How's yours?" Jeff asked as he drank more of his.

"It's, um, it's pretty good."

While I wanted to enjoy my drink, Jeff was eager to finish his and go dancing. While we watched, I noticed someone that stood out. She was about my height and looked human, with long white hair. When the lights flashed, I saw she was wearing a low-cut shirt showing off her chest. The woman weaved through the crowds like a dance. I couldn't explain it, but I felt something was wrong with her. Jeff elbowed me to tell me to finish my drink, and when I looked back to where I last saw her, she was gone. I finished my drink, and I wished I hadn't.

Jeff yanked me onto the dance floor. I didn't dance and people kept shoving me around. Jeff flapped about to the rhythm of the music while I struggled to breathe with all these people around me. At some point, Jeff started dancing with some alien and left me alone towards the dance floor's outer layer. I wanted out. My heart felt like it would pop out of my chest. I started making my way toward the bar. As I did, I must've tripped on something; I fell flat on my face. I also hit someone and got an ice-cold drink poured on me.

Someone snatched me by my collar and started yelling. I flinched. They didn't hit me. I saw the white-haired girl there. She had her hand on the angry guy's wrist. The creature holding me froze, and I saw his eyes widen. Then he dropped me and stepped back. Whatever she had said or done made him let it go. The woman turned back and smiled at me when I stood up. Her eyes were heterochromatic: one yellow and one red. Her long white hair was split into two tails.

"Sorry about that. Some people here can be touchy," she spoke.

I tried to thank her, but I found it hard to talk. For once, a pretty girl talked to me and didn't call me a dork. The girl grabbed my arm and pulled me off the dance floor and back towards the bar. The bartender got me napkins, and the woman ordered two drinks. When the bar lights flashed, I got a glimpse of her exposed long legs. She had legs like a model. I hoped she didn't catch me looking. The bartender handed her the two drinks. She took one and slid the other to me.

"Huh?"

"That one is yours," she smiled and took a sip of her drink.

Her fingernails were long and coated in a reflective, glossy black. With each dazzle of light, it became more evident that this woman was stunning and impossibly out of my league. I took the other drink and sipped it. I didn't care about the taste. The booze kicked in, and I relaxed somewhat.

"Thank you," I said.

She smiled and leaned on the bar back. Something about the

smirk made my heart skip a beat. She brushed her white hair behind her ear and kept smiling at me.

"You're not from around here, are you?"

"N-no, I got dragged here by a friend of mine."

She giggled and sipped her drink before crossing her legs. "I can tell you aren't used to places like this." Her long finger tapped the side of the glass in sync with the music.

On impulse, I asked her to dance. I don't quite know what happened after this, but I know Jeff saw us because he yelled "get it Todd" at the top of his lungs. At least, I think he did. I just remember this strange scent coming off her as we danced. The atmosphere was both eerie and calming. At some point, I felt her grab my flipper and pull me.

We weren't returning to the bar. She led me up the steps to an upper level. We stopped on the steps for a second, and she kissed the tip of my beak and then rushed higher up. The topmost level looked like some sort of VIP lounge. Android guards blocked the doors but recognized her and moved away. The lounge's interior had a lower level inside, with a big couch and a table with a giant bottle of alcohol sitting in a bucket of ice and water. The woman led me to the couch, and then the next thing I knew, she pushed me on top of it with surprising ease.

She reached up and began undoing the bands in her hair and shook her head, letting the full mane of white down. She looked more regal this way. I realized where this was going, and I realized I had no condoms. Before I could say anything, she was on my lap, and her boobs were at my eye level. This didn't feel real. I expected to hear my alarm go off any second now and for me to wake up with drool all over my body pillow.

But that wasn't happening.

"W-wait, I don't even know your name."

She smirked, put her finger against the tip of my beak, and giggled, "Thory."

She brought her head close to the side of my neck. Then I felt her kiss it. She repeated this a few more times, moving downwards. Her lips were cold. She put one of my flippers against her hip and under her shirt. She was colder than ice. That's when I noticed something strange. Her body didn't have that natural rise and fall you'd expect: she wasn't breathing. I couldn't feel her breath on my neck at all.

Then I felt something frigid pass into my neck, followed by something wet trickling down. Thory had a hand on my face. She shoved me into the cushion and twisted my head away from hers.

"What are you doing!?" I said.

I tried to shove her off, but she weighed ten times her size. She leaned in closer and used her other hand to pin my arm down so I couldn't get a grip on her. I felt something wet hit my leg, and I saw it. Blood. Mine. I tried to shake her off, but her grip only tightened, and the more I fought, the heavier she became and the harder she bit me. She eased off me, and I could look and see. She was sucking my blood!

I felt her teeth retract out of my neck, then she started licking the bite and looked down at me as blood dripped from her mouth. She started licking some of it off her arm while keeping eye contact with me. Both of her eyes glowed red. Her skin turned from pale to gray, and her fingernails had gotten even longer to the point of being claws.

"Not bad for poultry," she smiled as she licked more blood. "Wish I could take more, but I've got to run."

She climbed off me. I tried to grab her, but my body felt like cement, and I hit the ground like a ton of bricks. I only pulled at the back of her black miniskirt.

"Don't bother." She knelt and patted the top of my head like I was a pet. "My bite has left you paralyzed. You're not going anywhere for a while."

"W-why!?" I said, but it was getting harder to speak.

Thory laughed. "You're cute when confused like this." She then lightly slapped the side of my face as I tried to crawl after her. "Aw, don't worry, you'll be all mine soon."

Thory crept over to the balcony and leaned against it. She arched her back, let her hair droop off the side, and vanished after flipping over the railing. I tried to move, but Thory was telling the truth. My body wasn't responding. I could only twitch and flail, and then my phone fell onto the carpet.

"C-call...J-J-Jeff." I said before her neurotoxic venom stopped me.

I sat there, unable to move. I saw my blood coming out from the bite, but I couldn't feel it or respond. My phone kept dialing, but Jeff never answered.

I struggled to tell the phone to call Edgy, and it took intense strain to get my tongue to work. I waited with bated breath as I heard it keep dialing and dialing. No one answered. I was alone.

3. JEFF

Bruh, this club was off the chain. I wish I had more cash because these drinks were something else. The alien I was talking with wasn't interested in me, but there were plenty of other fish in the sea, and they were some fine ass fish. I wondered where Todd and that sexy white-haired chick went, but picking people out from the dance floor was hard. While wandering, I only got some dances here and there. I lucked up with a few girls that let me sip their drinks, so I had a steady buzz going, but the pressure was on to get with a chick. Todd couldn't show me up.

I had to go to the bathroom and heard people having sex in one stall. I wondered if it was Todd and that girl. That only encouraged me to want to get back out there and score. I hoped he had a condom, not that he could knock up a girl like that, but you know, for the other reason. I meant to give him some before we headed here, but it slipped my mind. While trying to fix my hair, my cell fell on the counter and someone was blowing it up. I checked it: Todd.

I called him back, and it took him two rings to answer. "Yo, what up? You got up in them walls, dude?"

"*H-help* me..." Todd whispered.

I had never heard him sound like that before."Where are you?"

"Top level."

"Alright, I'm coming man!"

I bolted up the steps. I had no idea what was happening, but it sounded serious. While running, I tried dialing Edgy, but he wasn't answering. He was probably drunk or blasting metal music, or both. Two super-hot androids blocked the way when I got to the top level.

"Yo, my friend's in there. I think he's in trouble!"

"Nice try, birdie." One robot said, shoving me away.

"Look here, pretty lady, I *ain't* lying. Why don't you just poke in and check? Your partner here can throw me out if it's a trick."

The robot in my face scowled and then looked at her partner. The other robot opened the door and revealed Todd lying on the floor, covered in blood.

"Aw shit!"

The robots and a nurse robot with bandages assisted me in getting Todd up. He was barely awake, and I can't say I blame him. He had lost a lot of blood.

"What happened man!?"

"S-she bit me," Todd whispered, barely able to keep his eyes open.

"Who bit him?" One of the security bots asked.

"Some sexy white-haired chick," I answered.

The robots stopped in their tracks and started blinking. "Oh, I'm afraid the two of you will have to leave."

"Leave? This woman done taken a chunk out of my friend here! Y'all got cops on this station!?"

"I'm sorry, but we cannot do anything."

"*Da fuck!?*"

The next thing I knew, they were pulling us out of the club, and they left us standing outside. Well, I was standing. Todd was lying on the curb and trying to sit upright. Now, I ain't the sharpest tool in the shed; Edgy will say I'm the dullest, but even I could tell something about this wasn't right. So, I helped Todd, and we limped back to the ship. The walk felt endless, but Todd improved as it went on, eventually being able to stand and walk without me.

"Dude, what the *hell* was that?"

Todd shook his head. "T-t-that woman, she's a vampire."

"She drank your blood?" I asked. Todd nodded.

When we got back to the ship, we heard loud as hell death metal and found Edgy slumped on the couch with a bottle of booze and a bag of chips. On the HD was a music video of some sort of metal band with a post-apocalyptic backdrop. I hardly understood their words because of the growling and heavy guitar riffs.

When Edgy saw us and Todd's bloody shirt, he sat up.

"What the *fuck* happened!?" He demanded, his words slightly slurred.

"Todd hooked up with a hot chick."

Edgy blinked several times and just stood there. "I'm sorry, say again? It *sounded* like you said Todd hooked up with a hot chick," he started chuckling.

"Oh yeah, she was bad," I said, laughing at that part of the story.

"How bad?" Edgy asked while raising an eyebrow.

"*Not* important now!" Todd groaned.

"Oh, right. It turns out she's a vampire. She took a chunk out of Todd, and we got kicked out." I explained.

"Dammit, where'd the bitch go?"

"Hell if I know."

Edgy ignored me and looked at Todd. "Todd!? Where did she go?"

Todd shook his head. Edgy and I helped him to his room, and then Edgy went into the fridge and grabbed a big ass bottle of water. Then he had me tell him everything. I tried my best with what Todd told me on the way back.

"I don't know shit about vampires, but we should get that bite checked."

"Checked?" I asked.

"The last thing we need is him *biting* us in the middle of the night."

Edgy started for the bridge, and I followed him. He reached into a compartment on the side, pulled out a silver can with a black and green label called NUCLEAR PEGASUS, and cracked it open.

"Are there any doctors that deal with vampire bites?" I asked.

"Don't fucking know, but I can ask the internet."

While Edgy looked for an answer, he asked me to watch Todd. I found Todd sitting in his room, shining a light on his neck. The skin around the bite was turning black.

"Oh, that's not good."

"What!?" Edgy called.

"Um, the area around the bite is turning black!"

"She said she'd see me again soon," Todd whispered as he covered the bite.

"What the hell does that mean?"

"It means he's going to turn into a thrall," Edgy answered while coming in with a device on his arm that showed a web page. "It says it right here, if bitten by a vampire and not drained completely, the person becomes a thrall within three standard days of being bitten. Once made into a thrall, they will become a mindless follower of the vampire that turned them."

"*Shit*," I said, breaking the silence.

"Yeah, shit."

"H-how do we stop it!?" Todd shouted, shivering as the words sank in.

"I see a post about a place specializing in many mysterious illnesses. It's run by some guy named Doctor Bernard Gee. He's got a clinic near a planet named Ocsid. It's not far. We'll get over there, and then we'll get Todd cured, then we find this vampire and kill her."

"Okay," Todd whispered.

"Todd, keep the light filters cranked to the max. UV light will hurt you soon."

He left, and I followed him out of Todd's room. Edgy readied the ship for takeoff. We left C15 by disconnecting the ship from the dock and going to the desert. Edgy then brought the ship into the atmosphere and put in the coordinates. He told me to watch Todd, so I checked on him. Todd was shivering and had a thermometer in his mouth. He turned on an anime. I don't know what it was about, but it kept him calm. The thermometer beeped, and he took it out.

"My temperature's a little low."

That felt like it was the least of our concerns, but it still bugged me. I kept my eye on him, but the booze, weed, and partying tired me out, and I fell asleep at some point. When I woke up, Todd was standing up and swaying. His eyes weren't open, and his beak was moving. I think he was trying to say something, but I couldn't understand him.

"Todd? Todd, you alright, bro?"

Todd said nothing. He just stood there and kept swaying back and forth. I stood up and shook him. Nothing.

"Todd! Snap out of it!"

His eyes opened, and they rolled into the back of his skull. Then his head went back, and he kept saying some gibberish. It was some straight-up Exorcist-type shit.

"Oh, *hell* nah! Edgy! Todd is *tripping* in here!"

"What do you mean!?"

"His eyes done rolled into the back of his head, bro!"

Edgy entered with a guttural groan. He appeared groggy and hungover. He looked at Todd before telling me to let go. Edgy grabbed Todd by his collar and lightly shook him. No effect. Edgy exhaled and released him. He slapped the shit out of Todd. He hit him with that front hand, then the backhand so hard Todd fell over. Edgy caught him and raised his flipper to pimp slap him again before he hit the ground.

"Damn dude!"

Todd started spouting that demon gibberish again. Edgy smacked him so hard I saw ton of spit fly from his beak like a spray bottle. Then he got quiet.

"Um...why does my face hurt?" Todd's eyes were normal again, and he looked around in confusion.

"You good?" Edgy asked.

Todd winced. "D-did you slap me!?"

"Yeah, I did."

"You were straight tripping," I said as Edgy let go of Todd.

He sat on his bed and looked confused and horrified. "I-I saw her! It was like she was calling out to me!"

"This woman must be really desperate to be sliding into your dream DMs."

"Jeff, shut the fuck up," Edgy said without looking at me. "Todd, try to stay awake. I think we're almost there."

"O-okay."

I followed Edgy out into the hall as he headed for the bridge.

"Yo man, how did you know slapping him was gonna work?"

Edgy shrugged his shoulders. "I didn't."

"You *guessed*!?"

Edgy nodded and climbed into the pilot chair. Exiting subspace, we faced a silver planet with many rings. When the light from the stars hit the rings, they were multicolored and changed constantly. The planet's atmosphere was the same way. It looked like a mirror ball.

"Nice place," I said.

"The clinic's not on the planet. It's in orbit around it," Edgy replied as he dropped us into one of the rings.

Inside the ring, we found clouds of ice and bits of dust. It was beautiful man. We weren't here for that. After steering the ship through the rings and into a big ass gap between them, we found the station. It was a large floating building with a light show going on. Without the giant pill and the word "clinic" on the holographic sign, I could have easily assumed it was an eccentric club. The landing pad was a bunch of squares lighting up in crazy colors. I could tell what Edgy thought when he turned around in his seat. This wasn't gonna be good.

4. EDGY

They say first impressions are everything, and mine was not good. Abysmal isn't a strong enough word for what I thought when we approached. I double-checked the address to ensure I hadn't fucked it up while drunk, but I was reading it right. Unfortunately, this was Dr. Bernard Gee's clinic. I landed the *Vermillion* on a pad that looked like a disco dance floor.

I grabbed my handgun, ready to use it if this was a waste of time. Thankfully, the clinic had an energy field around it so we could exit the ship and go inside without needing space suits or oxygen masks. Todd looked at me in surprise and asked if we were serious. I hoped I was right on this shit for his sake and the doctor's. When we exited the ship, they blasted us with funky music. Jeff enjoyed it and was nodding his head to it, while I found it beyond fucking obnoxious.

"Well, this place is...lively," Todd said.

I checked where Todd got bit. The feathers around the bite withered to a sickly gray, like they were dying. Todd noticed it too, and I could tell he was nervous. Someone came up to us, an android. She wasn't walking. Instead, her feet were roller skates. She wore a tight sleeveless jumpsuit that was the closest one could get to a wearable acid trip, as the colors kept shifting and swirling as she skated up to us. I could only tell she was a nurse because of the damn hat on top of her big-ass red afro.

"Hello," she said, giving us a warm smile.

"We're here to see Dr. Bernard Gee."

"I see." She pulled up a list of appointments on her arm. "Right this way, please."

She skated towards the entrance and opened the door for us. I don't think Jeff was paying attention. He was too busy listening to disco music. Todd looked at me, obviously asking, "what the fuck are we doing here right now?". I wish I had an answer other than "I'm wondering that myself" because I had no idea. We followed the nurse; her name was Nina, judging from the name tag. She led us inside and then skated behind the desk.

Even the interior looked like a goddamn disco. The ceiling had a mirror ball, and the floor changed colors and furniture was hard to see in the dark. No other patients were waiting there. I wasn't sure if that was a good or bad sign. Nina signaled me to come up to her while she interacted with the holograms.

"Please explain your friend's condition to the best of your knowledge."

"Some vampire bitch bit him."

Nina stopped, blitzed some commands into the system, and smiled politely. "Dr. BG will see you shortly. Please have a seat."

"Don't waste our time," I warned her, sitting down.

"I assure you, Dr. Bernard Gee is a licensed professional."

As she said this, a loud scream echoed throughout the clinic.

"Um, nurse, darling, I'm gonna need some help here," a smooth, chill voice said over the intercom.

Nina kept her smile, but it felt forced. "Please excuse me for a moment." She skated down the hall and into another room.

Todd's eyes were bulging out of their sockets. "I'm gonna die, aren't I?"

"If you do, they're going with you," I grumbled.

There were a few more screams from that room, followed by silence and a sound that reminded me of when I took a chainsaw to a mob boss' stomach. The sound horrified Jeff and Todd. I almost kicked the door in, but they came out shortly after.

Dr. BG was…something. Long, curly hair, a thick, short beard, and a flowing mustache adorned his face. Dr. BG was taller than us and wore an all-white shimmering jumpsuit that exposed most of his chest. He also had a giant necklace on with a crazy, heavy amulet at the center. The doctor appeared almost human, except for the blue skin and two antennae on his head. He also wore roller skates. He looked like some sort of disco singer. You wouldn't know he's a doctor without the gloves and mask.

"Well, howdy there, I'm Doctor Bernard Gee. Just call me BG. Everybody does."

This guy could not sit still to save his goddamn life. He was kind of dancing in place while talking. It was weird. I'm willing to bet this guy was higher than fucking Mount Everest.

"Yeah, um, can you help my friend? A vampire snacked on him." I told him.

His silver eyes lit up. "Aw, dude, a vampire, why don't you three follow me? Oh, and Nina, please clear my schedule."

"You don't have any other patients today."

He snapped and pointed at her with both hands. "Groovy."

We followed him into the room. Despite the medical equipment, the disco ambiance remained, complete with mirror ball and multicolored floor. He had Todd sit on the table, grabbed some of the usual medical stuff, and checked Todd. Even while doing this, I swear this dude was still fucking dancing. I wasn't paying attention to most of the tests, but I watched when he got to the UV black light. Todd's skin smoked, and the place smelled like grilled chicken. After turning off the light, Dr. BG jotted something down on his tablet.

Then he turned to us. "Well, it must be the Night Fever. We know how to cure it!" He spoke. Well, spoke wasn't accurate. More like he sang it in a pretty damn good falsetto. Credit where credit is due.

"He has a lovely voice, man," Jeff said.

"Right on dude," he smiled. "But yes, he is turning into a thrall which is not good."

"You know how to cure it!?" I asked.

"That's right, but there's a catch. The only way to stop him from turning is to kill the vampire that bit him. Once he's a thrall, well, we're gonna have an unpleasant decision on our hands."

"You've got to be kidding me!" I growled, pulling out the

handgun. "So there's really *nothing* you can do?!"

"Now, now, I didn't say that dude," he touched a device mounted to the wall. "Nurse, get me serum CV-127-B." He danced, skated back over to Todd, and grabbed a syringe. "Todd, I'm gonna hook you up with something that will buy you another twelve standard hours before you turn."

Todd stared at the giant needle in horror. The syringe was insanely large and longer than my arm.

"W-why do you *need* a needle *that* big?" Todd asked, cowering away from it.

"Here's the deal," BG winced. "It's gotta go into the bone marrow."

The look of sheer "I am about to piss my pants" level of terror on Todd's face was priceless. "D-did you say bone marrow?"

"Yes, I did. It has to go through the spine."

"Aw shit!" Jeff shouted.

"Butch up Todd," I said, trying not to laugh at him.

Nina came back with a giant vial of orange, glowing something. "Nina darling, please prep the patient."

I could tell Todd wanted to run, but Nina stuck him with a sedative that calmed him down. He had to take his shirt off and lie on his back. They strapped him down to keep him from kicking and squirming too much, then Dr. BG got the big ass shot and swabbed Todd's back. Todd mumbled and sobbed in absolute horror. Can't say I blame him. That was a big fucking needle. Jeff couldn't watch, but I whipped out my phone and filmed it. The needle had barely touched him before Todd started screaming like a little schoolgirl. I couldn't keep the phone steady because I was laughing so hard.

"Nina, the Friday Funk playlist, please," BG said.

Nina pressed a button, and funky disco music started blasting from speakers around us. Jeff and BG started nodding their heads to it. Nina had no expression and just watched. The music didn't diminish Todd's impressive screams. You would've thought we were water-boarding ducks back here. Todd relaxed briefly after being injected with the orange substance. Then he started flailing again, and his eyes turned red. I don't mean just the white part. I mean the entire eye. Veins popped out on his face and arms like a bodybuilder flexing and posing. The scream then got several octaves lower, so it almost sounded like a grown man screaming his lungs out. He returned to normal after a few minutes. The doctor took out the needle, put a pad on his back, and taped it. After setting down the syringe, Dr. BG ran his hands through his hair and leaned against the wall.

"That was...something," I said.

"Well, it seems to have worked. That's an extra twelve standard hours to find this vampire."

"Yeah, how do we find her?" I asked.

"Todd will do that for you," Nina answered while checking him.

"Huh?"

"When he wakes up, he should know where she is. They are linked now. That link will get even stronger the closer he is to turning," Nina spoke as she finished with Todd.

"How do y'all know so much about vampires?" Jeff asked.

"Oh well, I like to try and cure things people say are incurable. Have you ever heard of the Violet Plague on Kaon VI?"

I remembered hearing something about that. Two-thirds of the planet was dying from it. Then it stopped, and only a third of the people died. Which was still a metric shit load of people, but hey, it could've been worse.

"Well, my old team and I figured out a cure. We were going to try curing Night Fever next, but a vampire killed them. Now it's just Nina and me."

"Damn. That's rough bro," Jeff said while looking at Todd.

"I got a favor to ask. If y'all are going after this vampire, Nina and I want in."

"You're a doctor. How are you gonna help us?" I asked. He didn't look like a fighter.

Dr. BG smiled, and he and Nina led us into another room. I saw a wall of crazy weapons when Nina pulled the curtain back. Most of them involved metal stakes and bottles of water.

"Let's just say we have an unorthodox approach to treating those who have succumbed to the Night Fever around here." Dr. BG skated closer to the weapon wall.

"Damn," Jeff said.

I scratched my head. "How do you kill a vampire again?"

Dr. BG smiled and pulled a weapon off the wall. "Well, if it's just a thrall, shooting them in the head, hitting them with UV light, or blowing their bodies apart will do just fine. A full vampire, now that, you gotta get 'em in the heart with a stake or douse 'em in holy water."

"So, guns don't work?" I asked.

"Bullets will only stun them momentarily. Laser and energy weapons will damage them, especially if you can shoot their limbs off. But you can't kill them that way," Nina answered.

"If you let us come with you, I'll do you a solid and drop the medical bills for your friend there." BG said, while inspecting the guns.

That was tempting. Medical bills were the last fucking thing my bank account needed right now. "Alright, you got yourself a deal."

"Yeah!" He again said it with a falsetto, but this time, something weird happened. Clones appeared behind him. They were different colored and sang like he did, in perfect harmony.

Then they all vanished.

"What the heck was that?" Jeff asked, taking a step back like I did.

He tapped the amulet on his chest. "Oh yeah...that's something this amulet lets me do."

"You can make decoys of yourself?"

He nodded. "I can only do that for about a minute, maybe two, if I push it."

I remember thinking how strange that was, especially since the decoys weren't the same color as he was. Still, in the middle of a shootout or at a distance, you might fall for it. Even if only for a split second, that could be enough to end a fight.

"Neat," I said. Then I looked at Nina. I was about to ask if she had any useful skills, but something happened.

"Edgy!" Todd shouted.

We ran back to the room. Todd shook and squirmed in his restraints.

"What?" I asked.

"I know where she is! She's still on Noron!"

"Groovy, let's cure your friend," BG said with a grin.

"Oh, hell yeah!" I said as I drew my handgun.

Todd looked around the room, kinda confused about the whole situation. "Uh...can someone untie me, please?"

5. TODD

Upon finally reaching Noron, Edgy had everyone assemble in the armory to prepare for vampire killing. Hundreds of weapons filled the room as Edgy had weapons on the walls, in crates, and hanging from racks on the ceiling. I'm pretty sure several are considered WMDs. Everyone had giant lamps on their shoulders that emitted ultraviolet light. Edgy had me wearing a space suit to keep the light from burning me. Edgy then gave me one of BG's guns. It looked like a revolver but with a bigger chamber housing small metal stakes.

"Take it," Edgy said while he grabbed one rifle similar to the pistol, but bigger. I carefully took it and turned it over in my flippers. "Just don't shoot your eye out."

Jeff and I aren't good at firefights, but Edgy felt we needed as many people as possible. Nina opened a pouch and showed the grenades, but the sides were transparent. It seemed to contain liquid. It almost looked like water, but it had a strange white glow.

"What is that?" I asked.

"Holy water," she said. "Don't let that get on your skin. It'll burn like acid."

"O-okay."

The doctor grabbed a grenade for himself. "Hey man, you wouldn't happen to know what this vampire is called, would you?"

"She said her name is Thory."

Dr. BG stopped dancing and stared at me. "Oh, that *might* be a problem."

Edgy raised an eyebrow as he finished loading the rifle. "Problem?"

Dr. BG spun and anxiously scratched the back of his neck. "Vampires get more powerful with age, and Thory is an*cient*."

"H-how ancient?" I asked, fearing the answer.

He shrugged. "I dunno, at least three thousand years old."

"Shit," Jeff said before nervously drinking his soda.

"Okay, so we gotta kill a really old bitch, big deal," Edgy grumbled as he headed for the exit. "Wouldn't be the first time I've killed something over a thousand years old."

"A little cocky, isn't he?" Nina asked.

"Oh, he's serious," I replied as I felt the ship docking.

"It's go time," Edgy said, leaving the armory.

When we exited the ship, Edgy told me to lead the way. Many people stared at us; to be fair, we looked like we were about to walk into a warzone. That was not far off.

"Alright, Todd, where is the bitch?" Edgy asked.

I shut my eyes. I don't know how this works, but I could see her somehow. It was like mind-controlling a camera. Thory wore a backless white dress with her hair tied back in a large bun. She held a glass of blood in one hand and...what appeared to be someone's jugular in the other. Thory had the vein in the glass and used it like a water cooler. As she filled her glass, she looked around and tapped her foot as if waiting for something. Then she shoved her unfortunate victim onto the ground and stood up. From the balcony, Thory observed the dance floor. I could tell this wasn't the same nightclub she attacked me in; while searching, I found a name on a screen.

Afterlife.

As soon as I saw it, my view returned to her. Thory turned around to face me, leaned against the rail, and smirked.

"*Finally* come back to me, Todd?" Her voice echoed throughout my mind. She raised up the hand caked in blood and licked it. "Well, don't keep me waiting."

Someone grabbed me. I screamed and jumped. I was standing on the platform with Edgy and the others.

"You good?"

I ignored the question, accessed a wall display, and located it on a map. I pointed to it for Edgy and told him Thory was there, and she knew we were coming.

"Right on Todd, let's get this party started," Dr. BG said.

Dread built in my stomach as we got on the elevator. It felt like I had an ever tightening noose around my neck. We didn't waste any time reaching the club. Cadence was miniscule compared to Afterlife. It was a giant black tower covered in neon lights with buttresses and other gothic architecture across it. Holographic banners ran down the sides of the angular tower, displaying advertisements for drink specials and other attractions of the nightclub. Even if I didn't know about the vampire lord, this place felt evil. I grew increasingly ill as we got closer to it. I had knots in my stomach, and my head was pounding.

That wasn't the worst of it.

I started seeing her. She was there one moment, gone the next, when I blinked. Thory taunted me every time I saw her. The doctor believed she was trying to control me, but the medicine would temporarily prevent it. Instead of waiting in line, Edgy started threatening people with his gun. The security bots tried to stop us. Edgy nonchalantly shot them with stakes, impaling them against the walls.

"That was...brutal," Nina remarked while grimacing.

I refrained from looking at the aftermath. Edgy kicked the doors open and stormed inside. More security androids moved to stop us, but before Edgy could attack, the robots powered down. The club's music stopped, and then I heard clapping. Some lights shined onto the upper level. She was there, leaning over the railing.

"Aw, couldn't stay away, Todd?" Her voice, it wasn't just coming out of her mouth. I was also hearing it in my mind. She scooped up her wine glass filled with blood and took a sip. "And you brought friends, how sweet of you," she giggled.

Edgy fired the rifle. Thory moved to dodge it. He missed her, but he hit her glass. Blood coated her face, dress, and hand. Edgy fired again. She exploded into a cloud of mist.

"Ooh, a feisty one. I'll enjoy bleeding you dry."

I heard a ringing in my head. My brain felt like it was on fire. I almost fell over; I couldn't stand upright. Then I saw them. Almost half the clubgoers glared at us, and their eyes shone blood red. The other patrons stepped away from them. Thory descended on the bar back, became solid, and lounged on it, not looking at us.

"Kill them, but bring me those two alive," she pointed at Edgy and me.

The clubgoers started snarling, and I watched them transform. Their hands became bigger and clawed, and I could tell they were growing fangs. At least a hundred of them were looking at us like hungry teens eyeing a hot pizza.

"This might've been a bad idea," Dr. BG said.

We were severely outnumbered. Thrall bartenders climbed over the bar to attack. Edgy looked over his shoulder at us and nodded.

"Let's rock!"

Together, we faced away from each other and pressed our shoulder pad buttons. The UV lights activated, and a horde of thralls caught fire and screamed in pain. Edgy started unloading into the ones that dodged the lights. A bartender swung from the ceiling at me. I raised my revolver and fired twice, missing both.

I grazed him with the light, and the skin on his sides melted and burned away. The nightclub quickly filled up with vapor from the burning corpses. I'm glad I couldn't smell anything through the space suit. The bartender pounced. I fired again. I missed, but the thrall exploded into a pile of ash before it slashed me. Turning around, I saw Dr. BG there with a smoking gun.

"Now, this right here is a party!" He proclaimed while turning on his music and connecting it to the club's speakers.

Despite being in a battle, BG still danced to his music while shooting! Somehow, he was more accurate than me! Loud, funky disco music became the soundtrack to this intense fight. I looked around. Despite our UV lights, they were still coming and doing their best to avoid them. Edgy emptied his gun into them, killing several before he had to eject the cylinder. One thrall moved in to kill him. I raised the gun and fired.

The creature exploded into cinders and ash as the metal stake pierced its heart. Edgy nodded to me as he loaded another cylinder into his gun. The partygoers that were not vampires ran as best as they could. I steered clear of hitting anyone who wasn't one of those creatures, though it was a madhouse. I don't think Edgy cared who he hit.

I heard a snarl from above me. I looked up, and the lights hit the thrall. Not enough to kill him. He pounced on me, knocking me down and the gun out of my flipper. The creature snarled and struck the lights on my shoulders, destroying its own hands and taking away my primary defense. It reeled back in pain after shattering the lights. Then a vial of holy water hit it, and its body melted like a candle. Nina grabbed me by the shoulder and helped me up.

"You alright?"

"Y-yeah, but m-my lights are down!"

She tossed me a new pistol and told me to stay in the center of them. She and Dr. BG frantically attempted to make up for losing light, but this was not going well: they still outnumbered us. Edgy took the brunt of it from the front. He emptied his rifle into the enemy, dropped it on the floor, and pulled out two pistols. I came behind him to help as best as possible, but most of my shots missed. When the handguns ran out, he tossed them and drew another pistol that wasn't firing stakes. When he shot one thrall, the round exploded, only leaving a bloody stump.

"This is getting a little dicey!" Dr. BG called.

One of his lights was down too! Nina screamed and fell to the ground next to me with a giant slash to her chest. They disabled one of her lights. She kicked the thrall, and a stake sprouted from her foot mid-kick. She hit it in the heart, and it exploded into a pile of ash.

I looked back at Edgy. He fired two more explosive rounds and chucked the holy water grenades, but they were still coming! When the handgun clicked, I thought he was out of weapons. I was mistaken. He holstered the handgun and drew a shotgun from his lower back that was hidden under his coat.

"I'm running out of moves!" He announced as he fired a shell at several thralls. The little needles inside the shell exploded as they embedded in their targets.

"We need to split!" Dr. BG said.

"How cute. You think I'm going to let you leave?" Thory's voice boomed.

I shifted my gaze to her previous position. I was too late. A javelin of coagulated blood smashed into Edgy.

He went flying towards one of the couch areas.

"*Edgy!*" I screamed while running over to him.

I couldn't tell if the blood on the off-white couch belonged to him. As I got near him, Edgy sat up slowly, and I saw where it had hit him. It struck the light on his shoulder, but worse, it hit the battery pack. He was out of lights! Edgy ripped off the shoulder lights and stood up. He grabbed a bottle and drank from it. It happened so fast. Edgy grabbed me by the front of my suit, dragged me down with one flipper, then came forward and crowned the thrall behind me with the bottle. I spun around right as Edgy brought up the shotgun and fired. The blast knocked it across the club, then it exploded.

Before either of us could say anything, Thory chucked another javelin. This time she hit BG. Again, she went for the lights. She was toying with us! A shiver ran down my spine, and I gulped. More thralls came from above as we ran out of lights.

I realized Edgy's intention as he stood on a bar back and pumped the shotgun. He fired at Thory. The explosive flechette rounds didn't reach her. A wall of blood erected between her and the blast, absolutely insulating her from it. She didn't flinch or react to him.

"Over here, old bitch!" Edgy shouted at the top of his lungs.

Her expression changed. Thory's eyes narrowed as she hissed

and showed her fangs. Now she was livid, and my stomach was in knots. She raised her hand and pointed to him.

"*Bring. Me. His. Tongue!*"

The thralls snapped towards Edgy in scary unison. Without realizing it, I had done the same thing. Then Thory tossed another spear. Edgy dove behind the bar and began firing blindly over the counter.

"BG! Get them out of here. I'll buy you some time!"

I wanted to object, but BG snatched me while skating by. Nina had Jeff under her arm while she skated towards the exit. Panic ensued outside as the city's cops set up a perimeter.

"You gents *might* wanna clear out now." Dr. BG said while switching off his music.

They didn't have the time to speak. Burning thralls erupted out of windows on the upper level. They crashed amongst the cops and immediately ripped into them like a plate of ribs. Absolutely horrific. The surviving cops panicked and opened fire while we weaved past them. More of them poured out of the building as we escaped the perimeter.

Then the club exploded. The shockwave knocked us all down. My ears were ringing from the loud boom. I could still feel the heat even with the space suit's protective layers. I turned over onto my back to observe the situation. The explosion had blown half of the nightclub's lower levels to bits. Amidst the lull of the flames, I spotted him. Edgy stood there in the thick of it, shrouded in a fiery orange-red aura. He had his shotgun mounted on his back.

He didn't need a gun.

A thrall rose to attack him. Edgy kicked it. As he did, a wall of heat slammed into it, vaporizing the creature. Thory hovered above with a pair of bat-like wings sprouting from her back. The attack shredded and singed her dress, but her body was unharmed.

"Holy cow!" Dr. BG exclaimed.

"Yeah, he does that," Jeff said.

As Edgy stood there, I watched the remaining metal beams

glow orange like they were in a forge. The air distorted from all the heat. Edgy trembled with unhinged rage. I don't know how he got these powers, but they're fueled by anger and you don't want to experience them.

More thralls erupted out of the rubble to charge him. Edgy rushed them. He leaped into the air, brought both arms overhead, and slammed them on the ground. A shockwave of destruction traveled across the ground, disintegrating them on contact.

Then Thory attacked. I tried to shout, but the explosions, police sirens, and gunfire drowned me out. Thory slammed into Edgy, knocking him down. If the heat he put out affected her, I couldn't tell. Edgy rose to his feet, blood trickling from his beak. Dr. BG moved to assist. However, the thralls were too many, and they targeted us.

"Split!"

I got to my feet and followed his lead, but I looked over my shoulder, hoping Edgy would be alright. I couldn't shake the feeling that he was in trouble. Running, a voice in my head made me stop. I wanted to move, but I couldn't do it. Only my eyes moved.

"You cannot escape," her voice said.

It sounded like it came from all around us. My vision changed. I was high above the wrecked nightclub. Edgy was still fighting Thory. Her claws had torn up his clothes as she kicked him into what remained of a bar. Edgy erupted out of it in a berserk charge. He caught her by the neck, slammed her into the ground, then dragged her across it, ripping it up. She rose, and Edgy's flipper crashed into her jaw, dislocating it and sending her flying. Growling like a beast, he pursued as she crawled to her feet.

She kicked him in the ribs and knocked him back. Then, using her wings, she sailed into the air out of his reach. Edgy stumbled to his feet. His aura was fading, and he couldn't stand upright.

I heard a snarl, and somehow, I had control over myself.

I saw it a second too late. The thrall slashed my helmet and hit it so hard that he tore through the visor and almost ripped out my eye. The blow knocked me off my feet. I fumbled for the gun, but the thrall smacked it out of my flipper. I was good as dead. Then a stake slammed into its chest, and it exploded. I looked over my shoulder, unable to breathe. Dr. BG stood there.

"Whatcha doing on your back?" Before I could answer him, he summoned light clones of himself. "You should be *running*! *Yeah*!" They all sang in perfect harmony.

That's when I noticed the thirty thralls barreling towards me. I ran like hell. As we were nearing the ship, something flew overhead. It crashed into a car and a shop near us. We all stopped in our tracks, and so did the thralls. As the smoke dissipated, I recognized Edgy and Thory. Edgy rolled over and slowly tried to rise. Before he got up, Thory snapped her jaw back in place. With her torn, burnt dress and blood-red eyes, she looked like a demon. Thory raised her leg high into the air and brought it down like a guillotine on the back of Edgy's head, dropping him and cracking the ground beneath him. Thory extended her fangs. She never touched him. A stake went through her chest, almost taking her down. BG was the one who fired the shot.

Much to our horror, it didn't hit her heart.

Thory apathetically reached up and began pulling the metal spike out of her body with no signs of pain. As she finished, the damage to her body healed completely. BG tried to shoot again, but his gun clicked.

"Aw, man," BG said.

"Now you understand. You will *not* leave this planet alive." She crept towards us, her hands becoming claws, "I'm going to take my time killing you all."

No way we would get past Thory and her incoming army of minions. A hailstorm of gunfire erupted from our left. The city cops unloaded into Thory. Their shots were as deadly as snowballs and only made her flinch. It did anger her into ignoring us and attacking them by summoning more blood spikes, using her own blood to create them. While the cops distracted Thory, Edgy made his move. He tackled her. He failed to knock her down, but that wasn't the goal. When she opened her mouth to bite, he shoved something in there. I heard it crack, and then Thory screamed in pain. She shoved Edgy away and flew into the air.

I caught of glimpse of what had happened. Most of her face and throat were melting! He hit her with holy water. She retreated, and as I looked around, so did her minions. Jeff and I ran to help Edgy. He was barely awake as we dragged him back towards the hangar.

We quickly boarded the ship to leave the city before the police could question us. I knew Thory wasn't gone for good as we took off. She bombarded my mind with vulgar insults. I don't want to repeat the messed-up things she said.

6. EDGY

Well, that fucking sucked. I fought to keep my eyes open as I plugged in the coordinates to where we were going. We'd need more firepower to take her on again. A lot more. I then opened a menu to make a call, despite struggling to speak. As I was about to, Jeff brought me another ice pack. I placed it on my crotch. The ship made the call, and somebody answered almost instantly.

"HH Customs, my name is Helena. How can I help you?" A low and soothing female voice answered.

"Helena, you mean to tell me after all this time you don't recognize this number?"

I heard her chuckle. "Of course, I recognize my favorite penguin customer."

"Wait, are you saying you have other penguin customers?"

She laughed again. "A lady doesn't kiss and tell. What can I do you for?"

"I need several custom guns, all designed to kill vampires."

Helena paused. "Vampires, huh? That's a new one. How exactly do you kill them?"

"BG, you're up," I said, between coughs.

Dr. BG stepped up and began explaining. Despite her flirty, playful tone, I didn't have to see her to know she was jotting down everything. After BG gave her the crash course on killing vampires, she put us on hold for a moment.

"Oh man, she sounds kind of foxy," Dr. BG said.

"She's a harpy," I replied while shoving clean napkins into the nares on the sides of my beak.

"Oh, well, that explains a lot."

I looked at Todd. He was shivering and hugging himself. "You alright?"

"I-I'm fine."

I couldn't confront him because I was too exhausted. I grabbed an assortment of pain meds and ate them while waiting for Helena to come back. As Nina finished treating Jeff's injuries, I heard a click.

"We'll have something whipped up for you when you arrive."

I checked the route through subspace; it would take us a long time to get there. I asked the doc how long we had: roughly six hours left before the deadline, but with medication he could give Todd more time. I told him to do it and let Helena know we were on our way.

"Looking forward to it," she giggled as she ended the call.

"That move with the holy water grenade was a nice trick, but Thory will heal," Nina said while checking Todd.

"Fucking hag wasn't healing when she took off," I said.

"Holy water blocks it, but she'll override it by going to her lair. A vampire like that has a Blood Well."

"What's a Blood Well?" Jeff asked.

"Oh, it's exactly what you think it is," Dr. BG said. "Imagine a swimming pool, but take all the water out and replace it with fresh blood."

"Aw, that's nasty," Jeff replied, grimacing.

Can't say I blame Jeff for that. Didn't sound pleasant at all.

"If she goes there, she'll heal in a few hours," Nina explained.

"And thanks to Todd, she'll know where we are?" I asked.

BG nodded. "I'd put money on it. She'll try to come after us."

"Well, I'm gonna *try* to sleep off this headache," I said. "Somebody wake me up when we're close." I finalized the coordinates and set the ship to autopilot.

Then I limped off to my room and collapsed on the bed. I considered contacting Hylus for help, but I doubted Shard had any agents in the region that could come back us up. That, and I hated asking him for help. Hopefully, with Helena coming through with the weapons, we could handle it ourselves. I don't know how long I slept, but I woke up to a loud metallic scrape. I jolted awake and rose, upsetting my ribs. That's when I noticed what happened.

A metal spike protruded from my pillow.

My eyes followed the shot's trajectory. Todd was standing in the doorway with a smoking, shaky gun. There was something wrong with him. His eyes kept flickering from green to red, and his whole body twitched. He fought to keep the gun from aiming at me. Every time his eyes changed color, so did his aim. His face kept flipping between a state of panic and anger.

"Todd?!"

"I won't miss a second time!" He warned, his voice a mixture of panic and rage.

I leaped out of bed. Not fast enough. Todd squeezed the trigger as I reached him, and I felt the spike pierce my arm. I screamed in pain and almost toppled over as I got in range. I hit Todd way harder than I meant to. Adrenaline is a bitch. I heard the crack, and then Todd went rigid and fell over.

"Son of a bitch!" I yelled in rage and pain.

My vision blurred. I took the gun and ejected the cylinder. Then I grabbed Todd by his head and dragged him to the bridge. Jeff was high as a kite and listening to some trippy mellow music. He stood up, demanding to know what had happened.

"Get the *fucking* cuffs and wake BG!" I growled as anger and adrenaline flooded my bloodstream.

Jeff said nothing and left. I grabbed the spike in my arm and yanked it out, not caring about the blood I was getting on my clothes or the floor. I bit down to keep from snarling. Todd sat up. I weighed hitting him again, but I feared I'd crack something if I did. I turned on the safety harness so it locked around his chest.

Todd's eyes opened, and for a second, they were green. Then they turned crimson. He snarled and lunged at me like a zombie. The straps kept him down, but I didn't know how long it would take him to realize he could undo them. He kept thrashing and snapping at me, but I was out of his reach. Then he looked down at the release button at the center of his chest. Before he could, I hit him again. I tried my best to hold back. He lurched over to one side, still awake but dazed as his face turned purple.

"Jeff, where the *fuck* are you!?" I shouted.

"Here!" He called as he came back with a pair of cuffs.

"Cuff his ass!"

Jeff didn't hesitate as he saw Todd recovering. He grabbed his flippers and tied them behind his back. No way he would break those. Todd reawakened, still hissing and attempting to get out of that chair.

"That's not good," Dr. BG said, holding a box.

I glared at him while facing Todd. "Yeah, no shit."

He placed the box on the counter and retrieved a syringe and a bottle. The liquid inside glowed piss yellow.

"This right here should snap him out of the trance."

"*Should?*"

He winced and looked back at me. "I gotta level with you. I never had a clinical trial for this one."

"Oh *great*," I grumbled.

"Aw, it'll be fine."

He loaded the syringe into a dart gun and tagged Todd in the neck. He screamed and howled like we shot him in the dick. Within minutes, he collapsed in the chair as if sedated. Dr. BG sighed and pulled out a scanner to check him from range.

"He's alive," he looked at my bleeding arm. "We should get you checked out."

Todd sprang to life again and howled. His eyes flashed red again, and then he fainted. Jeff had a six-pack of soda cans raised over his head.

"If he gets up again, I'm hitting him."

Heeding Jeff's threat, Todd sat up. "Ow!" he groaned.

"Are you back to normal?" Jeff asked, slightly lowering the six-pack.

"I...I think so," Todd said. Then he noticed the bloody spike on the ground and the wound on my arm. "I'm so sorry! She was in my head! I felt like a puppet on strings!"

"Don't worry about it."

I told BG we needed to restrain Todd until we could kill Thory. Todd agreed with me and said he didn't want to hurt anyone else. Nina volunteered to watch him while she treated my arm. The good news was Nina's medi-gel accelerated healing. It would cut down the recovery time from a few months to a few weeks, but I wouldn't get full use of my arm until it healed. Nina had me sling it for now. Facing an ancient vampire lord with only one functioning arm was not ideal, but we didn't have a choice.

For the last two hours, I slept on the bridge. The seventh time the ship emerged from subspace, I woke up. We confronted a colossal ocean planet, nearly twice the volume of Jupiter. I could only see a few tiny pieces of land. The entire planet was one big ocean. A few rich people have made their own private islands and resorts here. This was Hydrus, but the planet wasn't our destination.

Instead, the *Vermillion* turned towards one of the twelve moons. This one had an atmosphere and a dense forest waiting for us. Beyond that was a large river with massive rapids ending in a giant waterfall. Many waterfalls cascaded into a central pool, surrounded by patches of land. Sitting at the center of this was a reflective chrome dome. As we approached, the ship emerged. Water curtains cascaded off its surface, creating an impressive sight. My ship looked tiny by comparison as it continued to rise above us. It looked like a metal jellyfish to me. A door opened on the front of it, and guiding holograms spun up, letting us know we could land.

Dr. BG whistled. "Wow, that's a fancy ship."

"Yeah, makes it easy for her to get materials from space debris and asteroids. It also can burrow into things to hide," I told him.

I brought the ship into the dock and activated the landing protocol. When we climbed out, a group of smoking hot harpies met us. The all-female harpy species almost entirely look like supermodels. In fact, most of their kind were pop musicians, models, actresses, or idols. To keep their species around, they have a very creepy ability. Their body converts their partner's genetic material into harpy DNA after sex to make children. A metric fuck-ton of children, usually. They multiply like rabbits on crack.

Despite being dressed like mechanics and wearing appropriate attire, the ones we saw were still drop-dead gorgeous. They almost look like human women, except their feet are bird talons and they can sprout wings from their arms. The ears have small wings on them. They have short curving horns on the top of their heads, usually only two horns, sometimes four. Their hair is multicolored, with many patterns. They also like to paint markings on their faces around the eyes and forehead. We left Todd on the ship with Nina. Jeff and Dr. BG followed me. One harpy asked if I wanted them to refuel the ship. I told them to put it on my tab. Smiling, she told me she'd get on it before walking away. Jeff snuck a peek at her ass. I did too.

"*Goddamn*, these broads are *fine*. Where does Helena find all these babes?"

"Most of them are her sisters Jeff," I told him, pretty sure we've had this conversation before.

"No shit!?"

"Yeah," I replied.

We started for the elevator. Another harpy, wearing a tight short dress, awaited us. She smiled and selected the correct floor.

"Helena's been ecstatic since you called," the harpy said. "We haven't been commissioned in weeks."

Usually, when I stopped by, I was the only one there, but I knew she had other clients. One of them is a former friend of mine. Emphasis on former. I'm just glad we've never run into each other here. It would be a real shitshow if that happened, and I did not need two right now.

"I see you girls moved again."

The harpy smiled. "We secured a deal on some rare materials for a project Helena is working on, so we're here for now. I hope we stay longer. Perfect place to get a tan."

If she hadn't said anything, I doubt I would've noticed the

tan. I couldn't see a single obvious tan line. Jeff tried to talk to her. Her name was Alicia, and I couldn't tell you if she was flirting back with Jeff or toying with him. Harpies are like that. When we got out of the elevator, she said goodbye. Her slow wave and big smile made me consider returning here for more than just guns.

Up the stairs, we came to a large, round area. From the dome's peak, we saw the massive falls and the vast water body it fed into. Dr. BG smiled at the view; it was insanely beautiful. The enormous area had carpets, with multiple lounge chairs and couches around us. Three stations offered their services: a bar, a food counter, and Helena's shop.

The hologram above her stand showed an animated logo and showcased her old commissions; many of them were mine. The minute she saw me, she grinned from ear to ear and gestured for me to come over.

Now, if every harpy I've seen is a twelve out of ten, Helena's a certified twenty.

Helena had long gray hair, ear wings with dark to light purple feathers, light brown skin, and orange-gold eyes. She had purple horns and purple markings on her face. The wings on her arms had the same colors as her ear wings.

As she leaned over the counter, I finally appreciated my height because of what was at my eye level. Helena's shirt exposed her stomach, so full midriff was on display, and I was beyond happy to see it after all the shit I had been through. She looked me up and down, and her lip curled into a sly smirk.

"What sort of wild fun have you gotten yourself into now?"

Jeff's beak was open so wide I'm surprised it didn't unhinge like a snake. Dr. BG stealthily pulled it up for him. Well, as stealthy as he could.

"Vampires, shootouts, explosions," I answered.

"Hmm, so your usual," she stood up and her wings vanished. "You'll have to tell me all about it."

She emerged from the counter, and I noticed her short shorts. I would have stayed longer if Todd wasn't in a life-threatening situation. Jeff's and BG's faces told me they were thinking the same. She put a hand on her hip to taunt us while leaning to the side to highlight just how smoking hot she was. She could boil a pot of water with just her looks.

"If I could, I'd love to stay and tell you, but we're in a rush."

Her smirk only intensified as she bent over to look me in the eye. She wanted me to look somewhere else. As she got closer, I smelled her perfume. It had a faint scent that felt soothing, hypnotic, and energizing. It made you want to stay close to her.

"Aw, well, that's too bad. I know a few things that might make your arm feel better." Helena stood up. "I always love your crazy stories." She then gestured with her head for us to follow her.

"Your handsome friend gave us a lot to work with. I think you'll find what we came up with to your liking."

I could tell BG was happy about being called handsome, especially by someone as fine as her. Helena put in the PIN and led us into the next room. I could hear guns going off as Helena's sisters tested weapons at the different ranges. This place was pretty goddamn close to heaven for somebody like me. Hot women, and ridiculous amounts of firepower. What's not to love? In the next chamber, we were at a range. We were on the other side of a glass wall. A big ass gun I couldn't use with one hand rested beyond the glass. Another harpy sported white and black wings with red markings on her face. She had the same color eyes as Helena but with paler skin. She wore jeans, a hoodie, a crop top, a red baseball cap, and a pair of goggles. Helena opened a compartment on the wall and handed us some goggles.

"This is the first weapon we made. You'll need those," Helena smiled and put on goggles. We all followed her lead. "Jesse, show them the launcher."

Jesse smiled, lifted the massive gun, and slid a disk into the side. Then she trained the gun on the dummies and pulled the trigger. I wasn't expecting a spinning disk of insanely bright UV beams that incinerated whatever they composed the dummies of. After thirty seconds, the disk fell.

"Holy shit!" I said.

"We call it the blacklight launcher. You like?"

I couldn't contain my smile. "*Hell* yeah!"

I felt Helena's long nails tenderly brushing the nape of my neck. It had an instant calming effect, and I felt my body unwind a bit. Out of the corner of my eye, I saw her lips curl up in a mocking grin. I was at war with myself over ignoring her taunts.

"Oh, don't you worry, we have more." She took her hand off my neck but put a finger on her lip. "Jesse, show them the second one."

Jesse grabbed another gun. This one looked like a shotgun, except instead of normal metal balls in the shell, what came out were small telescopic serrated metal stakes.

The next thing they showed was three stake guns, each of them bulky but housing twelve-round magazines. They were also much nicer as the handguns and shotgun had premium-looking wood with a nice finish. Helena reached up over my head and pulled down a box. Upon opening it, I noticed two types of stakes. One type had a hollow interior, and there appeared to be an empty vial inserted.

"Darlin', is *that* what I think it is?" BG asked.

She grinned and turned to him, leaning against the counter, and stretched her back. "I designed these stakes to inject vampires with holy water. We don't have any here, but I'm sure you can get it."

"Oh, don't worry about that. I brought four gallons of the stuff."

My brow raised. "*Four* gallons? Do they even *sell* holy water by the gallon?"

Dr. BG laughed. "You'd be surprised with what you can find at a Giga Mart."

He wasn't wrong about that one. Found a pretty sick bulk deal on anti-tank rounds once.

"Nice," Jeff said.

"Is that everything?" I asked.

"It is. Why don't you try them out?"

The launcher posed a problem; it was too heavy to lift with one hand. Thankfully, they gave me a harness with a controllable mechanical arm on the back to lift the gun, so my good arm was free to fire it. Shooting it felt more satisfying than observing someone else doing it. I grinned like a horny teenager seeing boobs for the first time.

"Helena, you have outdone yourself."

She chuckled. "You know I aim to please, so I take it you're satisfied?"

"Oh, yes."

I only had one issue and it wasn't her fault. Reloading the shotgun with only one arm was ridiculously difficult. Helena had the girls bring out several boxes of ammo for us. Unfortunately, she only had time to develop five disks for the blacklight launcher, so we'd have to be careful. She again if I had to go, and to say she was laying it on thick would be an understatement. As much as I would've loved to stay, and believe me when I say it was really fucking tempting, I had a friend to save. I paid for all the weapons. I suspect she gave me a discount because the bill was surprisingly light, especially on such short notice. We hurried back to the ship. Jeff seemed sad about leaving. Helena waved goodbye as we left.

"Damn dude, take me with you next time you come here. Holy shit, man," Jeff demanded while elbowing me and waving back.

I remembered something and smirked. "You were drunk as *fuck* last time we came here."

Jeff's eyes widened in shock. "Oh."

When we got back to the ship, I paid for the fuel and boarded. Todd sat in his chair while Nina fed him a cup of instant noodles.

"How's he doing, Nina?" Jeff asked.

"He's holding up for now."

That was good news. We showed Nina the weapons at our disposal, and she smiled at them. She and BG began loading the special stakes with holy water. Again, he played his damn disco music. I pulled the *Vermillion* out of the dock, and we slowly exited the giant jellyfish-shaped craft. As I brought the ship high into the air, I took one last look at Helena's ship and the giant beautiful waterfalls around it. I wondered if it would be a good idea to return after the job. I owed Helena one for that alleged discount and pulling this off on such short notice.

My arm erupted with pain. Releasing the controls, I grunted. I activated autopilot to leave the planet's atmosphere and return to space. Then I went to get the pills Nina had given me. I returned to find Todd screaming. His glasses lay on the floor in front of him. Everyone leapt to their feet and stared down at him, astounded.

"What's wrong?"

Todd stuck his beak into his shirt and started breathing into it; he was hyperventilating. He's done this before while freaking out.

"Todd, you good man?" Jeff asked.

Todd's breathing slowed. "I-I know where she is! I saw the planet's coordinates on a computer in her lair!"

"Nice work Todd." I moved to the console to put in the coordinates. "Alright, what is it?"

"TK-77-BZ-822-z-"

"Todd! Slow the fuck down. I can't type that fast with one flipper!"

He said it again, slightly slower, and he still lost me, "Todd, I swear if you *don't* slow down, I'm slapping the taste out of your mouth!"

Todd gulped. "S-sorry. TK-77-BZ-822-zeta-gamma-xi-omicron-B."

As I typed in those coordinates, the star map showed us nothing. I thought I made a mistake, but additional information appeared on the screen. Based on the known nearby stars and the way their gravity worked, the computer deduced a planet was there. I climbed into the chair and locked in our destination. Five-hour trip. Leaving us with roughly one hour before Todd turned. Not a lot of time.

I threw the ship into subspace and turned around in my chair.

"Todd, anything you can tell me about this place?"

"The entire planet's full of thralls and vampires! She's in a giant citadel in the center of the city. She's about to enter the Blood Well."

Dr. BG checked his blinged-out watch and started dancing in place again. "Aw man, this is about to be one wild Saturday night."

Going by Universal Standard Time, he was right.

I snickered. "There are worse ways to spend a Saturday."

Believe me, I know. I spent an entire weekend recovering from poison and parasites at one point. A lot of throwing up and mad dashes to the toilet. Destroying a city full of vampires sounded like my kind of night.

"Yeah!" BG sang in response, again summoning clones.

7. EDGY

I woke up when we had thirty minutes left of travel time. I went to check on Todd. He had a nervous twitch, like he had a bad drug trip, and one eye appeared red. We were running out of time. BG road into the room on his skates. He chose two pistols while I got the shotgun, a pistol, and blacklight launcher.

"Where's my gun at?" Jeff asked.

"You're staying on the ship," I told him.

"Why me?"

"Because you suck in a firefight."

"Hey!" Jeff objected.

"You missed a Union soldier at *point-blank* range *with* a shotgun," I reminded. Still not sure how the hell he did that.

Dr. BG tilted his shades down and stared at Jeff and me, surprised by that statement. "*How?*" He asked.

I shook my head. "Dog, I don't fucking know."

Jeff looked down at his feet without a comeback. "I guess I'll stay and fly the ship?"

"You'll stay on the ship, but I'll be *damned* if I let you fly it."

"Then who else is gonna fly?"

I picked up the remote control unit and stuck it into a pouch on my hip. Thankfully, with the new psychic linker I bought a month prior, I didn't need to use the buttons for some commands. So, Jeff wouldn't be doing anything but helping Nina, just the way I liked it.

"Oh, and I got a favor to ask. I hope it's not too much," Dr. BG said.

"What?"

"If we kill Thory, can we get the body in cryo before it turns to ash?"

"Why?"

"It might help with my research with curing Night Fever. I've never gotten the blood of an elder vampire before. It could be the key."

I shrugged. As long as the old bitch was dead, I didn't care. "I'll try, but no promises."

"My man!"

BG then pulled out a small metal case about the size of his palm and opened it. Inside was a plastic bag full of purple-blue powder. He made a line of it and snorted it.

"What *was* that?" Todd asked.

"Don't worry about it." He said with a smile as he prepped another line.

"Stardust huh?" I muttered as I got a better look at it.

"Yeah, the pure uncut stuff."

That explained a lot about his personality. Constantly dancing around all the damn time must take a lot of energy, and it must come from somewhere.

"You not gonna say anything man?" BG asked as he put his drugs away.

I turned back to him. "Dude, I *kill* people on a regular basis."

BG laughed at that. I grabbed the harness with the robot arm and saw that Helena had included an instruction manual with a lipstick kiss on it. I smirked and shoved my arm through the strap. Jeff had to help me with my bad arm. I triggered the back-mounted arm, linked to my nervous system. I used it to help me attach all of my weapons to the magnetic holsters and then grab the launcher. BG changed clothes into a white suit jacket with a black collar and black platform shoes with built-in skates. I don't know why, but I wasn't going to question it. I was still wearing what remained of my red jacket.

We soon emerged from subspace and confronted a dark gray planet far from a star. I sent out some probes and expected the planet to be beyond freezing. It wasn't. The planet had a breathable atmosphere with cold temperatures that didn't require suits. Todd told us where the citadel was, and the long-range scanners gave me a readout.

"Where is Thory?" I asked.

"Top level of the citadel," Todd said, while trying to sit up some in his seat.

"Something tells me it's heavily defended," Nina replied.

I went to the chair and activated the weapon systems. "Not for long."

I powered up the heavy cannon and armed the twin missile pods and the dual underbelly laser cannons. I looked at BG, Jeff, Nina, and Todd. They nodded, realizing what I was going to do. I couldn't hide the grin on my face as I grabbed the controls.

"Hold up a minute, amigo." BG said, syncing his phone with the ship's radio. "We gonna kick off this Saturday night right, with the Gee Jees."

I had no idea what the hell a Gee Jee was, but it was some more funky disco shit with impressive falsettos. I won't lie. The baseline was pretty good. BG started nodding his head in sync with the drums. I did the same.

"Not what I would roll with, but fuck it, it's Saturday night."

I sent the ship into a dive and entered the outer atmosphere. When the *Vermillion* broke through, I understood why the planet had warmth. The earth looked like a cracked eggshell, and I could see the piping hot magma beneath it. Nothing but black rocks made up the surface, and the dark city of spiky buildings. The citadel was the biggest building of them all and touched the clouds. Warnings flashed. They locked onto us.

"BG, what do you say we start the show?"

"Yeah!" He sang in a falsetto with his light clones matching key with the vocals in the song.

The ship auto-targeted their long-range AA guns. I fired the missiles, which struck the guns after branching out in unison. A ring of fire erupted around the citadel. More of their weapons came online around the tower. I fired the twin lasers, causing two beams of light to fire from the ship's bottom. Whatever they touched caught fire and exploded. As I made another approach, their defenses retaliated.

I steered the ship into a controlled spin. If I had two flippers or Todd could help, I could've dodged faster. I felt some of their weapons hit us, but the shields absorbed it. The citadel shifted. I broke off and flew low, using the buildings as cover. When I cleared a section of the city, I saw what it was doing. The top elongated, and large cannons extended. The rows of weapons opened fire.

I heard Todd hyperventilating behind me, and Jeff fell out of his seat. Thankfully, the mechanical arm helped me turn on stabilizers, so the ride became smoother. The shields displayed a warning and were taking a beating from those weapons. I charged up the heavy cannon. The ship rumbled as the structures on the top split open to allow the gun to rise. I watched the final charging sequence complete as I pulled up and tried to weave between their attacks.

As I got high into the air, the gun charged. I threw the emergency brake and flipped the ship upside down. When the *Vermillion* lined up with the tower, I fired the shot. A massive blinding column of blue-white energy shot from the giant rectangular barrel. The moment the beam collided with the structure, it erupted with fire and dust like a fireworks show on steroids. Huge chunks of it fell into the surrounding city. I smirked as I looked at the burning buildings.

I brought the ship closer to the citadel as most of the guns fell silent. Spying an intact platform near the top of the tower, I set the ship to remote and climbed out of the chair. Without a word to Dr. BG, I grabbed the cannon and left. He followed behind me, and we both jumped onto the burning platform. I grimaced as I hit the ground and felt a sharp pain in my arm.

A swarm of armored thralls rushed out of the single entry point to challenge us. Using the linker, the *Vermillion*'s smaller guns sprouted from the arms, and the two clusters of four guns fired into the advancing horde. A storm of blue energy rounds crashed into them, killing most of them. BG fired into the survivors. The new handguns cut through their armor like they were tissue paper.

I took my flipper off the cannon, pulled out my pistol, and joined in mopping up the stragglers. There was just one problem: the vamps activated the blast doors to keep us out. That was easy to solve. I had the ship rip it open with two missiles once we were a safe distance away. They blew the doors to bits after the loud explosive roar and clouds of fire, electricity, and smoke.

More thralls poured out. I flipped the goggles on and fired the launcher. To say it worked like a charm would undersell it. The spinning disk became a violet light show of death, leaving piles of ash and smoke when it finished. The place smelled like a barbecue.

"Oh, that is *nice!*" BG said with a smirk as he tilted his shades down.

"She's on the floor above you!" Todd told us through our coms.

"Got it."

We entered a creepy, ancient-looking temple. The arched ceiling was incredibly high up and seemed crafted for giants. With all the jet black stone, it would be an awesome set for a metal music video. I heard a hiss from above us. More of them dropped from the ceiling. I fired the launcher again.

Three shots left.

Like before, the spinning purple lights burned them to ash. More approached us from the other side. Others sought cover behind the pillars as I launched another disk. Those untouched by the light died by my pistol. BG skated ahead of me and unloaded into what remained. I pulled up a readout of the ship. The vamps were deploying some sort of fighters after it. The ship's new basic AI already marked them as enemies. I permitted it to use whatever weapons it needed to wipe them out.

"Over here, found a way up," BG said.

We stopped to reload our weapons beforehand, knowing we'd be dealing with Thory again. In my condition, I doubted using my rage powers would be helpful here. It already took a serious toll and the meds were the only thing keeping me going.

"Nina, how's Todd?"

"Not good, I'm afraid."

I heard frantic muttering and gibberish from her communicator. "What do you mean?"

She didn't answer. Instead, I heard her moving closer to the chanting: Todd. His voice was somewhere between a growl and a whisper. He spoke too fast. I couldn't understand it, and it didn't sound like any language I had heard. Todd repeated it like a mantra.

"Anything you can do for him?"

"I gave him another shot, but it's not working. You *need* to hurry."

I didn't need to be told twice. As we started up the steps, I understood why Todd started chanting like that. I heard multiple voices, not just one. All of them repeated the same words. Candles lined the walls leading up to the well. Recesses in the walls housed strange artifacts and skulls of varied shapes and sizes. We faced a large room when we reached the top of the steps. Robed creatures stood in a half-circle across the room. They kept their backs to us. I looked up at the ceiling and remembered how Dr. BG described this place. They strapped hundreds of bodies to the ceiling with tubes plugged into them, and I could tell what they were extracting.

I looked at BG. He drew holy water grenades, and I followed his lead. We tossed the most dangerous water balloons we could at them. Not sure how they worked, but they exploded and sent water in all directions. The chanting cultists weren't chanting anymore. They were screaming in pain. I fired another disk, and while it killed many of them, the others were true vampires.

We unloaded into them with stakes and easily defeated those who tried to attack us. With the room empty, I dumped the launcher on the floor and reloaded my handgun. Then we saw the well. A large circular pool brimmed with fresh, spiraling blood. I'd definitely catch every illness in the book if I went in there.

"How *dare* you!" A woman's voice boomed.

I knew it belonged to Thory. Her pale hair breached the red pool first, followed by her head. Whatever damage my grenade had caused to her back on Noron no longer mattered. Her naked form furiously rose, blood oozing off her as her crimson eyes gazed at the both of us and showed her fangs. I see why Todd was into her before the blood-sucking.

"What, not a fan of surprise parties?" BG said.

We opened fire on her. She dodged every single shot. I caught a glimpse of her before I felt her claws slash my chest. The strike knocked me on my ass. Her nails extended into long needle-like blades, and she prepared to stab me. BG tried to shoot her. Emphasis on the word try. Thory sidestepped his shots with no effort as she changed targets and walked after him.

Spears of blood flew from the well and sailed towards him. I stumbled up and raised the pistol. I fired. My shot didn't reach her. Instead, a claw of coiling blood formed and caught the stake. Then she threw it back. That stake would've been through my skull if I hadn't rolled. Dr. BG tried getting away from her. Wings of blood formed out of her back, and she instantly caught up and snatched him by the neck.

Her mouth opened. I winged her in the arm, causing her to scream and howl in pain. Dr. BG fell to the ground; judging from the loud crack, it sounded like he had broken something. Thory's arm began to melt and burn. The holy water was working its magic. She did something I didn't expect.

The crazy bitch tore off her own fucking arm.

Ripped it out of the socket like it was a band-aid.

"I will make you *suffer*!" She screamed.

A claw made of blood formed to replace the limb. This wasn't looking too good. My communicator picked up the sound of a fight.

"Todd broke free!" Jeff screamed. It sounded like he was being choked.

Yeah, this situation was fucked.

Thory sent me across the room and knocked the wind out of me. When I hit the ground, I landed on my fucked-up arm.

I suppressed a scream. I felt blood against my chest feathers. Her attack ripped through my vest. I looked up as Thory landed on the ground. She began licking the blood on her hand and smirked.

"Ah, so that explains it."

"Huh?"

She sucked on her fingers, sampling more of my blood. "Haven't tasted blood like yours in over a thousand years." Thory approached me as I forced myself to sit up.

"What the *hell* are you talking about!?"

"No point in telling you. You'll be dead in a second."

Her claws extended, and her pace increased. I pulled the trigger. The pistol clicked. She laughed. Shit. Then BG ran up behind her, but she spun at the last second and backhanded him. The decoy exploded into a pile of light. BG landed the shot and Thory shrieked. I watched as the shot pierced right above her navel. The holy water kicked in and her skin began to warp and melt like cheese in a microwave.

I drew the shotgun and squeezed the trigger. The spikes tore up her face and bare chest. She fell back and almost hit the ground. Then, like someone on wires, she pulled herself up. I saw the bones in her jaw and some of her exposed, rotten ribs.

We had her.

She rushed to the Blood Well. I desperately pumped the shotgun and zeroed in. BG fired too. We got her in the legs, and they both snapped off at the kneecaps. However, the rest of her got through.

A second later, the well stirred. Thory erupted out of it. Massive wings of blood gouged the walls of the chamber, and instead of legs, a vortex of blood swirled beneath her, keeping Thory aloft. New blood claws emerged from the pool.

I spoke too soon.

Now we were seriously fucked.

BG unloaded both guns into her.

"Aw hell," BG said between shots.

Whatever damage the holy water did no longer mattered.

The power from all the blood healed Thory faster than the holy water could melt her. I fired the shotgun, hoping the two of us could beat her regeneration. We couldn't. The claws attacked. I ducked and dodged some of them, but one caught me in the side, and I fell to my knees. She sent Dr. BG flying across the room. I didn't have a choice now. I grabbed the shotgun, growled, and forced myself to stand. Letting my anger over this situation boil to the surface, I funneled it through the gun rather than letting it out in all directions.

The gun glowed red, and the wood caught fire. The air around the weapon and my arm began to distort and warp. Embers danced off the gun as I pulled the trigger. The shell and all the stakes caught fire. When they collided with Thory's body, they erupted in a flash of blinding crimson light. I looked away from the blast. The shockwave caused me to briefly kneel.

When the light faded, I couldn't see what had happened through the smoke. I felt something slam into my chest. My gun flew from my flipper, and I sailed across the room. I vomited up blood as I hit the ground. My injured arm erupted with pain, and my vision blurred for a moment. I could tell Thory was still alive and somewhat intact.

"Your power is no match for me!"

I wanted to call her a cheating bitch, but I didn't have the energy to. Thory raised her claws to turn me into a mashed penguin, but disco music blared, and a stake flew through her skull. She turned and attacked Dr. BG as he skated around the room. She flattened him.

He exploded into light.

Decoy.

A purple-skinned version of him appeared on her right. She fell for the decoy again. This one lasted longer. I saw BG hiding behind a column and reloading his gun while trying to sit upright. He looked out of breath for once. When she impaled his second clone, he struggled to make a third one and almost fell over. This one lasted a few seconds. BG finished reloading, slicked back his hair, skated out into the open, and emptied the gun while cranking up his music.

His shots did nothing. Thory smacked him into the left wall, cracking it on impact.

"Enough with the *fucking* music!" She growled. Then she turned back to me. "Now, where were we? Oh yes, I'm going to bleed you dry!"

I heard something beep, and I looked at my arm. An external force hit the chamber, causing Thory to be thrown away from the Blood Well. The roar of fractured stone and the screeches of the metal were agonizing. It was louder than a gunfight, a fireworks show, and a metal concert, all happening simultaneously. I covered my head as bits of debris hit the ground near me. It only lasted a few seconds, but it felt like it would never end.

Whatever hit the structure came to a stop. I opened my eyes. It was the *Vermillion*. I saw some dented panels and scratched paint across the ship's body. The back of the ship opened and someone exited. I couldn't tell who approached. Then I heard movement from my left. I saw the claw before I saw the rest of them. Thory.

Without her connection to the well, she only had one arm left. The battle stripped her right side to muscle and bone in some areas. Yet she continued to crawl by throwing her arm forward and using it to drag herself towards me.

"Kill them both!"

My attention turned to the person who disembarked the ship. I saw they had a pistol in their hand. They advanced a bit, and the beanie confirmed my suspicions. His eyes were red, and his feathers didn't look right. The white parts had turned a sickly gray.

"T-Todd?"

Todd didn't answer me and raised the gun. This was one of the stake guns BG and Nina had supplied us with.

"Yes! *Kill* him! Kill him now!" Thory growled.

Each time she shouted, Todd shook. For a split second, I saw a change in his eyes. He was still in there.

"Do it!" She shouted.

"Hey Todd, you know that one body pillow you want? I'll get it for you if you shoot that bitch."

Todd lowered the gun.

"Are you *serious*!? Shoot him!" She roared, and the glow in her eyes intensified.

Todd raised the gun again. The body pillow bribe was worth a shot. Todd pressed the gun against my head. No way I'd survive this. I saw the claw on the underside of his flipper move to the trigger.

"You *fucking* weeb. You don't have the balls to kill me." I said, figuring I'd get one last taunt before I died.

The shot went off, but I didn't have a spike in my brain. Instead, I heard a scream from Thory. A stake pierced her head between the eyes. Thory gazed in disbelief as she comprehended what had just happened. Her eyes focused on the stake, and then she glared at Todd and hissed. Todd fired again, hitting her in the back. She flailed like a fish out of water, but she wasn't dying. He shot again, with no change, besides making her angrier.

"The *heart* Todd! Shoot her in the *heart*, for fuck's sake!"

This time, Todd shot her in the right spot. Her body ignited like the thralls and lesser vampires.

"Y...you were...mine," she said, looking at Todd.

Her eyes teared up as she continued to burn. She gave the impression of a girl that had just been savagely dumped by her boyfriend. I mean, I guess that's kinda what Todd just did. Then she lowered her head and shut her eyes. With that, she burned away, leaving a small pile of ash.

Todd dropped the gun and slowly helped me up. "So...that body pillow?"

"Not in a million years am I buying your degenerate ass a *fucking* body pillow," I said.

Todd looked down and sighed. As he helped me up, I had the mechanical arm jokingly shove him. "Fine, but *only* this one time."

"Fellas, I'd hate to ruin this moment, but uh, can someone get me to a hospital?" Dr. BG said, wheezing as he did.

Looking at him, yeah, he needed a hospital. And as I fell and lost consciousness, I did too.

8. TODD

"Well, Todd, you are officially cured," Nina told me as she looked at my blood with her enhanced vision.

She smiled and removed the other monitors. We were at a space station called PR-81. Glass and blue lights were the preferred aesthetic here, as every room showcased them. The medical equipment appeared top-notch and in excellent condition. Once Nina deactivated everything, she led me out of the room. I vaguely remember how we got here. I think I told the ship to get us to the nearest medical station, but I couldn't keep my eyes open either. As we passed through the glass hallway, I could see patients in other rooms being treated by different aliens and, sometimes, robots. Since Nina was a qualified medical android, she could treat all of us and use the equipment as needed. The hallway led to an open room with chairs and a reception desk. Someone was lounging in one of those chairs. I shook Jeff gently, and it took him a few seconds to recognize me. I noticed the bruises on his face that I had given him.

"You good?"

I nodded. "Yeah, no turning into a thrall for me."

"What about Edgy and BG?" Jeff asked, standing up and yawning.

"Somebody call me?" Edgy said as he came around the corner.

Bandages enshrouded his broken arm. He also had stitches and medical dressings for his other arm, neck, and face. His scowl revealed his dissatisfaction with the matter. Then we heard Dr. BG harmonizing with his light clones as he reached us. He shied away from skates, likely because the hospital

TALES OF THE EDGEWORLDS: VOLUME 1

disallowed that. He had bandages over his left eye and a cast on his left arm, and I saw bandages and stitches across his chest and stomach.

"How are you feeling?" Nina asked.

"I'm staying alive!" He sang.

"Damn, that chick did a number on y'all," Jeff said.

"Shut the hell up Jeff," Edgy growled. "How am I gonna pay for these medical bills?"

I smiled, "I uh...I already did." Edgy, Jeff, and Dr. BG all seemed surprised by that. "I grabbed some gold and diamonds from Thory's personal chambers and used it to cover the bills."

"Nice one Todd," Edgy said, smiling.

"There any left over?" Jeff asked.

I nodded. The gold coins scattered around still held a decent value in either units or credits, depending on the location in the EdgeWorlds.

BG smirked. "You sly dog."

"Oh, we recovered part of Thory's arm before it completely dissolved. It's in cryo on their ship," Nina said.

Dr. BG's silver eyes widened. "Aw man, I can't thank you all enough. With this, we can speed up cure research!"

I remembered one thing I saw when Thory had control over me. Other ancients existed, and Thory was particularly close to one. Based on her connection to him, he appeared more powerful, but his true strength was unclear to me. I sensed another vampire. They may have been close to Thory before, but not anymore. Despite my explanation, Nina was unsure about the ancient tied to Thory.

"So, what happens now?" Jeff asked.

"Well, I'm thinking you drop us off back at the clinic and then do whatever," Dr. BG said with a smile. "If you're nearby, don't be a stranger and stop by, especially if you have vampire problems."

Edgy nodded. "If we're heading out that way, we'll do that."

Edgy piloted the ship back to the clinic. Nina and Dr. BG saluted us and left, sliding back to their clinic with a partially melted portion of Thory's arm in a cryobox. Edgy exhaled, sat back in his chair, and opened the box of gold coins I had taken from the citadel.

"Alright, let's get these exchanged. Then I'm going to go to a liquor store and getting a big fucking bottle of whiskey."

"Man, screw that. What do you say we hit up a club?" Both Edgy and I just glared at Jeff.

"Jeff, sit your ass down and shut up," he growled. "I've got a better idea."

I saw the coordinates he was putting in, and when Jeff saw them, he grinned like a kid in a candy store.

"*Yeah!*"

"What? Where are we going?"

Edgy smiled gave me a big, devious smile. "A place where the girls won't bite you, unless you want them to."

THE CALLISTO INCIDENT

1. EDGY

I reclined in my beach chair and adjusted my shades as I gazed at the artificial sky and the false sun above me. Even if this entire beach was fake, it was just the getaway I needed. I reached for the frosted glass of bourbon on my left and took a heavy sip. The idea of a penguin crashing on an artificial beach in a space station may seem strange. Plenty of bars and a casino were within walking distance, making it the perfect place to hide and chill out. I used my flipper to move some of my red hair out of my face, it always covered my right eye, but I never cut it. I looked around at some other people. Oh boy, an abundance of hot aliens were in bikinis here. No one seemed to notice the short red-headed penguin in orange trunks and an unbuttoned red shirt. I was grateful for that. I needed to keep a low profile, especially after the bullshit bounty I had to deal with.

It should have been simple.

Kick in the door, kill the target, take his ring, and hand it to the client.

The client had other fucking ideas and decided I was a loose end.

Another body was added to the high body count, but that wasn't the issue. He was a broke-ass mother fucker, and he had ties to a crime ring in the EdgeWorlds, and they put a bounty on my head! To add insult to injury, the bounty was so high I'd turn myself in if it meant I could collect. Thinking about it made me angry again, so I took a deep breath and another heavy drink. Then I returned to the fried shellfish platter I had on my lap. My friends Jeff and Todd went up to the casino level of the station. I gave them some cash for gambling but not enough for it to hurt me. I sure as shit didn't need that.

As I dipped a golden brown tentacle in the red sauce and crunched on it, I felt myself unwind. I rarely felt like this, especially when sober. Mostly sober. The plan was to hide here for three days without any worries. Callisto Casino Station was ideal for that. As long as you didn't get too sucked into the gambling game and didn't provoke the mafia running this joint. The Golden Sevens are huge. Most of the big organizations in the EdgeWorlds are too chicken-shit to cross them.

I returned to my seafood and looked at the sea in front of me. It would look convincing if I couldn't see where the dome-shaped structure ended. The bridge from the resort led to a massive door at the room's edge. They tried to hide it by having the bridge's side made of panels that projected the wall behind them.

As I sat there enjoying my time, I thought about last night. The three of us went to the bars. Jeff got laid by some snake chick, I don't know how that works, and I don't wanna know. Todd kept an eye on us while I won money at the roulette table. Jeff had the biggest smile when we met for breakfast despite having a massive headache like Todd and me. Good times.

As I finished crunching another piece of food, a tall slim alien with pinkish-red skin and violet hair breached the water and flicked her hair back. She looked like a goddamn supermodel. I tilted my shades down to get a clearer view of her running her hands through her long hair. I looked around for a camera crew nearby because she was putting on a show. Judging by the whistles and the occasional "damn girl" I heard, I wasn't the only dude watching. She opened her eyes; they were red and had slit pupils like a cat's. Her ears were thin, pointed, and elf-like. As she climbed out of the water, I noticed how in shape she was. Something told me she'd been in a couple of fights because of some scars on her arms, legs, and rock-hard abs.

Then I heard footsteps coming towards me. I sat up a bit and slipped my right flipper under the towel I was sitting against.

The person approaching me blocked my view of the beach bombshell. He was some sort of humanoid wearing shades and a hat.

"You're coming with me, bird brain." He said in a grave voice.

"You mind stepping to your right? I was appreciating that *absolute* babe walking out of the water just now." I said, not giving this amateur bounty hunter the time of day.

He didn't seem fazed by my dismissal. I saw his hand inching for the obvious handgun in his pocket. If he was smart, he would've already had it out. If he was smarter, he would've acted like he didn't see me.

"Let's not make a scene, Edgy."

Did this moron know who he was talking to? Making a scene and causing mayhem was my bread and butter.

"Then go back to your chair and pretend you never saw me." I said with a smirk, "I'm on vacation."

He still wasn't budging. Beach babe somehow vanished from the entire area. Great. I had no eye candy to make up for the mess I was about to create.

"I'd rather not kill you. You're worth more alive than dead."

That got me to raise an eyebrow. "What's the bounty at now?"

The man paused, and I saw his gun sticking out of his pocket. "Thirty thousand units, alive, fifteen thousand dead."

I laughed. "Shit, I might have to pay to get a body double and turn myself in and collect with that kind of money."

He let go of his gun as a bunch of beachgoers walked past us and tipped his hat to them, trying to not make a scene.

"Look, just come quietly. People got families out here. They don't need to see us killing each other."

This fool thought I gave a shit. Another mistake on his part. I sipped my bourbon and noticed it was boiling. Not good.

"So I guess I can't convince you to fuck off huh?"

"Mighty observant of you."

I sighed as I drained the heated glass and sat it down. "Alright."

His head exploded before he could draw his gun. People

screamed and jumped in fear. Watching a man's head explode like a meat piñata will kinda do that. Time seemed to slow. I watched the contents of his gray brain split into chunks and shoot out like shards of broken glass. Unfortunately, some of those contents and his green blood got all over me, ruining my meal and clothes.

I'm supposed to be on vacation right now.

"God *fucking* dammit," I growled as his body hit the off-white sands.

Grabbing my silver and gold towel, I began wiping up the mess. As I did this, people stared at me and the body.

"What the *fuck* are y'all looking at?" I muttered.

After unscrewing the lid to the bourbon bottle, I drained it to try and drown out my rising fury. Then I kicked the body to vent frustration, packed up my shit and left. This son of a bitch ruined my seafood platter. Then I headed to the massive hotel at the center of the ring-shaped beach. A yellow hologram of the hotel's name formed above me, THE GOLDEN SEVENS HOTEL AND RESORT. I wasn't worried about security or the body unless the guy worked for the mafia. They wouldn't care, especially knowing he was a bounty hunter. My phone rang in my pocket. When I checked the caller, I almost considered not answering.

"*Shit,*" I grunted as I answered. "What do you want, Hylus?"

"I have an urgent assignment for you, and you are in the area." His booming, growling chain smoker-sounding voice grumbled.

"What the fuck?"

"I need you to support one of my squads. They're abducting an individual that stole vital data on one of Union's new weapons. They are trying to sell it to the highest bidder. I need them and that data. Union and others are coming for him. We must act."

Even though I hated Union for wanting to police all the EdgeWorlds and being douchebags, I wasn't about to ruin my vacation. Especially while I had problems of my own to deal with.

"No Hylus."

"What did you say?"

"Hylus, I am here on a *goddamn* vacation, and I'm *not* letting you or anybody else fuck this up! I already got a massive bounty on my head and plenty of bounty hunters gunning for me right now! I don't need this shit! Got it!?"

Hylus said nothing for several seconds. "The consequences for all of us will be dire if this job goes wrong."

"We'll cross that bridge when we get to it. For now, leave me alone."

I heard a growl through the phone. "As you wish."

The doors opened automatically to the lobby. A gold and silver android in a black suit sat behind the dark marble counter. She stood up when she saw me caked in blood and brain matter. That wasn't the only reason she stood up. The surrounding air shook and warbled and smoke came off the towel I had on my shoulder. I shut my eyes and took a deep breath, trying to keep it in check. After a few seconds, it stopped. Several aliens in the lobby gazed up at me as I approached the counter.

"Will you be needing our laundry service?"

"Yeah," I said, handing them my room key.

The android scanned it with her eyes and then blinked twice. She told me they would send someone to get it and for me to leave it outside in the blue bin. I returned to the room. It was nothing extraordinary. I ain't made of money here. I then climbed into the shower, not giving this shit a second thought. Little did I know how this day was gonna go.

2. TODD

I glued my eyes to the screen as the velocihounds raced down the winding metallic track. I gulped as the robot camera flew in front of them and showed their disturbingly impressive giant fangs and claws. They had six legs, with two pairs towards the front and one pair at the back. They also only had one enormous eye at the center of their head. The announcers were unable to predict the winner and went crazy.

I should mention, velocihounds are fast: their top speed is one-hundred-fifty miles per hour. Actually, calling them fast doesn't cut it. People around me cheered their hounds on to victory, but the outcome was uncertain.

I coughed as cigar and cigarette smoke wafted toward me. I returned to my noodles for a second. Then the commentators went nuts as one hound rocketed past the finish line. Some cheered, others fell silent around the screen. Better luck next time, I guess?

The bowl of noodles I ate was top-notch stuff. Better than the dehydrated instant noodle bowls I ate. It had the right amount of spice. The restaurant was integrated into the casino and included a small bar. Dozens of slot machines and game tables surrounded me. The casino and many machines and sub-areas had a gold and silver coloration. This tiny section boasted an abundance of shops and restaurants. We spent all day in a different sector yesterday, and I felt like we barely scratched the surface. After finishing my food, I adjusted my glasses, fixed my purple beanie, and headed over to Jeff's table.

I received strange glances from some. Given how rare

penguins are nowadays, I'm used to that. I dodged a couple of drunk aliens as they returned to a blackjack table. Then I saw the table Jeff played at. Jeff leaned forward and scowled at the board as people placed more chips into the pile.

Jeff is a penguin like me, but with blue eyes instead of green. He left his long blond hair untied, letting it cascade down to his lower back. As Edgy would put it, Jeff wasn't a scrawny shut-in like me. He was shorter and wider than me or Edgy. When I got closer, Jeff took off his blue hoodie, sat it on the empty seat beside him, and lit another joint.

"H-how's It going?"

Jeff looked up at me. "Bad question Todd," he said before inhaling his blunt.

Jeff's side of the table showed how much money he had versus how much he started with. When I saw how many units he lost, my beak hit the floor.

"How did you lose *that* much!?" I screeched at the top of my lungs. I realized it wasn't the crucial question. "Jeff, *where* did you get all that money?!"

He didn't answer me and flagged a waiter for a fancy drink.

"Jeff, *where* did this money come from!?"

He took another puff of his joint. "I uh...used the ship to get more chips."

My jaw dropped to the floor and vanished into space. My heart was about to explode out of my chest. My legs buckled, and I collapsed into the seat beside Jeff.

"You did *what*!?"

Jeff winced at my high-pitched scream. "Todd, relax. I can win it all back. I still got chips."

He only had two chips left, valued at a hundred units each. He had to win back three-thousand-three-hundred units to get his starting amount back. I imagined dreadful outcomes if he failed to recover it. Edgy would kill him. No, kill is too light. Edgy would do things to him that would make Jeff wish he were dead. I have seen it. He's done it to people for much less than losing his spaceship! As I sat there trying not to have a heart attack, the waiter returned with Jeff's drink. The beverage was green and carbonated with a sphere of ice and pieces of fruit peel.

"Um, waiter, i-is that strong?" I asked. The waiter, a small gray alien with an enormous head, nodded. "*Please* get me one as fast as you can!" I gave him a chip worth twenty units that Edgy had given me.

"Todd, calm down. The round ain't even started yet."

"E-Edgy is g-g-gonna *kill* you!" I said while trying and failing to not hyperventilate.

The dealer asked if everyone was ready. Jeff said he was, but I wasn't. I didn't understand the rules of this game, only that it involved dice. Everyone was rolling disastrously; then it was Jeff's turn. Jeff almost finished his drink in one gulp and stood up as he shook the dice.

"Bout to have a mean comeback!" He proclaimed.

My drink arrived right as he rolled the dice. Jeff then yelled.

"What's that mean!?" I exclaimed, almost spilling my drink.

The dealer handed Jeff all the chips people wagered. Now he had six hundred. He left only two chips after betting. The next round began, and everyone at the table flinched when the dealer rolled.

"Aw shit!" Jeff said.

"What?" I asked. "Is that bad?"

"Yeah, he rolled an *eleven*. Twelve's the max."

I did the probability in my head: less than three percent. Two-point-seven-eight percent. Everyone else at the table tried to beat that roll but couldn't. The closest they got was a ten.

I would've sweat bullets if I could. I couldn't keep the drink steady while I dreaded Jeff's turn. With how much was at stake, I hoped he somehow rolled that double six. Jeff finished his drink and then turned around, eyeing an attractive woman in a very nice red dress.

"Can you blow on these for luck? I need it right now."

He did. Blowing on the dice, the lady wished him good luck, laughed, and turned away. Jeff threw the dice. My heart skipped several beats. I thought I was gonna die as I watched them come to a stop. Seven.

"Goddammit!" Jeff said, now back to where we started.

As I tried to take another sip of my drink, I spilled some as I could not keep my flipper steady. Jeff gulped as people put their bets in. He looked at his two chips and then lit up another joint.

"Fuck it, go big or go home," he said as he slid his last two chips into the pile.

The dealer rolled this time. He rolled a nine. The next few people failed to roll higher. Jeff gestured to look under the table. I saw what he had typed on his phone.

IF I FUCK UP, WE RUN FOR THE SHIP.

I looked toward the nearest exit for a second. Hopefully, security wasn't nearby. The lady next to us, a tall creature in a white dress, rolled. She got a ten. I shivered. Jeff needed at least an eleven to win it all and the odds of rolling an eleven were five-point-five-six percent. Jeff took one last hit of his joint and rolled.

Time slowed while the dice flew. I watched with bated breath. If we won this round, that would cover half of the debt. Maybe Edgy could help cover the other half? That hope faded. Jeff rolled two ones.

He rolled a two!

Of all the things he could've rolled, he rolled that!

"Uh...bail!" Jeff screamed, bolting for the exit.

I followed his lead. We didn't get far. Men in silver suits and fedoras cut us off, and more caught up to us from behind. The leader showed the gold handgun in the holster of his suit jacket.

"Going somewhere?" He asked.

"Uh, just going to get your money," Jeff said, trying to diffuse this.

"Nice try. Either pay up or give us the ship."

Jeff scratched the back of his neck. "Can I make a phone call?"

We were so dead. Either the mob was gonna kill us, or Edgy was.

3. EDGY

Getting bits of bounty hunter brain out of my red hair proved way more frustrating than it should have been. My ultra-soaked hair felt like a thick blanket on my head as I stood in the shower. Despite setting the water to cold, it boiled by the time it reached me. I saw smoke billowing off the tile my flipper rested against. This was another reason for the vacation: my powers. Ever since they put that bounty on my head, it had been seeping out. Hell, I almost melted the controls for my damn ship. While getting supplies at a mall, I stubbed my toe and my powers leveled an entire aisle before I got it under control. As I continued to get chunks of brain matter out of my hair, I was still cussing out this entire situation. I cleaned up the mess and exited the shower. I didn't need a towel. Then I heard my phone ring. Sighing, I exited the bathroom and picked it up. In the thirty minutes I had been in the shower, Jeff had blown up my phone over twenty fucking times. My gut told me Jeff was in some shit. Deep shit. I tried to get my powers under control so I didn't melt the phone.

After a few seconds, I answered. "Jeff, what the *hell* is going on?"

"Uh, you need to come to the collections office now."

I squeezed the phone so hard I thought I was going to break it. "*What* the *fuck* did you do!?"

An awkward hush descended. Then I heard someone taking the phone. "Edgy! Jeff owes the casino money! They're holding us in the collections office, saying we gotta pay!" Todd blurted out.

I put a hole in the wall beside me. "You've gotta be *fucking* kidding me!" Todd dropped the phone in surprise. "Sit tight!"

I'm supposed to be on vacation right now.

Getting dressed, I grabbed my long red jacket and handgun. I eyed a bottle of booze on the nightstand and drank from it before I left. Automated shuttles transported me from the resort to the casino.

...

The collection office was far above the higher stakes area of the casino and overlooked everything. I had to weave through crowds to reach the elevator. Tall aliens with legs like stilts guarded a pair of silver doors. They were all in chromed, silver suits. The moment they saw me, they opened the doors and showed their weapons in case I tried something.

The thought of shooting my way in crossed my mind. But this station was swarming with mobsters and the handgun wouldn't cut it. I stepped into a large room full of people looking like they regretted their life choices sitting in line, in booths, or in cozy, lounge-like conference rooms. I was understanding the feeling. At least you could sit comfortably while they either took your shit or threatened to kill you if you didn't pay up.

I spotted Jeff and Todd in one room. They had goons standing behind them with their arms crossed and down in front of them like your typical bodyguards. The doorman allowed me in, and Todd rose.

"*Edgy*!"

Before he could say more, the guy behind him slammed him back into his seat. The green alien in the chair on the opposite end of the desk remained seated. He turned towards me in his rotating chair while puffing his cigar. In his other hand, he held a glass of bourbon on the rocks. The pudgy alien smirked and showed his piranha-like teeth.

"Ah yes, glad you could join us. Why don't you have a seat, son?"

One mobster pulled up another chair between Jeff and Todd.

Judging by the look he gave me, that wasn't a suggestion. I took the seat and glared at the piss-eyed creature in the large chair in front of me. He inhaled from his cigar and kept eye contact with me.

"Now your friend here ran up a debt of three-hundred-thousand-five-hundred units at one of our tables. He and twitchy over here tried making a break for it when they lost all the chips. Luckily for them, they came quietly, hate to get messy in front of the guest. Bad karma a few days before my daughter's wedding, ya know."

I felt like I had a jackhammer pounding inside my chest. Three-hundred-thousand-five-hundred units. How the fuck did Jeff run up that kind of debt!? Todd looked down at his feet. I then scowled at Jeff, and he was trying his hardest not to look at me. If looks could kill, he would've been a pile of ground meat.

"Jeff, how in the *absolute* fuck did you do that!?"

"I uh…" he scratched the back of his neck.

"Jeff, answer the *goddamn* question."

Jeff exhaled and looked at me. "I put the ship up as collateral."

I blacked out the second those words left his beak. One minute I was sitting. The next minute I had golden handguns in my face, and Jeff was on the ground with a bloody beak.

"Don't get blood on the carpets!" The collection agent shouted.

"You son of a bitch!" I growled, hoisting Jeff by his shirt collar. "I am going to *fucking* kill you!"

"If we *don't* pay them, they'll kill us bro!" Jeff said.

"No, *I'm* gonna kill you first!" I promised.

"Son, please let go of blondie and sit your ass down." The collection agent said, his voice having a slight growl to it.

I saw one of his goons cocking the hammer on his gun and noticed Jeff's collar was blackening. Exhaling, I released him and then sat down and turned to the fat fuck in front of me.

"Look, that ship is mine, not his."

"Tough shit, you pay us, or we take your ship or your lives. Simple as that."

So that's how it was going to be. "What if I save you the trouble and break Jeff's legs? Can we call it even then?"

The man chuckled and sipped his bourbon. "Well, I guess we got a joker here."

"Oh, he's serious," Todd said, knowing full well Jeff was a dead man either way.

"Yeah, but we need the money, so pay up or else."

Damn. No way in hell I would have the money for that. With the gun I had, a shoot out was not an option. The other option became increasingly tempting with every passing second. It slipped out just a second ago, I doubted they would've had enough firepower to stop me. They would be unable to respond in time.

Only one problem with that.

Jeff and Todd. The initial blast would melt or burn anything near me, including them. If it killed Jeff, it wouldn't be a total loss, but with Todd, no way. I was out of ideas. I had no cash and wouldn't give up my ship.

"How about I sell you some guns to cover this ass wipe's debt?"

The debt collector shook his head. "No dice, the Don doesn't want us accepting guns to settle debts anymore. Need something more valuable."

I glared at Jeff. "You just *had* to fuck up our vacation, didn't you?"

Jeff grimaced and looked down. "Sorry, bro."

"So, what's it gonna be?"

Another thought entered my head. "I might have a way to get your money. Let me make a phone call."

He gave me a nod, and I drew my phone and called Hylus.

"Have you come to your senses and changed your mind?" He grumbled.

"Sort of. Jeff's dumb ass ran up three-hundred-K in gambling debt and put my ship up for collateral. The mob wants their damn money, or else they're gonna take my ship."

"Say that again. It sounded like you said Jeff amassed *three-*

hundred-thousand units in gambling debt and put the *Vermillion* up as collateral." He replied after several seconds of silence.

"Yeah, three-hundred-thousand-and-five-hundred units to be exact. If I don't pay, they'll take my ship."

"You mean *my* ship?" Hylus replied.

"Hylus, don't start. I'm already in a bad mood. If I take this job, can you cover this debt?"

I heard Hylus saying something in a language I didn't know. The translator implant I had didn't understand it either. I needed to update the damn thing.

"*Fine*, are you with the gangsters right now?" Hylus growled.

"Yup."

"Put me on speakerphone."

I put it on the table in front of the debt collector. Hylus told him he would wire half the money now but would give the other half once I finished the job on this station. The mobster finished his cigar and his bourbon before considering the deal. He then added an extra rule, they were going to keep Jeff, Todd, and the ship under their control until Hylus wired the rest of the money. I could get weapons from it, but under their supervision. We agreed to that, and he handed me back the phone. Hylus asked me to take him off speaker.

"You owe me big time for this Edgy."

"Yeah, I know," I grumbled.

After that I hung up and faced the mobsters.

"No funny business, or my employees will beat you all so bad, death will look like a five-star massage parlor by comparison. We clear?"

I stood up and stared at him. "Don't get any funny ideas either."

I risked letting out some of my anger. A small wave of heat flowed from my flippers and onto the desk, causing part of it to burn and darken. The mobster pulled back. I saw my reflection in the mirror behind him. My eyes glowed a fiery orange. Taking a deep breath, I let go and headed for the exit.

"Stay here," I told Jeff and Todd.

4. EDGY

I inspected the black ether reaper gun I brought for this snatch-and-grab. I pressed the switch on the side of the large jet-black gun made of crystal. Black ether's name is derived from its complete absorption of light. I checked the pulsing core of black ether in its plasma state. Unlike the solid version, it gave off a faint and haunting red and purple light.

I smirked as I closed the protective housing and focused on my allies. The Shard team I assisted had seven members, each wearing black and red armor. Their gear looked like knight armor but futuristic. It hid their faces from me; I could only see their eyes. The squad leader had a large crest and a red stripe on top of his helmet. We gathered at the base of a silver tower with a bulbous top. It looked like a giant needle. The garden boasted well-maintained hedges and an impressive fountain plaza.

"So he's holed up in there?" I asked as I gazed up at the tower.

The squad leader nodded. "He's in the top-floor penthouse. Odds are he's hired security, so expect heavy resistance."

I smirked. "Figures, let's get this over with."

"We'll have to deal with the guard station first. Archer, you're up."

Archer raised a large rifle with an intricate holographic targeting system. He braced the rifle on top of one arm, and after a few seconds, he squeezed the trigger. A bolt of bright orange crackling energy sailed across the street and slammed into the unsuspecting guy in the box-shaped tower. The bolt melted the top of his head and left a spiraling hole. Before the other guard could raise an alert, Archer sent a blast through his ear canal. We crossed the street, and another squad member, named Switch, moved to hack the gate.

"Penguin, you're taking point," Novark, the squad leader, ordered.

That put a big smile on my face. "Hell yeah!"

I braced myself for a gunshot when we arrived at the plaza, yet nothing happened. That changed when I entered the lobby. All the staff members pulled out guns the moment they saw me. I unleashed the black ether reaper. The core spat out energized black crystal shards from the barrel and impenetrable black smoke billowed from the sides of the gun as it fired like a machine gun.

When the crystals dug into objects, the black ether went to work. The purple and red flash from the heart of the crystals signaled their activation. A black cloud spread out from them like an ant swarm. Whatever the darkness touched, they erased on the atomic level, leaving nothing left. I see why this thing earned the number two rank on the *Top Ten Evilest Guns* list in *Ordinance Overkill* magazine.

One survivor I missed rose to shoot me. He didn't get the chance. A loud booming sound accompanied a cone-shaped shockwave, then the man catapulted through the shattered window and into the office behind it. A squad member to my left held a pistol-like gun with a conical barrel. The second survivor tried to blind fire over the counter. He aimed for me, and two shots struck the shield. It flashed blue as it deflected each hit. I climbed onto the desk, stood over him, and struck him in the face.

I felt my power release as he caught flame the second I touched him. His body blackened and all that remained was a smoldering husk. As I looked at my reflection in a broken mirror, I saw my right eye glowing a fiery orange red from beneath my hair. I looked away and attempted to relax. The lobby had been decimated; huge chunks of it had been consumed, as if something had gnawed it away.

I heard the weird handgun fire again, and it sent a guy in

armor crashing through a wall. I figured out what it was: a kinetic launcher. Typically they're meant to knock you on your ass, not rearrange your internal organs. The squad member swept the hall, and everyone else entered the ruined lobby.

"What the *hell* is that gun!?" Novark asked, pointing to my weapon.

"A black ether reaper," I said while raising the gun.

"You brought *that* for this mission!?" One of the other squad members asked while watching the activated ether, still deleting parts of the walls, floor, and the reception desk.

"Yeah."

"Ever heard of the concept of overkill?"

I shrugged. "I'm supposed to be on vacation right now."

We entered the staff's office and found an intact penthouse key. While they did that, I wondered how this dude hired the hotel staff to protect him or if that was part of buying a penthouse suite. After all, this was a mafia station, so I'm sure you could pay them to protect you.

I didn't dwell on it. Getting this debt off my back was the only priority. At first, someone suggested taking the stairs, but then we realized how many fucking floors we'd have to climb. So yeah, taking the stairs was not an option. We all piled into the elevator and used the key to access the floor. The elevator music was unbearable, but I couldn't turn it off. I drew my pistol, aimed for the speakers, and shot it up. The rest of the squad jumped with surprise.

"What?"

They shrugged as I tucked the gun into the holster in my jacket. When the doors opened, two goons in silver suits greeted us. They didn't have time to draw their weapons. I took the one on the left and someone else took out the other with a machine gun. As I watched the black ether devour my target, I noticed the mobster suit. Novark blew open the doors with a grenade and ordered us to follow. The penthouse was colossal: a massive spherical chamber with an upper level filled with thugs firing at us.

I used my gun to get them to stop. My shooting hit at least two of the six. I just needed time to make it to cover. The column I hid behind started exploding as bullets, arcs of electricity, and plasma ripped through it. I spotted our target running into a room deeper in the penthouse as more gangsters entered the chamber from a set of gold double doors. As if I didn't have enough shit on my plate. I ducked, poked the gun around the corner, and let it rip into the newcomers. They too were mafia guys.

They returned fire, and I had to run for it as their attacks broke through the column. Without the shield, their attacks would have shredded me. Despite the dust and smoke, I attempted to shoot back. When I made it to a column, someone shouted about firing a grenade. I watched as the grenade primed in midair. Light erupted from it. I knew what this was.

The warp grenade sucked in everything nearby, including four mobsters. When the spinning disk of light finished, it closed with a flash, leaving some smoke and steam behind. That gave us all some breathing room. I focused on the guys above us and deleted their cover. We all directed our fire at them, and after another grenade, all was still. I looked around the demolished room: the cleaning staff was gonna have a meltdown over this shit.

Everything had been shot up or destroyed; nothing was spared.

Novark kicked the golden doors open, and we found our guy and two other mobsters. They didn't stand a chance and died in less than ten seconds. Our target aimed a revolver at us. When he saw how much firepower we were packing, he shat bricks, dropped the gun, and raised his hands. He was a short, scrawny alien with a head of jet-black hair. He wore a silver suit like the mobsters, but he had gold trim and gold sevens on his cuffs.

"W-who are you, and whaddaya want!?" He demanded.

Switch cuffed the guy, pinned him against the desk, and searched him. We found the chip with the intel. It had the thickness of a playing card, and the front of it was a screen that allowed us to see its contents. As Switch confirmed it, Novark pulled out a scanner and checked him.

"Aw shit," he grumbled.

"What!?" I asked.

"This guy is Volus, one of Don Nelvo's nephews!" Novark growled.

"Aw shit" was a fucking understatement. When the rest of the station found out, we would be up to our necks in mobsters. Our target laughed.

"That's right, you're *fucked*!" He taunted. "When my uncle finds out, he's gonna whack all yah!"

"Switch, shut him up," Novark ordered. He then took a small device and activated it.

Hylus' helmeted face appeared as a hologram. "Yes, what is it?"

"My lord, we have the subject, but there's a problem. He's the mob boss' nephew."

Hylus' face remained hidden, only his yellow eyes darting around. "Understood. Get him to the extraction point, make haste!"

Novark nodded and ended the call. "You heard Lord Hylus! Move!"

We didn't get that far. The moment we exited the office, a large force of mobsters greeted us. They had a small army's worth of guns trained on us. Novark approached the target, took out his sidearm, and placed it against the back of his head.

"Put down your weapons!" He growled, pressing the gun against Volus' head.

They weren't dropping their weapons. I guess they thought we were bluffing.

"Hey, do what he says! Don't be stupid!" Volus shouted. More mobsters poured in from the levels above us. They had us surrounded. Volus smirked and laughed. "Oh, never mind, drop your guns, and maybe my uncle will go easy on you."

I hated to admit it, but he was right. We were too exposed out here. I checked the readings of the black ether core. It had enough juice to make one hundred more crystals. We heard gunfire, but it was not from us. Then the roof and walls exploded and several mobsters got turned into pulp from the falling ceiling. We all ducked and got to cover as the smoke and dust cleared. Then I saw blue-targeting lasers sweeping the room. More people had arrived.

"Everyone! Hands in the air and surrender! This is Captain Zelvra Reza of Union! We outgun and outnumber you!" A nasally voice demanded. His helmet's speakers amplified his voice.

This went from sixty to two-hundred real fucking quick. They weren't kidding about having us surrounded; Union had guys on the second level and others descending from the rooftop with jetpacks. They wore Union's faction colors: silver, blue, and black. Each one carried body shields and had some top-of-the-line weapons, all energy-based.

Their commander hovered above. He was shorter than expected, about toddler-sized. I guess that's why he had a pair of thin skeletal stilts. He was so thin I doubt you'd need an x-ray to see his skeleton. He aimed a large pulse rifle at us while the rest of his squad pointed at the mafia guys.

"Final warning, and it's more than you deserve. Drop your weapons and bring us Volus!"

He looked so fucking smug. I wanted to pull him down by his horns. The mobsters weren't backing off either. This was a goddamn Mexican standoff.

"Buzz off, pig!" one gangster shouted.

Novark tightened his grip on Volus and looked around. An exit was nowhere to be seen. Blasting through them was the only way we could go back, but I wasn't confident. The rest of the group exchanged nervous looks. The gangsters were doing the same.

Then all hell broke loose.

Chaos ensued. Don't know who shot first, but a second later, we were all shooting. Bullets, lasers, and energy weapons fired this way and that, fucking up the room further. I aimed at Reza but he flew higher in the air and out of my sight. I watched as blue plasma crashed into several mobsters, killing them on impact. The gangsters hit back with a hail of bullets, and several jetpack guys fell out of the sky and hit the ground. I returned fire, hitting people on both sides without giving a damn. My cover eroded as this three-way shootout continued.

"We need to get out of here, captain!" The squad member with a machine gun shouted while dropping a Union soldier's body shield.

"I *know*! Switch, any ideas!?"

If Switch answered, I couldn't hear him over all the noise. I didn't know who had the advantage as it was all over the damn place. My shield took several hits and went yellow. It wouldn't withstand much more of this shit.

"I got it, boss! Fall back to the office!" Switch shouted.

"Torval! Give us cover!" Novark shouted.

Torval, the machine gun guy, nodded and unloaded at the upper floor. I fired at everything on our level. Doubt I was hitting anything, but it gave Novark and the others cover. I realized what we were doing when an explosion occurred behind us. We were going to jump from high up.

"Come on!" Novark ordered.

Torval got hit in the face with plasma. His head and neck were gone.

"Are you *fucking* kidding me!?" I roared.

I grabbed his machine gun and fired both weapons from the hip as Union goons gave chase. Two endless streams of gunfire ripped them to pieces. Those hit with the machine gun turned to mush as I backed into the office space.

"I am on *fucking* vacation!" Both guns ran dry.

Dropping Torval's gun, I ran for it. By the time I caught up, the rest of the team had already jumped out the window. Plasma rounds rushed past me, and several shots came close to frying me. I swore as I jumped out of the building. Yeah, that was a big ass drop. Even with the large lake below, this fall was gonna hurt like hell. When I hit the water, I felt like I had crashed through a brick wall at two-hundred miles an hour. My whole body stung.

The water around me heated up, and I felt steam coming off my body.

No time to worry about that now. The moment I breached the surface, I was under fire again. I turned around and drew my pistol, and started shooting. More Union goons with jetpacks pursued us from the rooftop. My pistol was pointless at that distance. I spun and ran like hell. Blue plasma globs collided with the ground and ate away at the concrete, making up the lake's edge. Switch started hacking a cab for us as I ran to join the rest.

"I need a moment!" He shouted.

Lack of cover was a big problem here. They dropped one of our guys as his body shield wasn't strong enough to block out the plasma. I clipped one's jetpack and sent the guy crashing into the street headfirst. I smirked about it, but something wiped that off my face.

The car beeped.

"It's good!" Switch shouted as the doors opened.

A flash of blue blinded me. Then I heard a sickening gurgling sound and smelled burning flesh. That's when I noticed Volus had a hole punched through his chest. He collapsed on his knees, eyes wide with shock. I looked behind us. Reza floated above, and he switched his aim to us.

"In the car!" Novark ordered, emptying his magazine at Reza.

When we all got inside, Switch had the robot floor it. One of the squad members swore in a language my translator implant also didn't know.

"We still have the intel! Switch, get us to the hangar. We're getting out of here!" Novark shouted.

"Copy that, boss!"

5. TODD

The mob had us sitting in a larger more luxurious lounge area with comfortable leather chairs. The lounge had a row of vending machines, pool tables, and holographic screens showing everything in the casino. Right now, it flashed an alert. Something was going on. Jeff looked up from the table he sat near and looked at the screen. We shared a questioning glance. We both wanted to find out what was going on. I knew Edgy had something to do with it. Jeff shrugged and returned to sipping his soda and chips. Mobsters in the room suddenly stopped talking and touched their ears. I started shaking as I watched them turning towards us. I nudged Jeff, but he ignored me. Then I elbowed him.

"*What!?*"

"*J-Jeff!*" I whispered as they all started approaching us.

"Bruh, what…oh," Jeff said.

"What do we do?"

Jeff winced, and the look in his eyes told me he didn't know. One mobster stepped forward, and I watched him reaching into his suit jacket. Not knowing what else to do, I raised my flippers and backed up. Jeff did the same as the leader trained his gun on us.

"Can we talk this out, bro?" Jeff asked.

The five gangsters laughed. "Get a load of this guy!" The one aiming at us said, lowering the gun for a second.

"W-why are you pointing guns at us?" I asked, noticing the others were getting ready to shoot too.

"Because ya buddy *kidnapped* the don's nephew, that's why!"

The leader answered.

"Ah shit," Jeff said.

We were dead. The ground shook, and everyone fell. The lights started flickering above us too. It only lasted a few seconds, then paused, and all the lights turned red.

"Hey, Paulie, what the *hell* is going on!?" One mobster asked.

"Warning the station has come under attack by hostile ships. Please remain calm and report to the nearest shelter. This is not a drill. Please remain calm and report to the nearest shelter." A female AI voice spoke. Her accent wouldn't feel out of place on a femme fatale in a noir film.

"Who the hell's crazy enough to attack this station!?" One of the other gangsters asked.

"Dunno," the leader stood up and looked at us. Then I saw him eyeing his gun on the floor.

His next move became clear to me. Running at him, I tried to get the pistol before he did. I grabbed the front of the gun, but he grabbed the other end. We both wrestled for control of it and I pulled as hard as I could.

The gun went off.

I froze. I wasn't dead. The bullet missed me and hit Jeff's soda. He tried to shoot again, but I ducked while still holding onto it. This time his shot went through my beanie. Then I felt a boot to my stomach. My glasses flew off my face as I hit the ground.

I looked up and saw the gun reflecting the red light around us. I was as good as dead. Then something hit the gangster from behind. He stumbled forward in a daze. I couldn't identify his opponent in the darkness, without my glasses. Crawling towards them, I put the glasses on. Jeff used a pool stick to strike the guy's stomach. Two mobsters approached him from behind.

"Jeff behind you!" I shouted.

Jeff spun around. He swung at one of them, but the gangster caught it. He yanked Jeff forward and socked him in the beak, knocking him to the ground. I got tackled. Suddenly, I hit my head on the counter. He had his hands around my neck. I couldn't breathe and my lungs burned.

Not knowing what else to do, I kicked at his stomach and ribs, making him choke me harder. He kept pushing me down; I couldn't overpower him. As I kept kicking, I felt my clawed feet cutting into his suit.

"You *little* shit!" He growled, lifting me up some before slamming me down again.

I started seeing stars. Everything spun. I felt myself falling over the side of the counter and hitting the vending machine nearby. I exhaled, and my lungs burned. The mobster vaulted over the counter and pulled a knife!

I swung at him, but he dodged me and slashed, cutting my shirt. This was a limited edition Metal Dragon Black shirt. I paid good money for it! Well, Edgy paid good money for it, but still! He slashed again, and I fell to the ground as the knife cut the vending machine. I felt my flipper hit something near me. I grabbed it, stood up, and swung.

The bottle broke against his head. The man appeared drunk, stumbling and wobbling. This was my chance. I hit him as hard as I could with my flipper. Which wasn't very hard, and he didn't flinch. He made another advance, but something changed. He flew forward and collided with a vending machine face-first. I realized he had tripped on a soda can a few inches before me.

Then I heard Jeff screaming behind me. One mobster had their arms locked under Jeff's while another punched him in the stomach repeatedly. I grabbed another pool stick and cracked one of them over the head with it.

"You scrawny bastard!" The guy screamed as he stumbled back.

White blood seeped from a wound to his head. He tried to rush me. I used the stick like a spear and hit him in the gut, knocking the air out of his lungs and making him keel over.

"On your left bro!" Jeff shouted.

"What!?"

I turned. I hit the guy in the head and knocked him away. Jeff then threw his head forward and then back, breaking the gangster's nose and freeing himself.

"Yeah son! About to beat dat ass!" Jeff taunted while spinning around.

He hit the guy with his flipper and drew blood. I heard someone getting up near me. The two guys I just hit looked at me with murderous intent. I froze.

Jeff yelled, then one gangster tackled him while the other approached. The two guys coming towards me advanced from different angles. I swung at one but he ducked. The other moved in. Pain exploded across my face and I tasted blood. The hit sent me stumbling, and I dropped the pool stick.

I got up and ran, putting a table between them and me. I pushed the table as hard as possible, hitting one guy in the chest and making him stumble. The other guy punched me before I could react.

A wall behind him exploded. The blast knocked me against the wall. My glasses fell off, and I couldn't see anything. I heard the hiss of an energy weapon and gunshots. The room became a flickering light show that could trigger epilepsy. I tried to crawl to where I thought my glasses were.

"*Todd! Todd!*" I heard Jeff shouting over the shooting.

I felt someone bump into me, and then someone tapped my shoulder. Jeff had my glasses. I slipped them on, but I noticed a chip in the lens. I glanced around and saw more mobsters clashing with guys in black, silver, and blue uniforms: Union soldiers. This was not good!

"Let's go Todd!" Jeff said, yanking me away.

I followed him out of the room. We rushed into the collection office and found chaos.

"W-we gotta get to the ship!" I squawked as a Union guy crashed into the wall next to us.

"Yeah bro, we bailing! Call Edgy!"

I tried, but I wasn't getting a signal.

6. EDGY

Well, this has all gone to shit. Switch told us that Union surrounded the entire station and were invading. They caught us in a turf war, with both sides wanting us dead. Getting out of here would not be easy. This place turned into a warzone. Tourists and vacationers were running for their lives while mobsters and Union shot at each other. Stray rockets spiraled out of control and crashed into the streets and nearby buildings. As the chaos unfolded, one thought kept entering my mind.

I'm supposed to be on fucking vacation right now.

"So what is the goddamn plan!?" I said, not hiding my anger at all.

Novark put his hand under his chin and looked around. He then turned on his communicator and tried to dial Hylus. The call never went through.

"Well, that's just great," I growled.

"They must have a ship equipped with a jamming device," Switch said.

"Oh that's just *fucking* great!" The rest of the squad looked at me and were dead silent.

"What!?" I asked.

That's when I noticed the surrounding leather was smoking. I tried to get my power under control. That was easier said than done. Best I could do was keep it from starting a fire.

"His ship is a Gentoo replica. It's designed for high-speed combat," Switch began, trying to figure out what just happened.

I knew where this was going, and I did not like it.

"If we get you to your ship first, can you cover our's out of the station until we can enter subspace?"

I sighed. "Yeah, but I've got two friends on this station I've got to get first. They should be in the collection office."

"What hangar are you in?"

"Hangar D."

"Alright, Switch, get us to Hangar D, then get us to our ship."

So, that was the plan. With no knowledge of Union's armada, we had no choice. By the sounds of it, their ship would not cut it if Union attacked them. I pulled out my phone and tried to call Jeff and Todd, but I couldn't reach them either. I guess the jammer blocked everything.

"Damn, even local calls aren't working."

"They want to prevent the mob from coordinating a counterattack on the ground or in space." Switch answered.

I closed my eyes for a second. A lot can happen in a second. The car spun out of control, and I felt the engine stop. While we continued to spin, we crashed into a liquor store, spilling gallons of merchandise everywhere. I did not have a seatbelt, so I slammed into the door and knocked it off the hinges. I felt a sharp pain in my arm, despite the door absorbing most of the blow.

Sparks of electricity and smoke danced off the car. I groaned and sat up while everyone crawled out of the vehicle. It was just one of those days. I grabbed one of the metal beer bottles, popped the lid, and chugged it.

"Is everyone alright?" Novark asked.

The squad sounded off. Then we all noticed what struck the engine. Several large black knives with violet energy coiling around them. We all drew our weapons and got to cover, expecting someone to attack us. Nothing. Only silence. I lowered my gun and grabbed my beer.

"Guess we're hoofing it," Switch spoke.

I heard a muffled scream from nearby.

"Where's Seren!?" One of the other guys shouted.

Something flew by his throat, and then a geyser of blood covered everything, and he collapsed on the floor.

"Holy shit!" Someone else shouted.

I heard footsteps, and I spun around. I caught a flash of movement and fired two shots, missing both.

"Someone's here with u-!"

I heard a groan followed by spilled guts. Before I could comprehend, someone vaulted over the shelf. They flexed their hands, and six blades appeared. The woman tossed them at Novark, Switch, and me. We all ducked. These throwing daggers were enhanced with magic. They cut through objects like they weren't there, and I felt one pass through my coat as I dived.

Standing, I opened fire. The woman chucked a bladed fan at me but I sidestepped it and watched it impale a handle of brown booze before vanishing. I had a clear view of the woman. Pinkish red skin, long violet hair tied back in a bun with two sharp hairpins. She wore a black dress with split sides, exposing her long legs. Novark and I unloaded on her, but she backflipped behind an aisle full of expensive wine. I emptied my magazine into it, hoping I'd hit her.

"Oh shit, that's *Lethil*!" Switch said as he stepped out of cover.

"Who?" I asked.

"Lethil, she's a member of the Unseen Knife, a group of assassins for hire!"

Novark and I circled her hiding spot from different sides.

"Your friend is pretty knowledgeable," a cold, flat female voice spoke.

The other side of the aisle was empty. I checked the ceiling, but she wasn't hiding up there. We heard a gunshot and ran around the side. I found her and Switch. She had a blade buried in his neck and held him by the back of his head. His blood coated her black dress, leggings, and gloves.

"Sorry, he has something in his throat," she smiled.

She then looked at me with her red cat-like eyes, showing her teeth. I recognized her: the bombshell from the beach! I raised my gun and opened fire. Lethil used Switch's dying body as a meat shield and put him in the path of my shots. She then kicked Switch towards me. I moved to the left to avoid him, but she vanished in that split second.

I noticed something on the floor next to Switch, a maintenance hatch. Novark ran up to me and we stood back to back. I prodded him and gestured to the hatch. He nodded. Then something landed in the street. Reza.

"Ah, there you are. Looks like Lethil has already earned her pay." His stilts activated, promoting him to an average human height. "Whaddaya say handing over that chip? *My* superior planning and intellect have obviously beaten you."

"Oh, shut the *fuck* up shorty!" I shouted, unable to keep my gun steady because of my anger.

"How *dare* you!" Reza growled.

Lethil walked out of the shadows. This was not good. Reza was behind me, and Lethil was in front of me. Lethil unsheathed a single blade, followed by a purple flash, and then multiple blades materialized between each finger. She seemed eager to kill us both, but Reza gave us a choice.

Novark nudged me, and I looked over my shoulder and saw him placing the chip in my pocket.

"Get out of here."

As he spun and opened fire, I ducked and pulled the hatch open with the manual release. Novark drew a grenade and prepared to toss it, but blades and plasma fire tore him apart as he armed it and dropped it in front of me. I dived into the tunnel. As I fell down the ladder, I felt the heat from the energy discharge. The tunnel muffled the sound but not the force of it as the entire shaft rocked.

Even as the grenade's heat faded, the metal vent felt warm. I realized that was because of me. The red aura billowed off me like smoke, and I was fighting a losing battle to keep it at bay. Now everyone was dead, and I had a killer assassin, Union, and the damn mob gunning for me.

Just great.

Just *fucking* great.

7. JEFF

We ran like hell. This station went from a nice ass vacation spot to a full-on battlefield! Somebody was going ham with a rocket launcher and blew up a restaurant above us. I think I had some glass stuck in me after that. Calling Edgy over the phone didn't work. I spun around after hearing Todd yell and saw him being knocked around by panicked people. Can't say I blame them, especially when a stray rocket hit a blackjack table and sent people flying.

I ran back and helped Todd up.

"We're almost there man!"

"W-w-what about Edgy!?"

Before I could answer him, a Union soldier coming up behind Todd had his head explode from a rogue shot. The blood hit both of us. Some of it got into my beak, disgusting.

"Todd, we gotta bounce man!" I shouted.

He nodded to me and looked at that guy's fucked up head. We were halfway out of the casino area. Another group of Union guys with big ass guns started opening fire on a bunch of mobsters using the slot machines as cover on the other side.

"Hit the deck!" Todd screamed, dropping to the floor.

I followed his lead and felt a ball of plasma sail over my head. It singed my hair. We crawled for it as lasers, plasma, rockets, and bullets flew overhead. I didn't know who was winning and didn't wanna know. We made a break for it when we reached the other end of the room.

Somehow the hangar area was even crazier. Numerous ships tried to get the hell out of there. Some hit each other while trying to leave the exit gates. When we got there, we watched two pod-shaped ships collide and explode. My eyes couldn't handle the blue explosion.

"Ah shit!" I said.

The hangar we were in, Hangar D, had multiple levels. Our ship was on a lower one. People fought over the staircase and elevators. When I say fight, I don't mean arguing or shoving, although that happened. I mean gunfights, fist fights, knife fights, you name it. Hell, I watched a dainty-looking lady suplex another chick, so we weren't getting through that shit. Todd and I had no weapons on us. Then I saw Todd running for a wall.

"What are you doing!?"

"Maintenance hatch!" He said, breathing like he had just ran a marathon.

I watched him type something onto a panel in the wall, and then it opened. After hearing more gunshots, I followed Todd without hesitation. The shaft had a long ass ladder leading to each level. The entire station shook several times as we made our way down.

"I hope Edgy's nearby!" Todd said.

"Knowing him, he's already there and mad as hell."

I didn't know it at the time, but I was right about both. It took us a while to reach our ship, but when we opened the doors, we had a problem. Glowing explosives lined the thruster arms, and a horde of mobsters swarmed the ship.

We both froze, staying in the shaft.

"W-w-what now?" Todd whispered.

These mobsters had rifles, not handguns, and they covered the ship from every angle. We had no chance of sneaking past them, and we couldn't risk shooting our way in without Edgy.

"Uh..." I said, trying to think of something.

Thinking isn't my thing. That's Todd's job. Todd looked around for an escape plan. He didn't have any ideas either and winced and shrugged. He tried ringing Edgy, but that failed again.

The room trembled; gunfire flashed from the corridor.

Something went flying toward the mobsters. Then someone entered the room. It was Edgy! He looked like he had been through some shit. Blood caked his clothes, and I saw cuts everywhere. The mobsters pointed their guns at him, and I recognized the leader.

The same guy in charge of collecting our debt.

"Well-well, figured you'd show up," he said, lighting a cigar.

Then he drew something else and pulled the trigger. With a bright ass flash, the bombs went off. The entire hangar rocked, as the explosions demolished the ship. Todd and I had to pull back as bits of it flew at us. As I poked my head out of the hole, I saw the damage. Orange and blue fire swallowed the red and black ship. I doubt it could fly now, not without some serious repairs. Especially as one arm came undone and broke off the main body. Despite all of that, Edgy didn't move a muscle.

"I'll be needing that data chip. You know, the one from Don Nelvos' nephew, the one *your* guys killed?"

I guess that explains why they tried to kill us. I couldn't see Edgy's face. His red hair and the shadows hid it.

"You got some *serious* balls to kill a mob boss' nephew on this own station. Now give me the chip, and we'll go easy on you and your pals. That's a promise from old Suul. It'll be a quick death. Two led pills to the head."

I think Edgy said something, but I couldn't hear him.

"What did you say, son?"

Edgy dropped his gun. Then pulled out a small card. Suul smirked.

"Giving up, are you? Hand over the chip!"

Suul's tune changed when he heard a growl from Edgy. I felt it from across the room. The place was heating up. The surrounding air rippled. Edgy was surrounded by a red-orange aura, and his coat and hair billowed as if caught in a wind.

Edgy looked up. His eyes glowed red. He was shaking, and the veins in his face pushed against the skin like he was about to pop an artery, or several. He was beyond pissed. I thought I knew what was coming next.

"Waste him!" Suul screamed.

Their bullets didn't touch him.

Whenever Edgy gets really fucking mad, things explode, melt, or burn. This would not end well for anyone. Edgy let out a giant red pulse and the entire station shook as the blast went off. Everything it touched exploded. The attack vaporized Suul and his people. My eyes stung from the brightness of it. Todd grabbed and pulled me back inside as the wave almost fried me.

I think he tried to say something, but I couldn't hear it over everything blowing up. Then the shaft exploded, and Todd and I went flying. I must've hit something because everything went black.

8. TODD

I woke up on a metal beam overlooking a dark pit. Large wires dangled from the ceiling above, electricity crackling off them. The cracks in the left lens of my glasses made it hard to see. Screaming and shooting sounded from nearby, but I also heard screeching machinery. I yelled when I realized how high up I was and almost fell over the side as my arms and legs wobbled. I couldn't breathe, shutting my eyes, I tried my best to slow my breathing. Distracting myself with a math puzzle I was trying to solve the day before, I felt my breathing slow. Please don't judge me. It helps me calm down sometimes.

I'm not good with heights. As I opened my eyes, I noticed something on the beam in front of me, a small data chip. The object was charred and ruined. I grabbed it and touched the screen. It ran diagnostics on the drive inside and a repair program to restore the data. A few seconds later it dinged and told me it recovered the files.

I stuffed it into my pocket. I felt Edgy would thank me if we ever made it out of here. The structure jolted. I looked up. I was in an elevator shaft! I noticed the elevator suspended high above me as the lights flickered. The station rocked again, and the elevator shook and lowered. Sparks erupted from the brakes and showered the bar I was on. Then I heard something else. Water. I peered over the side and saw water flooding the shaft. I surmised it came from the artificial beach.

"Todd!?" I heard someone call.

I looked behind me and saw Jeff lying on a beam above me. He had blood in his hair and bruises on his face.

"W-what happened!?" I asked.

"Edgy must've lost his s-!"

The station shook again and I heard the elevator scream. I looked down. The rushing waters were gaining fast.

"We need to get out of here!" I shouted while searching for an escape route.

Jeff then pointed to a pair of opened doors leading to a hallway. The doors were on a level above me and the elevator brakes were ready to snap. I gulped and started pulling myself along the beam.

"Don't look down, bro!" Jeff said as he swung around a support pillar blocking his way.

I attempted to take his advice, but it proved difficult as I had an involuntary urge to look downwards. The water was getting closer. I would not make it by crawling. My arms trembled as I realized what I had to do. I took a deep breath and forced myself to stand. It took me a few seconds to take the first step forward. I screamed as I felt myself swaying too far to one side, but I didn't fall. The station shook and the elevator descended once more. I almost fell over the side. I flinched as sparks from the failing brakes scalded me.

"Hurry man!" Jeff screamed from above as he was closer to the doors than I was.

The incoming water almost drowned him out. The live wire slowed me down, but I still managed to cross as Jeff climbed down to the door. Unfortunately, the grips for the ladder on my level were all gone, and I couldn't jump up and reach it. The station rumbled again; I heard a loud metallic snap. One brake had given way.

I had little time.

I jumped and grabbed onto a wire and a protrusion from the wall and started pulling myself up. I used some machinery as footrests. Jeff made it to the doors first by the time I reached the ladder.

"Come on, come on!" Jeff said.

When I was close to the doors. The elevator brakes gave out, and it fell. I had a split second to move. Jumping for the doors, I thought I was going to be ripped in half. At the last possible second, Jeff grabbed and pulled me inside as the elevator came down, and we both hit the ground.

We relaxed for a second, until we remembered the flooding.

I got up and tried to close the elevator doors, but they weren't budging.

"Stairs!" Jeff shouted and ran for it.

I followed him as he kicked open the door, and we entered a staircase. As we climbed the steps, the water flooded the area below. I felt myself slowing down. We couldn't outrun it. As the water gained, we made it to the hallway on the next floor. I got ahead of Jeff and opened a door. An emergency bulkhead loomed down the hall!

I reached it first and prepared to shut it as soon as Jeff made it through. The second he did, I pressed the button. The doors began closing as I saw the water coming. I feared they would not close fast enough.

They did at the last second.

We ran for it, unsure how long it would hold as the door began to warp. Judging from the fancy carpets and trimmings for the walls, we must've been in one of the premium hotels. We rounded the corner and ran into a squad of four Union soldiers. They trained their laser guns on us. Jeff and I put our flippers up. One goon reported it, and the responder's comment made me want to scream.

"They have the chip. Kill them." Before they could fry us, the ceiling collapsed on them, making them look like crushed tomatoes.

"Well...that was lucky," Jeff said, lowering his arms. "*Why* do they think we have a chip?"

I winced and showed it. "Because I do."

"Oh nah!? You better put that shit down!"

I shook my head. "If the mobsters and Union want it and Edgy had it, then it's probably important to Hylus."

"Yeah, and they'll all be *gunning* for us," Jeff replied while crossing his arms.

I grimaced. "D-do you want to tell Edgy you dropped the thing he needs for a job?"

The color drained from Jeff's face as he understood what I meant. "Okay, what now?"

"Head for the ship. Maybe we can call Hylus?"

Jeff nodded, and we started moving. We checked the map assuming the pathways held up. We had to cross over a nearby lobby and several other areas to reach Hangar D. The path to the lobby was clear. I thought we were safe. Oh how I was so wrong.

When we got to the lobby, something ripped my beanie off my head. I looked at the wall behind me. A black blade with violet energy was stuck in the hat and pinning it against the wall.

"The data chip, hand it over." A low female voice boomed.

I saw a woman, tall and red-skinned, walking towards us with two fans. She walked with unnerving confidence. When blades sprouted from the fans, I understood why.

9. EDGY

Everything was a red blur as I demolished everything and anything that came near me. Holding back this power was not possible. I didn't want to hold back anymore. Surrounded by melting metal in a fractured corridor, I had no clue where I was. A still breathing Union soldier lay at my feet. He turned to ash the second I touched him.

I heard more of them surrounding and pointing their weapons at me. Some can't wait to die. Then I heard that fucking midget's laughter.

"You're cornered! Nothing you can do now! You've walked *right* into my trap!"

I heard one of his men trying to tell him something wasn't right. Looking at Reza's smirk only made my blood boil even more.

"I did not *ask* your opinion! I have factored *everything* into my plans!" He boasted, relying on his stilts to tower over everyone.

He didn't know who he was fucking with. It was time to show him.

"Now, open fire!" He proclaimed.

That smirk on his arrogant face faded as my power flayed his men. Let's get one thing clear, this wasn't a fight. This was a slaughter. I charged head-first into their barrage of plasma and energy. I didn't do anything as I got close to them: my pure hatred turned them to ash.

All this bullshit cost me my vacation, and I was going to make these shitheads pay! Reza shrieked as I charged into the surrounding group. I smashed a guy's face into the ground and crushed his head like a grape.

His men opened fire. It only increased my anger. I looked at them and let the hate flow. The resulting blast of crackling red vaporized them. The walls, floor, and ceiling exploded all around me. Reza escaped as the heat scorched his face and arm.

"*B-backup!* I need backup! *ASAP!*" He squealed like a fucking pig.

I was going to roast him like one in a second. He tried to use his rifle on me. I scared him shitless and he couldn't keep his gun steady. Sniveling little bitch. I struck him and felt his ribs snap as my flipper connected. The air flew from his lungs as he crashed through a glass window. I followed him.

My powers acted on their own and lashed out at anything nearby, causing things to explode or catch fire. I wasn't in control anymore. I could only guide it; like controlling a supercar without brakes, the accelerator always floored. And I didn't give a damn. It felt good letting it out and watching everything shatter into millions of pieces.

Reza crawled to his feet and rose on his stilts to try again with the rifle. The blue energy slammed into a wall of crimson. This power of mine did something I'd never seen it do before. It suspended the energy from Reza's shots and then absorbed it. I felt Reza's attacks fueling it.

Learn something new every day, I guess. I extended my flipper and watched all that extra juice detonate into a pillar of crackling red that vaporized whatever it touched. Reza dodged part of it, but it devoured his stilts. He fell flat on his face near me. The red energy lashed out as whips and tore into his back. Pink blood splattered on the ground around us. Reza howled in pain and tried to crawl away. I stomped towards him, too angry to speak.

I was going to savor beating the ever-living shit out of him.

Then I felt something hit me. I stumbled to the side as I felt the bullet pierce my side. I turned, my rage rising to new heights. More of these fucking mobsters. Reza used his jetpack to escape down the hall.

I focused on the mobsters and yelled. A pulse of destruction followed. I felt the entire station tremble again. Everything exploded like we were on a set for a summer blockbuster. More moved to stop me. More bodies to add to the pile.

10. JEFF

I stepped towards the lady with the fans. I saw a spinning blur and suddenly found myself on my knees, facing a scared and confused Todd. My face stung like crazy.

"W-what just happened?"

"She…kicked you."

"Roundhouse?"

Todd winced. "Y-yeah."

I looked back at her while she stood on one leg. Damn. She had some nice ass legs.

"The chip, hand it over."

I stood up. Man, I thought I was drunk. The world spun for a few seconds and I almost fell but Todd caught me. I shook my head and snapped out of it.

"Nah," I said.

The insane lady clicked her tongue on the roof of her mouth several times and shook her head. She reached us in less than a second. I tried to swing at her. She dodged, and I felt her knee slam into my back, almost knocking me over. Then I heard her fan open, and the blades extended.

I jumped back. She sliced my shirt and the skin beneath. The calm expression on her face scared me more than the blades. I couldn't catch my breath as she tossed the fan. Somehow I dodged it, but the fan returned like a boomerang from hell and I ducked as it almost took my head off. A thick pinkish-red thigh crashed into my face, which knocked me back, then a spinning kick to the chest sent me flying into a shop's table.

"You're either brave or stupid to challenge a member of the

Unseen Knife," she said. "Now, be smart and hand over the chip. Killing you would be no challenge and no fun."

My lungs started working again and I picked myself up, using the table to do it. Todd tried to strike her. She hit him with two kicks that were so fast it took me a second to realize she had hit him in the stomach and jaw.

She turned to me and pulled out a blade. I ducked as a knife flew over my head. Another somehow phased through the table and cut my arm. I screamed and grabbed my flipper. Goddamn! That shit hurt! I heard Todd yelp in pain and watched as she flipped him over her shoulder. She then hoisted her leg up to her chest. Crazy lady was about to give Todd the meanest axe kick.

I grabbed a random mug and tossed it at her. Somehow, I hit her in the head, and got her to stumble. Her face registered surprise for a moment before her red cat-like eyes narrowed and I caught a glimpse of her sharp teeth. Before I knew it, she flipped over the table I was hiding behind, and I felt her leather boot colliding with my face.

Everything was spinning. I ran for it and felt a knife slice the side of my leg, making me fall. I rolled over on my back. The crazy lady reached for her back and drew another knife. I was dead. Todd grabbed me and pulled as she threw the blade. It missed me by a hair. She threw another, aiming at Todd. He ducked.

She spun like a ballerina, pulled out more, and chucked them. Todd got me near a table as more knives almost hit me. One pinned my shorts to the ground, and I had to rip them.

"How many knives do you *have* woman!?"

My answer was a knife landing right in front of my crotch. Todd yanked me around the side of the table. We did not get a second to breathe. She chased us down and axe-kicked the table in half.

She was sick of our shit.

Her bladed fans returned to her, and she raised them to cut us to pieces.

Then the place shook. The lights above us flickered. Panels

started falling from the ceiling and walls around us. The crazy bitch in front of us fell to her knees as the station careened on its side.

"Oh, not this shit again!" I shouted as Todd, and I began sliding down the hall.

The woman pulled out a blade and stabbed it into the ground, stopping her fall. Grabbing her ankle, I tried to catch Todd, but he slid out of my reach, screaming at the top of his lungs. I looked up at the lady. She was not happy to have me hanging onto her leg. The station continued to tilt.

"Wanna call it quits for now?" I asked, trying to smile.

She kicked me in the face and sent me tumbling.

11. TODD

I groaned as I sat up. I landed on the reinforced glass, arm and face first. My body stung, and I felt bruises everywhere. I couldn't find my glasses. Everything appeared hazy, as if I were looking through a foggy window, unless it was near me. I found the source of the water by looking down. In his fit of rage, Edgy sent the entire station crashing into the ice world we were orbiting!

I looked down at a large canyon that made me shake. I didn't want to know how high I was. I was very close to finding out. The panels cracked and fractures formed on the other side of the large window. Enormous machines and furniture pressed against part of the glass. Squinting, I searched for a way off the window. As the cracks worsened, I ran for it. Anywhere had to be safer than here. The glass continued to break.

I was going to die.

Then I saw something dangling above me. I jumped and grabbed it. Holding on for dear life, I heard the window shatter and a blast of ultra-cold air slammed into me. The temperatures on this planet would be unbearable, if I wasn't a penguin. I realized I was holding onto a cable connected to something in the ceiling. I swung forward a bit, felt solid ground with my toe claws, and released the cable, falling flat on my face.

Something nudged my flipper, and when I snatched it, I discovered my glasses. Despite the cracked lenses, they were better than my natural eyesight. I was lost and disoriented. The presence of shops and glitching holograms told me I wasn't in the lobby. Some sparks fell from malfunctioning equipment above me.

I don't know why, but I confirmed I had the chip. Finding a way out of the sideways room, I entered a disorienting hallway. Gunshots, explosions and screams echoed throughout the halls. I suspected Edgy's involvement. As I continued, I found what remained of his aftermath.

Bodies. Bodies everywhere.

They were all burned or melted. The majority were in pieces and resembled abstract art. It smelled like overcooked meat on a grill. One of them had an energy pistol on hand with an almost depleted energy cell loaded. I grabbed it and kept moving. Then I noticed the giant melted hole in the wall and more decimated corpses. My arms wouldn't stop shaking; I've seen Edgy rampage before, but this was on a different level. As I kept moving, the path reoriented, making the walk forward awkward. Well, more awkward than it already was.

I worried about Jeff, I recalled him hanging on to that assassin's foot, but I doubted that would end well. I found a mostly functional map terminal nearby. Half of the buttons didn't work, but I could see my location. I didn't know if the stairs or hallways to the lobby three levels above were accessible. I feared none of us would make it out of here alive.

I don't know why, but I tried calling Jeff. No signal. I followed the route on the map. Didn't take long to come to a roadblock, and by a roadblock, I mean a collapsed ceiling. I couldn't find a way through it, but I found another corridor that led around it. As I walked, I heard more of Edgy's rampage. His powers never last this long. He tends to power down after a few minutes, but if I had to guess, it had been at least an hour. That realization made me tremble. The last time he pushed it this far, he ended up bedridden for weeks at a clinic.

I found myself outside of a ballroom. A host of bodies dotted the landscape, none slain by guns or energy blasts. Something crushed them. I almost threw up.

"Ah crap!" I heard someone yell from the ballroom.

I recognized the voice: Jeff! I bolted into the large room. I winced as I had to make my way through broken glass and plates. Jeff dangled high above me, tangled up in loose wiring.

"Jeff!" I called up.

"Todd!? Is that you!? Oh man, you gotta help me get down."

I noticed one wire holding him up was giving way. From that height, a fall could kill him. There had to be a way up there. Noticing the intact upper walkways in the ballroom, I realized I could get closer to Jeff.

"H-hang on, I think I have an idea!" I shouted. "Try not to move!"

The station rocked again as I spoke.

"Uh…that might be easier said than done bro!"

The room shook again, causing ceiling paneling to fall around us before I could say anything else. That wasn't the biggest issue. No, that was the sealed doors on the far side of the room. I could hear water crashing into them, and the doors started to warp and bulge.

"Aw shit!" Jeff said.

This entire room was about to flood! I bolted for the upper level, monitoring that door. When I reached Jeff's level, I tried to reach and grab the wiring, but he was too far away. I panicked even more. I scanned the area, searching for an alternative. Then I spotted something, a kinetic manipulator, likely used to move props onto the stage that were too awkward to carry. The manipulator sat in a room nearby on my level.

"Hold on, Jeff, I have an idea!"

"Alright, man, just hurry!"

I made a break for the room while the bulkhead door screamed and shook. Spinning, I observed a small hole in the door. The water spread quickly across the floor. The door to the kinetic manipulator was locked, posing another issue. I armed the pistol and shot it. A cone of cyan energy punched through and let me inside. The kinetic manipulator was a large device with a slot for your arm. The end looked like a box. A holographic display spun up and said the absolute worst thing it could in this situation.

CALIBRATION REQUIRED.

"Oh no, no, no, no!" I said, cycling through the calibration menu.

"What's going on over there!?"

"T-they *never* calibrated it!" I shouted while skimming the text in the initial setup window.

"What's that mean!?"

"It means I have to go through setup before it works! Give me a minute!"

"Oh sure, I'll give ya a minute. It's not like I'm *dangling* here for my life while the room is about to flood!"

As he said this, the door had another breach. Now the room was seriously flooding. I thought I finished the setup, but it asked me to install the latest drivers for the components. I frantically looked around for a data chip.

"Yo, Todd, no pressure, but that water is rising fast man!"

"I know! I know! I'm *trying*!"

Opening a box labeled ASURA INDUSTRIES, I found the data chip, and slammed the thin rectangle into a compartment on the bottom. It recognized the chip, and a progress bar slowly filled. I exited the room and looked below. The water almost consumed the stage.

"What's it doing now, dude!?"

"It's installing software! I can't make it go any faster!"

The bottom level was flooded. Even if I got Jeff down in the next few seconds, we'd need another way to the lobby. I looked at the progress bar. It finished the first of three software installations.

"Come on! Come on!"

The wires holding Jeff snapped. He screamed and fell closer to the rising waters. Jeff and I were both freaking out. Another wire broke. Jeff fell. He grabbed onto a cable and hung from it.

"Don't let go! It's almost done!" I shouted.

"Bro I'm about to *die*!"

I heard the device beep and turn on. The wire snapped. I

squeezed the trigger inside the device and aimed. Somehow I caught Jeff at the last second. A cube of purple-blue energy formed around him. Jeff's eyes were on the verge of popping out. Mine were too. Loose live wiring electrified the water, making it dangerous to put him on the ground. I brought Jeff up to my level and let go.

"I almost shit my pants!"

I said nothing. I was preoccupied with hyperventilating and finding a way out without being electrocuted. Jeff saw it before I did. Another maintenance shaft.

"Man, they got these all over the place, don't they?" He said as he pulled the manual release.

12. JEFF

We got close to the hangar despite taking detours. Every so often, I heard shooting, screaming, and explosions. Edgy was still wildin' out there somewhere. We exited another shaft and found ourselves in a big part of the casino. I remembered losing a hundred bucks here at the craps table the night before. To my surprise, the very nice gray-brown statues were still intact. Rows of stone aliens, brandishing sharp metal swords, lined the path. I also saw a glitched-out hologram for the strip club three floors above us. I should've gone there when I had the chance. The place shook, and I heard someone screaming in pain.

"Hey, what do we do about Edgy?" I asked Todd.

Todd grimaced."Get the tranq guns and hope we can stop him?"

"I was afraid you were gonna say that." I noticed the pistol in Todd's pocket. "Is that thing loaded?"

He nodded. "Yeah, but it only has one shot. You want it?"

Neither of us was a good shot, but with Todd's cracked glasses, I could use it better than he could, hopefully. He was right about only having one shot. Better than nothing, I guess. The hangar was on the opposite side of the room. The upper walkway and the shop above had fallen and crashed in front of us, blocking the way.

"Oh, that's not good," I said.

Todd raised that kinetic manipulator and pulled the trigger. He started moving some of the rubble away with it and sat it down nearby. This was gonna take some time. I looked around and saw a functioning drink dispenser nearby. I grabbed a cup and began sipping some soda, then I started looking for food. I was starving. Then I saw something that made me drop my half-full cup. I raised the gun and fired. While moving, she tossed a knife. I felt it cut my arm. My shot caught her in the thigh, and she growled.

Todd looked in the direction I fired, and his jaw hit the floor. "Oh no!"

"Todd, how long you need?!"

"A couple more minutes!"

"Alright, keep at it. I got this," I said.

"What!? She'll *kill* you!"

"Todd, I got this."

Yeah, I was lying like a motherfucker. The assassin chick stepped out into the open. She jammed a syringe into her leg and scowled. I would say she wanted me dead, but she wanted to do more than just kill me. I had to stall for time.

"Look, lady, can we just chill out? The soda machine's working. Why not grab a drink and move on? We just trying to get out of here."

She didn't pull a blade. She started walking towards me with her fists balled. Somehow, that scared me more, but I needed to keep her from butchering Todd. I did the stupid thing and approached her.

"We don't have to do this. You don't want these flippers."

She did. She came at me with a flying karate kick that sent me into a craps table. I couldn't feel the right side of my face. She tried to stab me in the chest, but I rolled out of the way and onto the floor as the crazy lady pulled the knife free and tried again.

I grabbed part of a roulette wheel and raised it like a shield. The knife went through and stopped in front of my eye. I tossed the shield to the left, knocking her off guard. Getting up, I swung at her.

I missed. I hit a statue and felt a sharp pain in my head and ribs. Assassin lady ripped one sword out of the hands of a statue and was looking to turn me into fresh deli meat. She kept slashing, and I kept backing off, ducking and trying to keep a statue between us.

That's when I heard a beeping from Todd's end. "Todd!? What was that!?"

"The manipulator's overheating! I can't use it for another five minutes!"

I avoided another blow to my head as the lady attacked me. I doubted we had five minutes. The woman cut my shirt several times and drew blood, but I got her to hit a statue and get the sword stuck. I grabbed a sword from the statue behind me.

"Yeah! What's up now!?" I taunted while swinging.

I didn't get very far with that. She caught the blade between her palms and yanked it out of my flippers after a couple of swings. Before I could do anything, she kicked me in my chest and knocked me into a slot machine.

I ain't even gonna lie. This was a one-sided ass-beating at this point. She was whipping my ass up and down the casino floor, and I stopped feeling it. She was too fast and not giving me any time to breathe. I couldn't see anything and had blood coming out of my beak.

She didn't let me go down either. She'd grab and lift me up or hit me under the jaw with her knee, knocking me back up. My body felt ten times heavier as she kept laying the hands on me. My team would've thrown in the towel two minutes ago if this was a sports match. She knocked me on my ass and pulled out a long black knife.

"Time to die," she growled while wiping my blood off her face.

As my vision focused a bit and I had a bit of clarity, I had one last trick up my sleeve.

"Can I say one thing before you kill me?" I asked.

She paused, her eyes got narrow. "What?"

"Damn, you *fine*. Like seriously, your face is a twenty out of ten, and your body is too. I mean, and pardon my language, but you put the double '*ass*' in assassin, holy shit."

She glared at me. She wore a look of shock and fury. You'd think calling her drop-dead gorgeous would calm her down.

Somehow, she wanted to murder me even more.

"What is *wrong* with you!?" Todd shouted.

"Hey man, I'm stating facts," I turned back to her. "Absolute bombshell."

"Do you think *that* will keep me from killing you?"

"Will it?" I asked after a few seconds of silence.

"Yes."

"Really?"

"*No*." She smiled and raised the knife aiming for my heart.

I shrugged. "Worth a shot."

The entire station rocked again, and the lights above us flickered. Then the ground gave way. Both of us were plummeting. My fall stopped, and I saw a purple energy cube around me. The assassin kept falling but then dug her knife into the surrounding machinery. She came to a stop a few feet below me. The look on her face told me she still wanted to gut me like a pig.

"Are you alright!?" Todd called while keeping me suspended.

"Yeah, I'm just peachy, bro. Get me out of here."

Then I heard something screeching from above. One of the big bulky machines on the ceiling was falling. Todd pulled me out of the hole right as it fell. The assassin let go of the wall to avoid being flattened. She had nothing to grab onto and fell deeper into the station.

The rest of the floor collapsed. Todd tossed me towards the door and ran for it. I limped through and waited for him to catch up.

"Hope that's the last we see of her," Todd said while adjusting his busted glasses.

I spat out blood and coughed. "Yeah."

We reached the hangar and located the ship. It was beyond fucked. The *Vermillion* had multiple holes and lost an arm thruster. Todd reached the airlock doors first. The console still worked, and Todd had his key on him. We made it inside the red and black room and entered the rest of the ship. The ceiling collapsed in many places, and the living room looked like a warzone.

"Aw man! Not the SlayStation!" I shouted, noticing the broken black and blue box-shaped console.

Todd sighed and headed for the bridge. I went to my room and retrieved my weed stash before following him. When I got there, Todd was seated in Edgy's chair and looking at the ship's damage.

"Can this thing fly?"

Todd turned away from the console and shook his head. "Let me see if I can reach Shard."

I stepped around the hovering chromed-out chair and looked at Todd as he kept typing in commands.

"We have a signal!" He exclaimed, his eyes getting all big.

"Sweet!"

A holographic screen popped up, showing several Shard ships in the area. Todd sent an SOS to all of them. One answered us.

"Edgy, *what* in the blazes is going on down there!?" A deep voice answered.

That voice belonged to Edge Lord Hylus. He was one of several lords, but he's the one Edgy answers to, sometimes. He was a giant figure in black, red, and orange armor. Hylus had these giant red crystals sprouting from his shoulder pads. More crystals rested in the crown on his head. His armor was spiky. Wouldn't surprise me if he cut himself while putting it on. His helmet hid his face. All we could see was a pair of yellow eyes, and they were mad as hell and surprised to see us. Checking the window in the corner, we both were a hot mess.

"Edgy's powers are going out of control! The mob damaged our ship, and we can't leave!"

A low growl sounded from Hylus. "That explains why the station fell and collided with the planet below. You must escape. It is teetering on the edge of a massive glacier. Union's fleet is preventing my men from approaching. They are deploying ground troops and forming a perimeter around the station."

"Oh, that's not good," I said.

Hylus' ship rocked, and the screen distorted. "We're going

to try punching our way through. We intercepted their communications. Todd, do you still have the data chip?"

Todd pulled it out. "Yeah."

"Excellent, then this operation is not a total loss. Listen, connect that to the ship's console and transmit the data to the address I'm sending you now."

"What about Edgy?" I asked.

Hylus paused for a moment. "If his powers are out of control, you must avoid him and escape the station. It's unstable and could fall any second now. My men will handle him as soon as we break through Union's forces."

After a few minutes, Todd transmitted the data.

"Data received. You have my gratitude, Todd. Based on the schematics my men have, there is an airlock near your position. That will put you atop that glacier. Use that to escape. Take whatever weapons you can from Edgy's arsenal. You will need them. I will send you the route now."

Both of our phones beeped, and I saw the directions on mine. "Alright."

"Good luck, Hylus out."

We each grabbed a tranquilizer gun, and then I grabbed a sonic rifle and a vest. Todd grabbed a combat visor and an energy pistol. The visor helped him see without his glasses and made shooting easier. At least, that's what he tells me.

"You ready Todd?" I asked while downing some pain meds.

"Y-yeah, let's get out of here."

13. EDGY

More shooting. Gunfire roared all around me. I was having the time of my life, even as I felt my insides rip apart with each passing second. The anger fueled me and blinded my vision. All I heard were screams. I recognized one: Reza. He was here! I felt pain. They were shooting at me again.

My power absorbed it. I couldn't keep still as the hatred poured out like a broken dam. Everything was a haze as I felt my power annihilate more. The haze parted, and I saw Reza trying to shoot me.

He still didn't fucking get it. He was a dead man walking. The red aura absorbed it. I jumped. The bones and muscles in my legs broke. I caught up to Reza and dragged him back to the ground, smashing his face into it and leaving an imprint.

I didn't want him to burn like the others. No, I wanted to have some fun with him. More reinforcements entered from a junction behind us and started shooting. Some of their shots hit me. My powers dulled the pain. I tossed Reza into them and heard his bones snap.

The haze thickened. I felt more pain in my chest. My mind felt like it was on fire. Only one thought carried me: kill them all. I couldn't see who I killed. I didn't care. Only screams. Never stopped attacking. Then it all became silent again. Where was Reza? I chased him down.

"*K-k-kill him!*" Reza shouted.

Pain followed. My power tried to protect me, but I fell. I couldn't breathe. Bleeding everywhere. I heard something. Laughter.

"Running out of gas!?" Reza shouted. "Finish him!"

As I regained some clarity, I realized what was happening. My powers were ripping me apart. I had gone too far this time. Or had I? Something frightened me. I was still holding back. My power begged me to let go of the leash. I agreed.

Who gave a damn what happened to me? I wanted them dead. Let it burn.

Shutting my eyes, I gave in. The chains shattered. No stopping it now. I had no restraints.

Everything shook. I stood and attacked. More shouting. More gunfire. Only one goal, slaughter. There was no escape. They could not stop me. There was only one thing they could do, die. I smelled melting flesh and smoke and tasted heated blood as I erased them. I heard something. A voice? Familiar. My vision cleared. I stood over what remained of a Union soldier. Entrails and blood caked my flippers.

"*Edgy!* You gotta calm down bro!"

Jeff. I snapped towards the source of the sound. He had a pistol trained on me, and so did Todd. They were trying to sedate me. They wanted the murder genie back in the bottle. I didn't want that.

They opened fire. The special darts didn't melt in time before they reached me. I felt the injectors do their work. My heart rate slowed. The crackling aura faded. I felt the full weight of my injuries. The pain was unbearable. I fell to my knees, gasping for air as I vomited whatever was left in my stomach and more blood.

"E-Edgy!? Are you...okay?" Todd said as my lungs sucked in air between coughing and vomiting fits.

"I didn't think that was gonna work," Jeff spoke.

My heart rate spiked again. The red aura returned, as did my anger. I realized something that made me go cold before it regained control. The tranquilizers weren't working. It could not be stopped. I heard the hiss of an arming plasma weapon and spun. Reza attacked. I absorbed the plasma's energy, causing him to run. As the rage blinded me, I pursued. Felt something melting under my feet. Outside. I saw more of them from afar. I charged.

14. TODD

I couldn't believe it! Jeff and I had dumped enough tranquilizer into him to subdue an entire herd of large horses, and he was still going! In fact, it seemed to have made him worse! Watching him rush Union's frontlines was something out of a horror movie. He ran at them like a beast. Even as the high-energy cannons of the tanks opened fire and made craters in the surrounding ice, he didn't slow down. His powers seized and tossed some of their energy blasts away.

Jeff and I exchanged looks as he reached them. He leaped into the air, brought his arms over his head, and descended upon them. I would've believed you if you told me someone just detonated a small thermonuclear warhead.

My visor dimmed and protected me from the bright red flash, but the sounds made me cover my ear holes. Jeff was doing the same. Even at a distance, I could feel the heat. The snow in the air vaporized from it. Enormous cracks formed in the glacier as I felt the ice beneath my feet turning into slush.

I used the zoom feature on my visor and saw him. Edgy stood atop a destroyed hover tank, surrounded by blue fire. The fuel cells must've ruptured from the explosion. His torn, burning jacket billowed like a torn cape. As the red aura coiled around him, he looked like a demon, and his body trembled with unhinged anger. He turned towards us, and I saw the glow from his eye shining through his blood-soaked red hair. Every vein was forced against his skin and glowed like molten metal. There was so much blood covering him I couldn't see his white feathers anymore. Edgy then slammed his flippers into the metal, denting it with each strike. He was trying to kill the surviving pilots inside!

Some soldiers shot at him. Their energy rounds hit him, and he seemed to feel it. He pounced them like an animal and began pulling them apart. My stomach was in knots as I watched a few panic and run in terror. Edgy ran them down like a rabid dog.

His rage intensified again, and red whips ripped them apart and incinerated them.

The other tanks opened fire on him. I lost sight of him in the smoke, steam, and ice clouds. I had other problems. The ground shook. No, it was considerably worse than that. The glacier was breaking!

"Run, dude!" Jeff shouted.

I booked it as best as I could. Cracks formed all around us. The station screamed as it sank deeper into the frigid waters below, taking more of the glacier with it. The ice shook, and I fell on my face. Jeff almost fell, but he helped me up. The cracks spread further and further out. We would not make it in time.

I heard something swooping down from above. A small red ship. The door on the side opened, and armored men snatched us as the ground gave way. I thought I would have a heart attack. I watched half of the gigantic glacier break apart and fall into the ocean, taking the massive station with it.

"*Holy shit!*" One of the Shard agents shouted.

I looked to see what he meant. Edgy was still going. He set out another pulse, slaughtering at least a dozen people and flipping a tank. As the ship continued to rise, I saw more of the battle. Edgy's powers had left gargantuan craters in the glacier. It looked like someone had shelled the place with orbital artillery. More tanks moved to open fire on him from multiple angles.

"What did they do to make that little bird *that* mad!?" One of them asked.

"Its...its a long story, bro," Jeff whispered.

"We've gotta help him!" I shouted to the pilot.

"We used up all our rockets just getting here! Hang on, we're gonna get you to Hylus!"

I watched as the seven tanks unloaded on Edgy. I questioned how much more his body could endure.

15. EDGY

I was dying. Body felt pulled in all directions at the same time. Insides burned. I collapsed on my flippers and knees as the tanks continued to attack. Power protected me even so, pain. I tried to stand. Legs failed me.

Broken. Everything became clearer. While I couldn't keep going, my power could. It still wanted to level everything in sight. Maybe I imagined it, but I felt it taunting me. Questioning if this was my end. Was I about to fall here and now? That pissed me off. I punched the ground, fracturing it and sending fissures in every direction.

I tried to stand, ignoring my broken legs. Another barrage of tank fire sent me back down again, making me vomit more blood. I comprehended the situation. The aura thrived on their attacks' energy, even if it was too much for me.

It didn't care; it needed more fuel to keep the fire alive, and I had little else to burn. That wasn't all. I felt all that energy building up inside me like a bomb. It would take them all out, including me.

I heard Reza laughing. "*This* is power, you little shit! Keep firing!"

They kept shooting, and I couldn't keep my eyes open. My body felt numb. A lull in their shooting occurred. I could see. I sat in a giant crater. Several craters surrounded me. A primal roar was building inside my mind and throat.

"*What* are you doing!? Keep shooting. He isn't dead!" I heard someone shout.

"Sir, the guns are overheating, and the ice is already under enough stress. This entire area could go at any minute! Another voice said. "He *must* be dead after all that!"

He wasn't too far off. I felt like a puppet on strings.

"He *isn't* dead, trust me! That...*thing* is not dead! Keep firing, and do not question me again!" Reza shouted.

Their bickering bought me time. I took a deep breath and stood. Reza saw me, and the look of horror on his face was fucking priceless. The glacier trembled and the red aura intensified. I watched the energy form a crackling thrashing red-orange dome around me. This fool thought he knew what power was. He was about to learn.

"Fire *everything*! Contact the *Liberator* and tell them I need orbital bombardment now!"

That never happened.

I felt the old injury to my skull rip open. I let out the roar as my power and the pain intensified. Despite being close to death, I never felt more alive. All that pent up energy detonated. A column of red light erupted from it, and the ground exploded around me. I howled until I felt my voice box rupture. I was slipping in and out of consciousness due to the searing pain. While the massive pillar of destructive energy poured out of my head, an ever-expanding dome of red radiated around me and swallowed the entire glacier.

I couldn't hear anything and couldn't see anything besides the blinding red light. Every fiber of my being was coming undone. When it faded, I saw the skies above. Red embers floated around me, carried by a harsh spiraling wind. My vision kept losing focus like a broken camera.

Dark clouds had formed above. Burning destroyed ships rained from the skies. Pieces of a large white and silver starship crashed into the ocean. My lungs gasped for air as I tracked pieces of it. Each shallow breath sent surges of pain throughout me. I watched the front portion of it collide with another glacier in the distance, shattering it. Everything felt angry. Huge waves crashed into the remaining ice and the fallen ships. I was perched on a fragment of glacier, which was slowly dissolving beneath me. A wave of beyond freezing salt water smacked me in the face and stung my eyes, wounds, and mouth. Then I heard a loud mechanical screech. A damaged tank breached the surface.

Reza was still alive and hung out of the tank's access hatch. As he sat up, I saw his broken horns and left arm. Reza's face had lost its skin on the left side due to burning. He looked half dead. Reza's eyes widened in shock when he saw me. He slammed his fist onto the top of the tank.

"Operator! The fucker's *still* alive! Shoot him!"

I expected a face full of plasma but there was no response.

"Operator!?" He snarled.

Blood from my head wound obscured my vision, but I saw him retreat into the tank. I heard a static hiss coming from the vehicle and felt the heat of charging plasma.

"Fry you little bastard!" Reza screamed.

With two broken legs, ruptured muscles, a massive head injury, and no energy left, I couldn't do a damn thing to stop him. Through the blood, I saw the cannon light. I noticed more than that. Smoke billowed off the tank and I saw and heard safety warnings. I forced myself to smile.

"*W-what*!?" He screeched, realizing the mistake he made.

It was too late for him. The intense heat from my energy discharges had rendered the plasma unstable. Adding more energy to it to weaponize it was like pouring water on a grease fire. The tank swelled and the pale blue light from the plasma leaked out of it for a split second. The resulting explosion sent me hurtling through the air and onto the sinking wreckage of a starship. Somehow causing me even more pain. Forcing myself to roll over, I saw the giant black and dark blue mushroom cloud rising from the smoldering wreckage of the tank. If I had the strength, I would've laughed maniacally. Wished I could've seen the look on his face as it detonated. I looked up at the darkened skies above.

As more blood seeped into my eyes and my vision started to blur, I saw a black and red ship descending.

My eyes shut.

16. HYLUS

I exited the small transport ship and entered the medical vessel in a system neighboring Callisto Station. To be exact, the location of the former Callisto Station. The disaster had a silver lining: the recovered data was utilized effectively. That beam of energy that radiated from Edgy traveled into space and destroyed a Union vessel leading their forces in the area. But it also took out ten of my ships. We estimated the combined casualty numbers for both sides to be in the ten thousand range.

It would take me an eternity to find replacement ships and people to crew them. The loss of life on that station had to be factored in. That was at least thirty thousand. The majority were uninvolved civilians. I could attribute some of those deaths to Union and their attack on the station. The majority came from that dreadful penguin.

I had seen his powers before firsthand, but nothing like this. The other lords were astounded by the damage he caused. Lord Noxilus appeared unsurprised but curious to know more. They inquired about my intentions for him.

Several suggested having him killed.

As I entered the medical vessel, I saw the triage teams hard at work. The doctor bowed to me.

"My lord, are you here to see him?"

"What about his injuries?" I asked.

The doctor seemed unnerved by that question. "My lord, his injuries are like nothing we've ever seen."

"Elaborate, please."

"Well, he's torn apart nearly every muscle in his body. He

has massive trauma to almost every other organ. And several wounds attributed to gunshots and lasers. The oddest thing of all, the open wound on his skull is not responding to any healing accelerants we have tried submerging him in."

"Submerged?" I asked.

The doctor's four eyes blinked several times. "With as much damage as he's suffered, it's the only way we can do it. We repaired the damage to his skull, but it seems like it didn't open because of any external trauma."

I paused. "What do you mean?"

"I've never seen anything like it. It's as if it opened on its own from the inside."

"How long do you estimate before he will recover?"

The doctor was silent for a while. "It's going to be at least several months. Might even be a year."

"Has he woken up at any point?"

The doctor paused. "He vaporized one of our surgeons. We must keep him sedated, or his powers might reactivate."

We entered the elevator and headed for the secret deck beneath the intensive care wing. I ordered everyone who witnessed that battle to remain silent. I did not tell them who caused the destruction. I wasn't sure what they would do knowing that I was keeping Edgy sedated and treating him.

"Speaking of his powers, what can you tell me about them?"

The doctor shook his head, his antennae twitched.

"Outside of what we already know, very little. It seems the injury to his skull reacted to it. There was noticeable trauma to the part of the brain in proximity to it. Whatever these powers are, if he doesn't get a handle on them, they will kill him. This stuff is not my field of expertise, my lord. You may need someone who knows magic to look at him."

"Hmm."

I expected that. Edgy's powers seemed far more magical. Lord Noxilus wanted to study him, but I didn't know what he'd do if he had Edgy in his care. I relied on one magic user for answers, and I had to trust she could keep him in check.

The doors opened, and we entered. The room contained several consoles, all monitoring vitals and information related to it. Beyond the consoles was a large vat of white-green fluid and a viewing platform. I stepped up to the platform and lowered it to the base of the gigantic vat of healing accelerants. I constructed this chamber in case I ever needed extensive medical treatment. Never imagined using it for this abominable bird. He lay suspended towards the bottom. A large gray mask covered his mouth and fed him oxygen. Long tubes connected to his arms and legs and kept him sedated. As I approached, I watched his brows twitch. As I gazed at his scarred, broken body, I wondered how he was still alive. That was not the real question. Why was I keeping him alive?

He inflicted more damage to my forces than Union did. Not to mention, Union would use this as a lightning rod to fire up their brainwashed populace and drive more witless fools to join them. Our situation was still dire, despite the weapon data we collected, all due to Edgy. As I watched him sit in the vat, I felt my grip tightening on the sword on my back. It would be so easy to slice him in two as he slumbered. The majority of lords had a good reason to desire his death. He was far too dangerous to turn loose. It wouldn't be long before he returned to attacking us as well.

The communicator in my gauntlet beeped. I glanced down and identified the individual. Lady Corvix, one of the Edge Lords like myself, appeared as a hologram beside me. Her massive black wings stretched out as she turned from me to Edgy.

"So...that's him?" her voice whispered.

She obscured her face behind a dark gray mask with four black eyes. While black feathers covered one pair of wings, the other set was like a bat.

"Did you find anything else about his past?" I asked.

Lady Corvix turned to me, "I can't find any records of his birthplace or parents. I can't give a concrete date of birth either. I have to conclude that he originated from Aves before its destruction. Most of their records were lost and could not be preserved."

"I see."

Lady Corvix focused on him. "So, what do you intend to do with him? Eclipse thinks he should die. Viltrax and Noxilus want him alive. Noxilus, I understand, but Viltrax, why?"

"Viltrax's entire force comprises gangsters and thugs. He started off not so differently from Edgy. I recruited him, and he proved himself worthy of the title of Edge Lord."

"I suppose that explains it." Lady Corvix shrugged.

"You never stated your answer. Should he live or die?"

Lady Corvix remained silent for several moments, looking at his scarred body floating in the vat. "He's too dangerous to be kept alive. He's like a rabid dog, if you let him off the leash, he'll turn on you. What's your plan for him?"

"I have not decided yet."

"You intend to send him to Peridae, don't you?" Her ability to sleuth and infiltrate others' networks was uncanny. "You want to understand his powers before Noxilus does."

"If he cannot control them or becomes an enemy, he will die. He will remain contained by Peridae and her witches until I either learn the secrets of his powers, he learns to control them, or I have need of them."

"You think she can contain...*that*, especially with the Crusaders knocking on her door? Or do you intend for him to aid her in driving them back?"

"If she cannot contain him, then he will die by my hand."

Lady Corvix nodded and turned her attention elsewhere. "He won't be pleased, even if it's for his benefit."

"Verily, but those are our options."

With that, Lady Corvix ended the call. I turned my back on Edgy as I reviewed the plan. When he healed, Peridae's people would come. They would transfer him to a Negacite coffin to ensure his powers remained suppressed and put him under a sleep spell, then take him to the witch Peridae and place him in a Negacite containment cell. That would block him from using his powers for now. I stopped at the viewing platform and turned back. I thought about killing him again, but something stayed my hand.

He was a weapon, and we were at war.

With Union growing more powerful, Edgy's power would be needed, but only if controlled.

MINER RESCUE ON VERDI IX

1.

When our ship came out of subspace, I realized how bad things were. Even from afar, my optic sensors spotted dense rings of debris and chunks of ruined blocky starships. Upon zooming in, I analyzed the damage to one of the severed auxiliary boosters. The destruction profiles matched my records and logs. Death Head's pirate fleet did this. I tightened my grip on the black and silver controls and pushed forward. The giant thrusters at the side of my ship, the *MSLF-Stratis*, hummed to life.

"Is that the pidae tal defense fleet?!" My mechanic, Choo-Choo, said.

Judging by the cadence of her voice, she had just finished exercising in her room.

"Yeah...it is," I answered.

As my mechanical hands steered us closer to the large blue and green planet beyond the debris field, I couldn't help but feel we were too late to do anything. After pulling back on the controls, I turned the oval chair to Choo-Choo, the ship's only organic.

Her real name is Niyarla, but everyone calls her Choo-Choo for a very specific reason. Unlike many other organics I had encountered, she looked human aside from the dull green scales on her back, arms, and the sides of her neck. Her white hair contrasted with her tawny skin. Her large pinkish-red eyes surveyed the debris field. Taking it all in, she adjusted the stained and sweaty tank top she wore.

"Uh...what do we do?" She asked in a soft voice that didn't

match her lean and toned body.

"The distress beacon is still on. Maybe there are survivors on the planet?"

Choo-Choo folded her arms. "Meeka, this smells like a trap. Doesn't the mining company have its own fleet? We should sit this one out."

"But what if they're still survivors!? We can't leave them to fend for themselves."

Choo-Choo sighed. "We can't save everyone."

Despite that being an accurate, logical statement, I still wanted to take action to save them. I paused and brought my hand under my chin. I'd seen many organics do this to signal that they were thinking. Shaking my head, my long artificial black hair with a glowing violet interior got in my optics for a moment.

"This is right out of their playbook," Choo-Choo continued, putting her hand on her hip. "They set traps using distress beacons to lure in ships that they can ambush and rob."

I examined previous reports of pirate attacks and immediately noticed a pattern. Employing an SOS as bait was not unfamiliar to them. From what I saw, they used it to great effect. She was right. Ignoring the high probability of a trap was impossible. Turning away from someone in need felt wrong.

"QUEEN, what do you think we should do?"

A holographic face appeared. It appeared as a female humanoid with a crown. Her eyes were a featureless, ghostly white.

"We are in the Epsilon Sector, and there is a Shard outpost near us. The safest option would be to let them investigate and spring the trap."

I stood up. QUEEN, my maker, may have been right. If the beacon was real and they were still alive, they may not be there when Shard arrived.

I had my answer. "We're going in. What kind of hero would I be if I let people die?"

Choo-Choo nodded and scratched the left hair puff on her

head. "I knew you'd say that."

QUEEN nodded, "MEEKA 2-27. Your naivety will get us killed one of these days."

"You can just call me Meeka. I'm the only MEEKA unit here."

She smiled a bit. "Sorry, force of habit."

I activated the ship's stealth systems, and the chromed silver and purple panels changed to mirror the surrounding space. As we entered the debris field, my neural processor entertained the idea that this was a trap. I checked for unusual thermal readings, but my scans saw nothing. I hoped the ship's biosensors would detect survivors in escape pods, but I found nothing. Using my optics, I inspected the damage to the defensive fleet. Pidae tal were small organics that resembled moles known for their impressive mining operations, and this planet, Verdi IX, was one of them. Their starships were much more bulky and simplistic in design. From what I could find, they were usually box-shaped and utilitarian. Whereas the *MSLF-Stratis* was sleeker and far cooler. I had QUEEN to thank for that. While leaning on my chair, Choo-Choo touched a half-read comic on the desk and got sweat on it.

"Be careful! That one is a limited edition variant cover."

"Oh, sorry," she apologized before sliding it aside. "So, nothing on the scanners?"

I shook my head. "No. No signs of any pirate ships, either."

That's what worried me the most. The pidae tal always had several ships equipped with formidable armaments around their mining operations. Small cruisers wouldn't stand a chance unless they were in large numbers. As I continued looking, I didn't see signs of Death Head's ships among the wrecks. They must've taken the fleet out without losing a single craft. Despite being an android, that thought made me shudder. This resembled the last issue of Captain Photon, where he ventured into a trap to save a building full of innocent people. Only I wasn't on the edge of my seat reading it and watching the drawings move as holograms in real-time. I was living it.

We continued toward the planet and entered the deepest part

of the debris field. I stood up and grabbed my short, thin black jacket with glowing neon purple on the inside. I also adjusted my buttoned-up shirt and the skirt I wore. Choo-Choo laughed at me.

"For a bounty hunter that tangles with criminals, you sure pick the cutest clothes to do it in."

I smiled. "All heroes need a recognizable costume."

Aesthetics before practicality. It complimented the feminine form all the Meeka units had. The ship rocked, red lights flooded the cockpit, and sirens went off.

"Mines!" QUEEN shouted.

I raced back to the controls and grabbed them. The damage readouts quickly streamed to my CPU, and I saw massive damage to the left thruster. More mines decloaked near us. The red icosahedrons then exploded, and the ship shuddered violently. We spiraled out of control.

"Oh no! Oh no! Hang on!" I shouted to Choo-Choo as I fought with the controls.

"Activating stabilizers!" QUEEN announced.

I had a moment of control and stopped the ship by the belt's edge. Although I didn't need to, I took a deep breath and relaxed all my servos.

"Okay...that was close. Niyarla? Are you alright?" I asked, turning around.

I saw the twin puffballs before I saw the rest of her. "I want off this ride," she groaned while rising. "How's the ship?"

"We have suffered moderate damage, but it has not impacted our core systems." QUEEN answered.

Unfortunately, that statement aged like fresh unprocessed milk left outside during a heatwave. The ship's back kicked like a mule, and we tumbled through space toward Verdi IX. I tried to stop it, but the right thruster wasn't getting power. We were also now well within the planet's gravity field. Escape was impossible.

"Brace yourself! Gotta land this bird!"

I did what I could as we entered the atmosphere, and I

watched flames billow off the ship as it continued to spiral. QUEEN and I coordinated with the stabilizers and the still working booster to regulate our orientation somewhat. My comics flew around like a startled colony of bats. The more the ship trembled, the more my figurines, model kits, comics, and toys loosened and hit the two of us like hail. It felt like we were in a washing machine going turbo. A fierce rainstorm pelted the damaged vessel as we cleared the dark clouds. I saw a dense rainforest beneath us with large branching rivers all around and colossal mountains. Under any other circumstance, it would've been a gorgeous view. The g force sent me flying back in my seat. One of my statues struck me in the cranium and knocked my head back.

"Ow!" I watched the figure slam into the wall to my right and bounce around like a pinball.

Thankfully, the protective packaging prevented serious damage to it. I was just glad it hit me and not Choo-Choo.

We came down towards the river. I pulled up as high as I could. I felt the ship's underbelly strike and bounce off the river and smash into the muddy riverbank. We continued to slide across the thick mud, dirtying up the chromed vessel as we neared the edge of the rainforest. The ship's long neck tilted forward and nearly hit the ground. QUEEN fired the stabilizers, and the ship leaned back and remained upright. The messy cockpit made me wince, and Choo-Choo seemed to feel the same way. As she removed her harness and stood, I switched my vision mode and checked to ensure she had no broken bones. Luckily, I didn't detect any fractures.

"Well... at least the ship's in one piece," she said, forcing a smile. I identified bruises on her arm, likely from one of my statues.

I smiled back. "You are too." I looked around the ship at the loose wiring from the ceiling and my scattered comics, figures, and model kits. "QUEEN...how's the ship?"

QUEEN blinked twice and sent me the damage report. Good news: ship could fly. Bad news: repairs would take hours and limited flight range. I connected to a map of the system. We could make it to the repair depot if the ship avoided further damage.

"That bad huh?" Choo-Choo asked.

I projected it as a hologram from the palm of my hand. Choo's eyes zoomed in her head as she took it all in. She then smiled, shook her head, and scratched her scalp.

"Well, it's a good thing I didn't shower before we arrived."

I checked the distress signal. With my average running speed, I could reach it in two hours.

"Can you manage without me?" I asked her.

Her smile widened, and she rolled her eyes. "Go on, go do your hero thing."

I nodded and touched her shoulder. "Thanks, I owe you one."

"Yeah, you do, more than one. Now get going."

That was an accurate statement. I'm unsure what I could do to repay her. As I thought about it, I raced through the ship, grabbed my energy spear and a small rapid-fire plasma gun, and exited the ship.

2.

The fauna on this planet was incredible! I almost wanted to slow down to further analyze them. QUEEN accessed the feed from my optics and took in everything. I observed armored insects marching in convoy and transporting pieces of a fallen tree back to an enormously large burrow. I switched vision modes and detected them beneath the ground in tunnels. Organic life, except for bacteria and occasional off-world plants, is rare where I come from. I backed up all the footage and images of the bugs and kept moving. I spotted several peculiar organisms perched in the trees. Each had four arms and twin prehensile tails, and four gigantic eyes. I heard them communicating through beautiful chirps and clicks. I suppose they were as perplexed by the sight of me as I was of them. As I examined them, a call came in: it was Choo-Choo.

"Choo?" I asked. "Is everything okay?"

"It's going well, despite the humidity and nonstop rain," she said amidst the sound of the rain and her repair work.

If I weren't an android, the rain would have been unbearable. Nonetheless, it was a new experience. Then I remembered Choo-Choo grew up on a space station; she wasn't used to rain either.

"How close are you to the signal?"

"Thirty minutes away," I replied while effortlessly vaulting over a fallen tree.

"Any signs of Death Head's pirates?"

"No updates, but ensure you have a weapon. The pirates are bound to investigate the crash."

"I sent out the recon drones. If anything gets too close, I'll have a heads-up. Don't worry, I have a mag rifle."

"I hope you don't have to use it."

"Same, I don't want to be seen by anyone right now."

I paused. "Um…what do you mean?"

Choo-Choo laughed. "I'm fixing the ship with… no top on."

That was not what I expected. "W-what!? Why!?"

"Because it's hot, and my shirt weighs a ton with all this rain. You'd know if you weren't an android."

I checked the humidity in the air. Yeah, I guess an organic would find it unbearable. "Uh…be sure to stay…hydrated?"

She laughed again. "Think I'm getting enough of that with all the rain. I'll let you know how it's coming along."

"Okay, be careful."

"Shouldn't I be saying that to you? You're the clumsy one."

"I am not clumsy!" I insisted.

Choo howled with laughter. "Did you *forget* when you tripped and fell into that *Morlac* nest on Grelis?"

I grimaced. "That was *one* time!"

"And the time you accidentally backed up into a *geyser* in Hydro City?"

I still had that damage report saved somewhere in my file directory.

"Well yeah, but-"

"And that time you pulled too hard and took the fridge door off the hinges."

"Okay! You've made your point!"

She laughed and closed the coms channel. I kept going, and eventually, I came to a picturesque waterfall surrounded by brilliant green plants with bits of red here and there. I spotted a piece of metal emerging from the pool's mire. I drew close and identified it, a damaged scouting drone. When I grabbed it and tugged it, the drone wouldn't budge. I tightened my grip on it and exerted more force. No dice. I tried harder. This time I pulled it free of the thick yellow-brown mud, but I lost my balance and fell back and onto the ground, dirtying my clothes.

I grimaced, sat up, and looked at my muddy clothes. "Aw

man."

I shook off the mud and then turned my attention to the drone. The teardrop-shaped machine had four arms, two of which were attached to the bottom and two that branched into thrusters. Energy emanating from the back of the head and eyes of the mechanical skull indicated its pirate origin. I noticed a deep puncture wound in the face. Soot covered the edges, and as I reached into the hole, I fished out what remained of the projectile.

It belonged to a pidae tal spike gun.

The spike's temperature indicated someone had fired it in the last fifteen minutes.

"Choo! There might be a survivor out here!"

I failed to see it.

The massive jaws swallowed the drone and my left arm. It yanked me into the murky water along with it. I could barely see its body, but I felt the intense bite force squeezing the plating on my arm. I would have marveled at the large predator's strength if it wasn't attacking me.

It then spun around underwater, twisting me with it. The force exerted would've easily torn off or broken my arm if I was organic. It shook its large diamond-shaped head, swinging me like a chew toy. The predator then breached the surface, bucked, and slammed me onto the rocks, setting off my pain sensors and making me grimace. The animal paused, allowing me to get a good look at it.

The creature was enormous and had eight eyes in a row on its head. The color of its rocky scales shifted to match the surroundings. It then corkscrewed again, trying to break or rip off my arm.

It thought I was food. Unfortunately, for this magnificent animal, I was not on the menu.

I transformed my left arm into cannon mode and charged it. The large reptile shrieked, opened its shark-like mouth, and recoiled as I landed in a crouch and trained the energy cannon on it. It seemed perplexed by my presence.

The animal hissed and lunged. I fired a low-powered shot and watched the violet energy shred the larger spikes on its back. It howled and screamed, flailing about and displacing the mud and water. I didn't lower my arm cannon as it finished thrashing. It held my gaze and continued to growl, and then I watched it pull back into the water and submerge. I needed thermal vision to detect it lurking in the pool.

"*Meeka!* Are you alright!?" QUEEN asked in my head.

I ran a diagnostic as I retreated, and my left arm exited cannon mode. I needed to thank QUEEN again for making us MEEKA 2s as durable as she did. The arm had minor dents, but my jacket sleeve was another story.

"I'm fine." I then contacted Choo-Choo. "Hey Choo, if you ever wander away from the ship, stay away from the water. There are these *really* cool, large camouflaged predators lying in ambush."

"I didn't plan on going for a swim, thanks anyway."

"They're strong enough to pull me into the water and throw me around like a rag doll. Then I used my cannon on it and sliced off one of its dorsal spines! It was so *cool!*" I explained, unable to contain my excitement over this.

"Well, I'm glad being a chew toy was fun for you. You mentioned something about a survivor?"

"Oh, yeah! I did!" I realized that had completely slipped my mind and began searching for tracks. "They shot down a pirate scouting drone. They must be nearby." Sadly, I didn't see any tracks in the mud. "The rain washed away their tracks. I'm almost at the beacon."

With that, I kept moving. I found evidence of a shipwreck. Broken and uprooted trees, a huge scar in the dirt and mud, and dislodged metal panels littered the area. It wasn't long before I found the wreckage. The escape shuttle was a large box-shaped vessel with four cylindrical boosters attached to its rear.

Attached was a bit of a strong word. The boosters barely held on, while the wings were stuck in the dirt yards away. An internal fire filled the cleared-out section of the forest with smoke. I entered through the open side door. Warning lights flashed and showed me the four dead pidae tal inside.

One of them was close to the door, and I saw a dried bloody paw print on the door control. He must have survived the crash, but bled out because of the puncture wounds to his bulky environmental suit. His tiny dead black eyes gazed up at the open door. I knelt in front of him and gently pulled his eyelids down. By my estimations, he hadn't been dead for more than an hour. I moved to the pilot's chair and the shattered front of the shuttle. The pilot died from a piece of metal impaling his heart. The co-pilot seat was empty, and I found the distress signal. It relayed the same transmission my ship detected.

Death Head's pirates had attacked and seized control of the mining platform. I accessed the terminal and looked at the logs. The logs recorded five had boarded and left the mining platform. Something shot them down, and they crashed here not too far from the platform. They hoped to escape the system and head for a pidae tal station three systems away.

Wait. Five.

I only counted four.

Then I noticed the blood trail: someone had gotten off this ship. I followed it outside and found a damaged helmet. I patched into the external camera. The mole-like creature attempted to rescue the dying one by the door, but the injured one instructed him to leave before the pirates arrived. He hesitantly left his friend behind and stumbled out into the rainforest. He tore off the damaged helmet since it wouldn't do him much good and headed the way I came.

"I'm at the beacon. It's a crashed escape shuttle. Looks like one survived the crash and-"

A ball of energy grazed my shoulder, making me stumble back against the wrecked ship. I tracked the shot, crouched, and drew my plasma gun. Another green energy blast struck part of the ship behind me and pierced the hull. I returned fire. I heard a grunt of pain from the tree line. Switching to thermal vision, I counted four pirates, but a fifth energy signature was among them, sitting by a rock.

"That bloody hurt!" The one I struck shouted as he clutched his arm.

"Shut your trap and get her. We'll bring both of them to the captain!" Another commanded.

Both. Did they capture the survivor?

I checked the damage to my shoulder. Thankfully, it only damaged the outer plating, nothing serious. The pirates repositioned for a better shot at me. I ran for it. More energy blasts erupted from the forest. I transformed my left arm and fired a medium-powered shot. The blast punctured a tree, slammed into one pirate, and knocked them down.

One of them emerged from the tree line. The pirate was a lanky alien covered in spiky chitin armor. Like all members of Death Head's pirate army, his head was a mechanical skull, only his looked insectoid. He snarled and fired a long energy weapon that looked like a flintlock rifle from a pirate movie, but with holographic sights. I aimed at him and fired the plasma gun.

My shots collided with his chest, and he screamed and retreated behind a rock. Another pirate emerged from his left. This one was almost completely cyberized and fired a pistol. I ducked at the last second and fired the arm cannon. My shot punched a hole in his chest, causing blood, sparks, and fluids to erupt from his mechanical parts.

I was at the tree line now, and the insect pirate slashed with an energy cutlass. He would've decapitated me with that green blade if I had been a second slower. I dropped my gun, reached for the collapsed spear on my back, and activated it. The rod transformed into a spear with an energy blade. I gripped it with both hands and lunged.

The insect didn't realize how fast I was, and despite him being larger than me, I had the reach advantage. With a few swings and jabs, I brought him to his knees. I one-handed the spear and pointed it at his neck. I heard the pirate I shot in the arm, reaching for his gun.

"Don't even think about it," I threatened, stealing a quote from a heroine in a schlocky action movie I love.

He reached for the gun. I armed my cannon and shot him. It was a paralysis blast, nothing more. Then I turned to the kneeling bug man in front of me. Searching my memory banks, I tried to think of a tough line to get him to talk. Interrogating people was a novel concept to me, especially with pirates. Perhaps I could tell him to talk, but that wasn't specific enough. I could've tried asking him to tell me what he knew, but that seemed too pedestrian. Maybe shout and tell him to spill the beans? I saw it in a detective show once. No, that was lame. I remembered a line from a Lady Midnight movie that could've worked.

"Well? You're gonna say something tin can!?" He growled, disrupting me and showing the rows of saw-like teeth.

"What!?" I asked.

"You have a blade to my neck and haven't killed me yet, so you clearly don't want me dead. What do you want!?"

"Tell me everything about Death Head's fleet!" I demanded, pitching my voice down a bit.

He paused and stared at me. "You're bad at this whole interrogation thing, aren't you dollface?"

Maybe that only works in movies?

"Who's your captain?" I asked, trying to maintain a tough persona.

I watched his small green glowing eyes look at the blade at his neck. His eyes shifted to the pistol with the curved grip on his side.

"By the time you draw that gun, I will have already moved the spear into your neck. Death would be instantaneous." I said without thinking about it.

He froze, surprised that I predicted his intentions so well. "Fine, that would be Captain Iron Claw."

I checked the database. Iron Claw was one of Death Head's trusted lieutenants, and he had been behind multiple raids in the Epsilon Sector in the past few months, this being one of them. I could sum his methods up in a single word. Ruthless. Ruthless would be a gross understatement.

I looked at the reports of a cargo ship raid. Those that died fighting were luckier than the rest that surrendered. After getting what he wanted, Iron Claw flooded the ship with lethal nerve gas. None survived. I feared even more for the miners now at his mercy. I needed to put a stop to him before history repeated.

"Why is he here!?"

His eyes narrowed. "You really think the captain tells us everything?"

His vitals didn't rise as he answered me. He might have been telling the truth.

"Where are all his ships?"

"We only brought one, came out of subspace, and fired a graviton bomb right at the heart of their fleet. Then we deployed stealth mines in the debris field in case any schmuck came to stop us, and I guess it worked. What's the matter? Didn't think to check for mines? Maybe you need a software update."

I paused. I hadn't done a full sensor check! If I had, I could've avoided the crash landing. The pirate continued to give me a smug look. I wouldn't admit it aloud that I hadn't done that. I set the cannon to paralysis mode and shot him. I then switched modes to a capture shot, creating energy restraints around the still-living pirates. It would keep them immobilized for twelve hours. Then I found their prisoner. A small creature with brownish-red fur and long arms that seemed disproportionate to his short, stout-looking body.

The pidae tal miner looked up at me. "Who the *fuck* are you?" he asked gruffly.

"My name is Meeka. I'm here to rescue you and the other miners. Pleased to meet you," I said while smiling and extending my hand to him.

His dark black eyes narrowed. "Lass, how am I supposed to shake your hand while I'm tied up?"

"Oh! Right. Hold still," I activated the small plasma cutter built into my left arm.

"Is it just you?" He asked as I cut the first cable.

"Just me."

"Oh well, that's just *fucking* great. They send one damn doll in a skirt and thigh socks, figures the mining union would only send a single bounty hunter to save some cash."

"Oh, uh… no one sent me," I said as I cut the last cable and freed him.

"You came on your own?" He asked while stretching his long arms and short legs.

I nodded. "My ship's close to here. You'll be safe there. Well, safer anyways."

He didn't reply to me and instead hobbled over to the more humanoid pirate I had shot in the arm. He then kicked him and swore at the pirate.

"Is that necessary?"

"Little bastard *almost* killed me!" He growled before grabbing a boxy, heavy-looking rifle off the incapacitated pirate's back. I saw a name written on the side.

"Hello beautiful," he whispered to it before turning back to me. "Alright, lead the way."

"What's your name?"

"Halgar."

3.

Traveling with Halgar was...interesting. I don't think I've heard someone swear as much as he did. He groused about the rain and the mud, and I don't think he directed it at me. He was talking to himself. It's an odd trait I've seen Choo-Choo do when trying to repair things on the ship. Perhaps it helps them think? As we kept walking, I noticed he struggled to keep up with me and I heard him panting, and he kept pulling at his body suit. Forgetting how easily organics tire out, I decreased my speed.

"It's hotter than a treligaran's ball sack out here!" He complained between heavy breaths.

I blinked twice as I processed that and checked the ship's zoology database. Treligarans are colossal, belligerent mammals typically bred for their meat. Their gonads maintained an average temperature of one-hundred degrees Fahrenheit, much higher than the core temperature of the body. Their testicles were also eaten as a delicacy on certain planets. I wished to forget what I had looked up, but I had a question for Halgar.

"How do you know how hot their testicles are?" I asked.

Halgar didn't answer me, he just stared and blinked repeatedly. Eventually, he looked away and sighed, "I don't...it's just an expression."

"Oh...right, a figure of speech...yeah."

As we kept walking, I heard Halgar stop and rest against a tree. "Need a minute, ya fembot."

I stopped and watched him unzip the upper part of his body suit, exposing the simple gray sleeveless shirt underneath. I looked down at my clothes. My shirt had holes and cuts to it, and so did my skirt. Mud caked the black thigh highs I wore and the simple shoes I had on.

"You sure picked the weirdest getup to go wandering around in a rainforest. You look like you're going to a damn nerd convention!" He muttered.

"I am *not* a nerd! I am a bounty hunter and a hero! Well, at least I'm trying to be."

His small black eyes widened, and then he howled with laughter and threw his head back. "You are a *massive* fucking dork!"

"No, I'm not!" I lied.

"Never heard of a robot dork before. What will they think of next? Whoever programmed you must have a sense of humor or very specific taste."

"I didn't get my personality through programming! My brain is a self-learning neural net processor!"

He continued to laugh. "Whatever you say, whatever you say."

I scowled at him, but I didn't have much of a retort. QUEEN listened, unamused. Trying not to think about it, I checked for more pirates, but saw nothing. I didn't find comfort in that. The pirate's explanation suggested that they may not have a strong presence on this planet.

"Hey, Halgar, what did you see during the attack?"

Halgar took a deep breath. "It started while I was in the mining rig's lower levels doing cabling maintenance. Alerts were blaring, and then the rig rocked something fierce. When I reached the upper levels, those pirate bastards had already made it inside. Security didn't stand a goddamn chance."

As he spoke, I switched vision modes to see his small, rapidly beating heart. It was much higher than when I initially found him. He was also breathing at an elevated rate.

"How did you escape?"

"One of the security guys, Narwin, got us to a shuttle. He activated the distress beacon you homed in on. When we fled the platform, we saw the aftermath of that graviton bomb...I doubt anyone survived. We didn't realize they had control over the automated defenses, and they shot us down, and well, you know the rest."

I climbed over a fallen tree but realized Halgar was too short to make it over. I extended a hand toward him and pulled him up.

"Do you know if there are survivors?" I asked as I pulled him up.

"Yeah, they were taking the miners hostage. I'll bet they're forcing them to keep mining the ore vein we found."

"What did you find?"

He climbed off the tree, and we continued towards the ship. "Don't know, company wouldn't say. They're pretty tight-lipped about operations, but I heard from one engineer that we struck gold. Wouldn't say much else."

I tried to figure out what he could've meant. What would make Iron Claw assault the mining platform with only a single ship? The reports I read showed he had a sizable armada. So why only one ship? I did another query and found my answer. Due to a recent ambush, Iron Claw was only able to attack the mining platform with one ship since most of his fleet had not yet rallied. He must have learned whatever the miners had found by pure luck. I needed to resolve this quickly before more of their fleet arrived. I realized we were near the ship and recalled Choo's words.

"Hey, Choo, we're almost there."

"Great," she muttered. I detected annoyance in her tone.

"Oh, and please have a shirt on," I whispered.

She didn't give an answer and closed the channel. When we arrived, I found Choo-Choo sitting on a crate taken from the ship. Her hair was so damp because of the rain that it drooped. Her clothes looked to be the same. Despite that, she smiled at the sight of me.

"Hey!" She said before standing up.

I noticed she wasn't hiding her thin, split tail and let it sway behind her as she approached us. I noticed Halgar was focused on that.

"Halgar, meet Choo-Choo."

"A *kaleon*!?" He grumbled under his breath. I guess he didn't think I could hear him.

"Just him?" Choo-Choo asked while removing her oversized stained gloves.

Halgar crossed his arms. "First, I got saved by a dorky android, and *now* I got to hang out around a kaleon nimetran hybrid. Just great."

I saw her left brow twitch for a second. Halgar may not have noticed, but I recognized the subtlety and desperately wanted to avoid the usual aftermath.

"Um...Halgar, do you know of a way into the mining rig?"

Halgar put his clawed hand on top of his snout, and he grumbled to himself for a few seconds. I heard Choo-Choo take a deep breath, and she relaxed a bit.

"There is a way in. It's pretty fucking dangerous, but since you're a robot, you might not mind it."

"What do you mean?" I asked.

"Well, our survey teams found a bunch of ancient ruins near the platform, which leads to a large cave system with an entrance to the surface. That entrance leads to the ruins, which will take you right below the platform. Problem is that cave is full of lava, doubt much can withstand it."

"Never easy, is it?" Choo-Choo asked while smiling and crossing her arms.

Halgar touched the device on his wrist, and a holographic map showed the entire rainforest and a crude 3D model of the large platform. Then a single strip of white drew a path from the ship to a random spot near one of the mountains.

"I can sync the data with your map."

I took the data and calculated the travel time on foot.

"Alright, wait here. I'll figure out what they're up to and free the miners."

"You want me to stay with a damn kaleon *mutt*!?"

Choo-Choo turned to him, her brow twitching faster than

before. "I'm not too thrilled to be stuck with you either."

"Um... am I missing something?"

"You must live under a rock. Our species have been fighting for the last twenty years! Hell, we only recently negotiated a cease-fire!"

I did not know that at all. "Why?"

"Because his kind *attacked* one of our colonies for no reason!"

"No *reason*!? You *claimed* a planet in our territory as your own and chased out our ships from the system! That's an act of war!" Halgar shook with rage and stood on the tips of his toes to get closer to Choo's face.

I saw the rage building in her face, and her tail lashed at the surrounding air. I needed to diffuse this now.

"Right now, it doesn't matter who started the war. Neither one of you fought in it, right?"

Halgar took a deep breath and a step back. I saw his muscles unwind. I wish I could say the same about Choo.

"It *matters* Meeka! Some of my friends enlisted to fight, some returned in boxes, others were not so lucky! You want *me* to be cool with one of his kind like that?!"

Halgar flexed his claws and grumbled. "You aren't the only one who lost friends in this damn war! I watched my best friends get blown to bits by one of your ion cannons! So quit acting like you're the *fucking* victims here!"

"Shut up!" Choo boomed. "Don't pretend like your people aren't heartless! All you care about is your damn bank accounts and corporate profit margins!"

"And all you scaly *fucks* care about is expanding your pathetic empire! Wonder how long it will be before you piss off someone worse than us, and they wipe your asses off the face of the E-!"

In that instant, he learned why she earned the nickname Choo-Choo, because she hit him like a freight train and dropped him with a single punch. He hit the ground like a plank of wood. As I saw blood gushing from his nose, I hoped she didn't give him head trauma. I witnessed a spark of anger on her face, but it dissipated, and she inhaled deeply and grinned.

"*Niyarla!*" I said as I checked for any lasting damage.

"Sorry about that."

"You can't blame him for what his people have done. You should know that." I said, looking her in her eyes.

She broke eye contact and turned away. "Yeah…I know."

"I didn't think you cared that much about being a kaleon."

Outside of her tail and scales, she could pass off as a nimetran, and she often kept those hidden. Nimetrans aren't much different from humans, at least not from a distance. Their eyes and the natural colors of their hair would give them away. They can also create hybrid offspring with many species. Even ones that don't share any obvious traits with them.

"Most of the people on the station were nimetrans and weren't a fan of me being part kaleon, but the kaeleons didn't care." She looked back at Halgar as he woke up.

"Damn, what the *fuck* hit me?"

Choo-Choo smirked, "I did." She took a deep breath. "I'm sorry about that. Why don't we start over and try to be nicer to each other?" She then extended a hand to him.

To my surprise, he took it, and she pulled him up.

"Not bad for a kaleon," he said, rubbing his face and spitting out blood from his gums.

The next thing I knew, he was laughing. I don't know why. Punches like that don't usually elicit laughter. She started laughing, too, and that left me even more confused. There was no trace of the argument. I do not get it. I almost wished to ask them what was so funny, but I definitely didn't want them to go back to fighting, particularly if Choo-Choo knocked him out again. We were supposed to be rescuing them, not giving them brain damage. Making sure they were okay, I left them alone and headed towards the path.

"Organics are very strange," QUEEN said.

"Yeah…"

4.

The cave entrance was...not very inviting. Survey spikes ran down to the bottom, illuminating a large hole in the ground with green light. As I scrutinized it, none of it seemed natural. The sides of the walls were too precise and uniform for natural erosion. I then calculated the distance to the bottom, half a mile down.

I took a step towards the chasm's edge. The ground gave way beneath me. I screamed as I plummeted through the air, and my arms flailed about in a panic. My trademark clumsiness reared its ugly head as I slammed against the rocky wall with a booming thud and bounced off it like a pinball. The ground was coming up fast. I activated my stabilizers, but I didn't have enough time. I crashed into the bedrock face first, leaving a deep imprint in the ground. Marinating in my clumsiness, I lay there for a few seconds.

"Well...that's one way to land, I suppose," QUEEN remarked.

"Yeah," I winced and stood up. I did a quick system check. No damage besides my pride, I guess. I headed for the corridor ahead of me.

The deeper in I went, the higher the temperature became. Even with the survey spikes, I had limited visibility until I switched to ultraviolet. I also found remnants of research equipment, including lights, terminals, and other excavation gear. I patched into one of their systems and found data on the ruins. They estimated the ruins to be sixty-thousand years old but knew little else.

"Hey, Halgar, any other info on the ruins or lava?"

"I don't know if it's true, but one guy mentioned a probe being eaten by a giant worm coming out of the lava, but he was drunk as shit when he told the story."

"Did…did you say a lava worm?" I asked.

"Yeah, I did."

"That's so *cool*!"

"You and I have different definitions of the word cool," Halgar muttered.

"She's like that," Choo-Choo laughed. "Don't get too close. I'm a good mechanic, but I'm no miracle worker."

"You're pretty close," I said, hoping I'd get to see it, at least from a safe distance.

I found a large door incorporated into the rocky tunnel ahead of me. I saw an airlock-like door and detected a sudden temperature increase behind it. The rocky doors had intricate symbols carved into them as arrangements of dots connected with lines.

"QUEEN, have you ever seen this writing before?"

"Negative."

Their writing was fascinating. I couldn't find a match for it in the databases back home. The miners didn't have time for me to investigate it; I needed to get to the mining platform and save them. I tapped the open command, and the doors hissed and then opened. A heat wave clobbered me, and I felt the temperature skyrocket. I entered the tunnel of black, glassy rock and saw embers in the air. Halgar was right about the temperature. Most organic life would not survive the heat here. Even I felt my cooling systems working overtime to prevent overheating, and as I traveled deeper, it only worsened. As I followed the jagged rocky path, I came to a large open cavern flooded with churning, boiling lava. I had luck on my side- rocky platforms were within reach, allowing me to cross.

"Meeka, now is certainly not the time to make another mistake. Please go slowly," QUEEN warned.

I nodded and jumped off the ledge, landing on a rock sticking up from the lava. My cooling systems flashed a warning. I couldn't stay here for long. I jumped to the next rock and continued towards the exit. It felt like I was playing the deadliest game of hopscotch ever. I mean, that's not terribly far off. I had to engage stabilizers to keep from losing balance and falling. The lava's reddish-orange glow illuminated the chamber and allowed me to see without night vision.

"Any signs of the lava worm?" Choo-Choo asked.

"No, unfortunately," I replied, quickly jumping across three rocks before each sank into the lava.

I reached the exit, and I had to remove my jacket momentarily. Vents on my arms opened up and expelled hot air from my internal components. It was ineffective in dealing with overheating. I kept moving and found something strange, small animals with jagged black rock coating their bodies like an exoskeleton. They scaled the walls and ceiling using their six legs while eating the rocks on the walls. One hunkered down into a ball when I got too close to it, and it camouflaged seamlessly with the surroundings. I questioned if they would be the worm's prey, should it exist, or food for something else. The next cavernous room led to a lava fall and a deep pool below. I checked the map and realized I would have to scale the lava fall to reach the exit.

The question was how.

I noticed a few rocky platforms leading to the wall beside the lava fall. I needed a running start, but I could still make the jump. As I ran for it, the entire cavern shook, and rocks fell from the ceiling and walls. I stopped in my tracks.

"Um...QUEEN, Choo, are you all reading any seismic activity?" I asked.

"No, why?"

I dodged a rock as it hit the ground beside me. A wall of lava erupted from my side, and I had to roll to safety as it threatened to coat me. The erupting lava traveled in a circle around my rocky platform. Circling. The lava worm. It was real! I powered up my arm cannon to the highest setting and tracked its movement. My thermal vision was useless thanks to all the surrounding heat. I watched it continue to circle and shake the entire cavern, but I could only catch a glimpse of it, and not long enough to shoot it. Then it all stopped. I remained immobile.

"The worm is real. It must be *huge!*"

Something punched a hole in the platform's center. I shielded my face from the lava spray and I felt bits of it hit me and cause my jacket to ignite. As the lava cleared, I saw it. Dense hardened rock covered its segmented body, and its face opened like a blooming flower, exposing rows of serrated teeth.

I hated I was right about its size.

Even the bit of it I could see almost scraped the ceiling. The enormous creature snapped towards me, and its booming roar made the entire cave tremble and dislodged rocks from the ceiling. I looked past the colossal animal. The platforms in the lava I intended to use to get out were gone. The massive creature looked down at me. I felt like a small flea compared to it.

I raised my hands. "Hey, nice, giant...alien lava worm." I slowly approached the exit, hoping it hadn't noticed me or would become disinterested. "I'm just gonna g-"

I felt something slam into my chest and knock me across the room to the platform's edge. Looking up, I spotted long whip-like appendages sprouting from recesses in its skin.

The whips lunged again. I rolled to my feet as they crashed into the ground behind me. Running towards the worm, I fired at the face. I watched the blinding bright purple blast collide with its head, creating a dense cloud of smoke. Its entire body recoil back from the impact, but it wasn't dead! It righted itself, and the whips lashed. I jumped onto one and ran up its length while drawing my spear.

One of its limbs slammed into my face, knocking me out of the air. I flipped and dug the spear into the wall on the opposite end of the chamber, far from where I needed to be. The worm bellowed. I saw that the high-powered blast only shattered some protective rock around its face but nothing more. I aimed and fired again.

Not fast enough. It submerged into the lava, taking the rest of the platform with it. I needed a way out without landing in the molten rock. I could only think of one thing. When the beast leaped out of the magma with its mouth agape. I planted my feet against the wall and kicked off as hard as possible while freeing the spear. I was on a clear trajectory for the inside of its gigantic mouth full of spiraling teeth.

I aimed the gun, but not at the worm itself. I fired the shot at a downward angle, and the recoil carried me over its mouth. But I had another problem. The tendrils. I activated the second energy blade on the other end of the spear and set my wrist into a three-hundred-and-sixty-degree rotation, slicing through any approaching tendrils. I landed on its back and ran down the length as it crashed into the magma. When I got to its tail, I jumped as high as I could.

As I sailed through the air, I calculated my trajectory: I would not make it. Firing the cannon again, I propelled myself higher to the left, towards one rock jutting out of the lava fall. I misjudged my flight and slammed into the rock wall, sliding down it as if it were greased. I peeled away from the wall, fell, and bounced off and shattered the rocky spikes on the way down. My foot passed through the lava, and I felt it searing my metal body. I stretched out, seized a piece of rock, and arrested my fall about halfway down the wall. I felt the stone fracturing under my weight. No time to think about that. I heard a low roar behind me and swiveled around. The worm was back.

It rammed the magma fall with its gigantic face. I swung to a nearby glassy rock and caught onto it as the worm shattered the stone wall. Its whip appendages lashed at me again. I jumped and landed on a rock atop the lava fall. The worm rose above me, and the rumble emanating from it shook the cave. Warnings flashed across my vision, telling me about the lava still eating at my leg. It had made it through the paneling on my foot and shin and started damaging the internal mechanisms.

The worm struck. I jumped and landed on another piece of rock sticking out of the lava. My weight caused the rock to sink, so I had to hop off it or risk further damage. My jumps were getting weaker because of the damage to my right foot. I stumbled to the glassy rocky land at the edge of the magma flow. The worm snarled and gazed at me. I quickly rose, armed my cannon, and trained it on the head. I was not confident in my ability to fend it off. After a few seconds of a standoff, the beast spun away and fiercely burrowed onto the lava. Something tells me it was salty about missing out on a meal.

I questioned if I would even taste good to it. Maybe it didn't have taste buds at all. I checked my foot and saw the damage. I had to scrape the bits of rapidly cooling rock from the holes and execute deeper diagnostics. The complex artificial muscles suffered damage, so I needed to fix them to restore full functionality.

"Meeka, are you okay?" Choo-Choo asked.

I winced as I looked at my foot. "Uh…yeah, I-I'm good."

"You *sure*?" She asked, sounding like a mom that suspected something.

"Yes, I'm perfectly fine, just had a close encounter with the worm, is all, but I'm good."

"You stepped in the lava, didn't you?"

How did she know!? I nodded, even though she couldn't see me. "Kinda."

"How do you *kinda* step into lava?"

I explained everything to her. As I finished, I heard a sigh.

"Well, at least my mechanic skills aren't gonna dull anytime soon."

"Sorry!"

"It's fine. Can you walk on it?"

I stood up and started walking around a bit. I could move around, but I walked with a slight limp.

"I can manage on it." Then I noticed something else, my hair. The lava had roasted the ends of my hair on the left side. "Oh man, it singed my hair!"

"Ouch. Did you get a good look at the worm?"

I transmitted images and footage of the fight to her. "You could say that."

"Oh shit, that thing is huge!" She exclaimed a few seconds later.

"Yeah...huge. Might be an understatement."

I heard her laugh, "I'm glad you're alright. You should be near the ruins now."

"Huh, well, I'll be damned. Rukan was telling the truth about a giant worm," Halgar remarked.

"I wonder how old it is?" I replied as I crawled through the rocky tunnel.

I found an opened door similar to the one at the entrance. As I climbed out, I found myself in a large rocky hall of stone.

"Well, I'm in the ruins," I told them.

"Not bad, robo dork. Follow the survey spikes and excavation equipment, and you should be right at the platform's base."

"I am *not* a dork!"

"And I'm not a pidae tal."

5.

The runes were amazing! Despite its stone structure, advanced technology shone. The carvings on the walls had a language I could not decipher. I wished I didn't have to run through the reddish stone octagonal halls. Some writings on the walls would display as holograms whenever I approached; the ruins must've still been getting power. I noticed they had a lot of depictions of the lava worm, and it seems like they both respected and feared it.

Can't say I blame them. As I entered a huge antechamber, I spotted large pillars of energy erupting from the ground. As I approached, I identified what it was. The energy pillars contained data and fed it into a device on the ceiling. I saw more than that. A small construct loomed near the pillars. It had a single ball in the center of its body that I'm guessing it used as an eye. I spotted ten more. From the center of their spiky bodies, they projected energy from a single eye and seemed to alter the data streams. They floated off the ground and glided and swam through the air. They didn't seem all that interested in me, thankfully.

"Hey, Halgar, are you seeing this?"

"Yeah, the eggheads called them custodians. They seem to repair and adjust those data streams. Don't touch or change the data. They'll get irritated if you do."

"Define irritated?"

"One scientist tried to extract some data, and they zapped him so badly he pissed his pants."

"Noted."

I took Halgar's advice and avoided the data streams, despite wanting to know what they contained. As I stepped around a data stream, one custodian spun and turned toward me. The orange eye at the core glowed brighter for a second, and I detected a build-up of energy.

I put my hands up. "Easy...easy, I'm not gonna touch the data, be cool, you small...kinda cute robot."

I doubted it understood me, but the orange glow died down, and it turned its back on me. I relaxed and lowered my hands and kept moving. One followed me. It had a distinct color from the others. While the others were dull brown, this one was more orange. I observed it transmitting data by light to the other custodians, so it had to be some type of command unit. As I reached the other end of the antechamber, the commander unit stopped following me, but it didn't stop watching me.

"What? I'm just passing through."

"Just...passing...through," it said, mimicking my voice. That caught me off guard. The commander left, turning their back. "Cute robot."

It returned to the others and didn't acknowledge me further. I wondered what would happen if I gave it access to a language database. Would it reach a point where it could carry a conversation rather than mimicry? I didn't have time to test this: the miners needed me. The chamber beyond contained some artifacts the excavation team had already cataloged for further study. I found a rocky staircase with a massive door at the top.

"You'll be near the lower levels of the mining platform," Halgar told me as I raced up the steps.

When I exited the ruins, I faced a massive cylindrical chasm and a beam of white light striking the ground below. The output revealed that the laser was a D9-VTZ mining laser designed to penetrate the deep rock. The platform was a wide cylinder with a mushroom-like cap. Long spidery legs were on the sides, and embedded in the walls for stability. Looking at one leg, I found my way inside.

I encountered a problem.

The defenses were still active, and the targeting lasers for the energy cannons swept the area.

I zoomed in on one of the smaller cannons. Yeah…that had enough power to shred my starship's armor; getting caught by one of those turrets was not an option. Luckily, I spotted a solution. I ran for the leg, weaving between green targeting lasers and running on the rocky walls to get past the gaps. As I reached the limb, I climbed to the underside and grabbed onto the pipes and hydraulics.

I looked down at the giant crater. While the mining laser dug deeper, small gravity beams pulled up large chunks of rock and ore. That was something that still bothered me. What did the miners find? It obviously wasn't the ruins, since the pirates had no interest in it.

I tried to identify what they were extracting, but my databanks did not have an answer. QUEEN didn't know either. I deactivated the glowing in my hair and my jacket as I continued to climb. I entered through a gap at the socket connecting the limb to the platform. Once inside, I spotted more of Iron Claw's men. Most of them were totally cybernetic. I watched some miners operating the machines to process one chunk of rock the gravity beams had brought up. I needed to get control over the platform's systems, then maybe I could help them. Uncovering what they were harvesting was a pressing issue.

I circumnavigated the turret as I made it to the upper balcony. The pirate overseeing the area wasn't looking at me. I stealthily landed behind him and moved to the shadows. I bumped into a storage crate. The pirate noticed. Smooth.

"What was that!?" He snarled.

I slinked around the corner and hugged the wall as I heard him stomping towards the crate. I transformed my arm as he got closer. He stopped a few feet from where I hid, and I watched a green scanning laser sweep the crate. Then he deactivated it and turned away. I moved away without making anymore noise.

Sneaking down the corridor, I heard many voices and a

rhythmical banging like a drum. The closer I got, the clearer it became. These pirates sang a shanty like they were out to sea or space.

I spotted them all in the mess hall with mugs full of a bubbling black ale. While shouting the vulgar song lyrics, they smashed their mugs together, spilling ale on the floor. I did my best to ignore it and focused on a way through them that wouldn't cause me to be captured. I thought about shooting down one crate hanging from above to get the pirates to investigate, but I realized that was a stupid idea as my cannon would give off light. Then I contemplated a maintenance hatch, yet none were in the vicinity, ruling out that possibility.

I figured out a different route, which was stupidly obvious. Staying low, I could get to the table without alerting the pirates. I crawled under the table as the rowdy pirates continued to sing and yell. Every time they shook the table, it made me freeze for a moment. Then one of them bumped into something and spilled their drink, which got in my hair. Lovely. I encountered a problem at the end of the table. The next table was too distant, and the dancing pirates would spot me if I ran for it.

I hunkered down under the table and waited for an opening. They fell silent as a door opened on the far side of the room.

"Captain Iron Claw!" They all shouted after a moment.

I heard a metallic rumble, followed by a loud explosion and a crashing sound close by. From under the table, I only saw Iron Claw's mechanical clawed feet and the bottom of the long jacket he wore.

"Glad to see you scum are wasting time!" He growled in a guttural, mechanical voice. "Get these planet lubbers to work! Our treasure here will not mine itself! And our reinforcements won't be here for another twelve standard hours!"

"Aye-aye captain!" They answered while standing.

"Now get to work, or I'll *rip* you all apart!"

All of them left through the doors on the far side of the room. As someone else entered, I repositioned to get behind a table, and the remaining pirates halted and watched. They carried a miner in each hand by the scruff of their necks.

"Captain! These two were trying to escape!" The pirate answered while tossing his captives onto the ground before Iron Claw.

"Escapees, you say?" He snarled. He turned back to the remaining gathered pirates. "What do we do with escapees around here, lads!?"

They answered with growls and yells. Iron Claw turned back to the prisoners. I saw the serrated hook that made up his right arm. He placed it under the jaw of one miner and lifted his head. The trembling miner's eyes looked in my direction, and our eyes met. I charged my arm cannon and prepared to fire. I had to save them!

"*Meeka!*" QUEEN shouted. "If you attack now, the *entire* facility will go on alert! You can't fight them all directly!"

"But!"

"Look around you! You will get them, and yourself killed!"

I paused and looked around the room. Engaging them head-on would be pointless. QUEEN was right. I had no choice. Lowering my cannon, I powered it down. I knew what was coming next. I saw the hurt in their eyes. They knew I couldn't help them.

It happened so fast. Iron Claw's hook skewered his brain like a twisted, bloody kabob. He then separated his head from his body like pulling a cork from a wine bottle, showering the other with blood. To add insult to injury, he tossed the severed head on the floor and stomped it. It looked like a bloody cracked eggshell when he was done. His horde of pirates cheered like this was some sort of sick concert or live show.

"Unless you want to *die* like your friend, you'll answer my next question! Was anyone else with you!?"

"N-no. It was just us two!"

Iron Claw put his hook under the jaw of the other miner and brought his mechanical face closer to his victim, and reached into his long ripped black jacket.

"*Please!* I'm telling the truth! We planned to steal a ship and leave from the landing pads above us! Please let me go!"

"I believe you."

His curved emerald energy saber ignited, and he plunged it into the panicked miner's chest. The miner's eyes widened in both shock and pain as he dug the blade deeper into them. He ripped it out, and the body crashed onto the floor. Deactivating his sword, he turned to his minions.

"Hang them up for the rest of these *fucking* moles to see!" He commanded. "Shows over. Get your asses out of here!"

He stopped the one that brought the miners. "Not you. One of the scout teams sent to investigate that pidae tal ship never returned. Rally a team, go to their last location and be quick about it! Send another squad after that other ship that crash landed here too. We can't afford distractions until the rest of the fleet arrives!"

"Aye captain!"

I waited until I was certain I was alone and came out of hiding. The pirates had taken the bodies and only left blood and the crushed skull. I wanted to chase after Iron Claw and kill him! I stood up and opened a channel to Choo and Halgar.

"Iron Claw is sending men out into the forest. They might find the ship," I warned.

"I still got the recon drones up," Choo answered.

"I've got my spike gun. I've been itching to shoot more of them bastards!"

"Choo, how goes the repairs?" I asked.

"We're neck deep in them and need more time."

"Okay, stay safe."

I lingered for a moment, contemplating if I could have saved them. Niyarla's words echoed in my mind. You can't save everyone. Reluctantly, I turned away. I needed to focus on the ones I could save.

On the far wall, I found a maintenance hatch. This would bring me closer to a major terminal, according to Halgar. The hatch tunnel was definitely designed for an organism much smaller than me, and I got stuck on some of the machinery and bumped my head into them several times. Eventually, I crawled over a grate and saw some pirates chatting below.

"How much *more* amplicite do we need before we can get out of here!?" One pirate complained. "Sick of dealing with these damn moles!"

Amplicite. My database query yielded no results.

"Halgar, what is amplicite?"

"Huh?"

"Amplicite. That's what the pirates are harvesting."

"Hmmm, the name sounds familiar. I think I overheard a corporate guy mentioning it. Whatever it is, it's really valuable. They bragged about having so many buyers since they announced they had it."

Whatever it was, I knew it was bad. I eavesdropped some more, but the guards' conversation didn't give me anything noteworthy, so I moved on. It didn't take me long to find the terminal Halgar mentioned. I had to cut through the grate and enter the large, empty room to reach it. I tracked down all the miners; freeing them would be difficult, as they were in clusters on multiple levels.

I tried to access the automated defenses, but unfortunately, I couldn't control them from here. I would need to reach the main security station four levels above me in the mushroom cap section of the platform. Doing another query, I learned about amplicite. Those files required security clearance, but QUEEN and I attacked the security key and cracked it in ten minutes. I guess the mining corporation was cutting corners with its cyber security. Then I had all the answers I needed.

Amplicite was an extraordinarily rare mineral that magnified the characteristics of any material it was combined with. The file detailed combining it with a common alloy for starship hulls. The alloy combined with amplicite exhibited increased durability compared to the non amplicite version. I found another file where they tested it with energy rifle components. This vastly improved the rifle's cooling and the amount of energy it could handle, resulting in more potent shots. I could only imagine how much damage an armada of immoral pirates with amplicite-infused weapons and ships would do.

I detected movement, spun towards the doorway with my cannon, and drew the plasma gun. I switched to thermal vision and swept the area. The movement source was so faint I couldn't pinpoint its exact location. Checking the upper level, I saw nothing. I knew my sensors weren't malfunctioning; I increased the sensitivity of my audio sensors and moved away from the terminal.

I watched an emerald blade pierce my abdomen. Before I could react, something tossed me into the wall. I felt the metal panels crumple against me and Sparks erupted from the stab wound. I spotted something coming towards me and raised the arm cannon.

A spike impaled my chest.

Then everything went black, and my systems shut down.

System failure.

6.

System failure detected.
Critical damage to primary nuclear power cell.
Solution?

....

Solution found!
Auxiliary power cell intact.
Initiating backup power.
Rebooting systems

I activated my optical sensors first and looked around. I spotted two pirates. The first wielded an energy sword with a slight curve, the other was empty-handed. He must've been the one that rammed the spear into my chest and damaged my primary power cell. Thankfully, QUEEN endowed me with a backup. Both pirates were completely mechanical, had skeletal bodies, and wore no clothes. Their armor differed from the ones I had seen before. I saw evidence of stealth systems installed but questioned why my thermal sensors couldn't read them. I switched on my auditory sensors.

"We found some girly android in a *weird* getup snooping around," the one without a weapon spoke. "Don't worry, she's scrap."

I reactivated the rest of my systems and did a quick diagnostic check on my arm cannon: it still worked. Transforming my arm, I grabbed the spear in my chest. I fired a full-power blast at the unarmed one and watched as the shot punched a massive hole in the pirate's chest, showering the area with sparks. I aimed at the other one and fired a second shot.

The blast didn't strike him. A barrier made of glowing hexagonal tiles intercepted my shot, but the force of it knocked him back. I tore out the spear and crawled to my feet. As I grabbed the plasma gun, the pirate with the sword rushed me.

He was much faster than the ones I clashed with in the forest. His sword sliced through my already torn-up and burnt shirt. I fired the plasma gun and watched the barrier eat all of it.

"Not gonna work!" He hissed before slashing.

I didn't have time to dodge. I used the plasma gun as a shield and watched the energy blade chop it in half. Crap! That gun was a gift! I dropped the broken gun and readied the spear. I then noticed the one I shot wasn't where he landed.

I spun and felt his fist collide with my face. I get why he didn't carry any other weapons, as a surge of electricity flooded my system. My optics glitched and froze several times. I couldn't see his second hit until I was on my knees. He electrified both his fists and prepared to smash them into my head. I still had my spear.

With calculated precision, I thrust my spear deep into the pirate's power cell. The sword-wielding one moved to attack. I shot him with the cannon, buying myself time to free the spear from the dying pirate. As I shot at the other, I noticed where his barrier came from: the circular pads on his shoulders. I then put both hands on my spear and focused on him.

"You'll pay for that *bitch!*" He snarled.

Even with my reach, he was still lethal and rushed me while dodging my jabs and strikes. One of his slashes almost took off the synthetic bangs covering my forehead. I backflipped out of range and landed in a crouch. He ran me down before I could rise, snatched me by the neck, and lifted me into the air. He made a critical error. I planted my arm cannon into his forearm and fired a high-power shot. I watched the violet blast shred his arm and make him drop his blade, causing him to scream. At this range, the barrier couldn't activate in time.

I aimed at his torso and fired again. His armor seemed more durable than the others. I swung my leg and rammed it into his face, knocking him over and getting him to drop me. I landed on my knees, targeted the nearest shoulder pad, and fired three shots into it, shattering the device. Embers and electricity flooded my vision. He grabbed his sword and raised it. I jabbed with the spear and embedded it in his wrist, stopping him mid-swing. I fired six shots into his chest and sent him flying across the room.

I stood up, inspected the gaping holes in my chest and abdomen, and realized I hadn't activated my communications unit. I reactivated that.

"*Meeka!* Come in Meeka!" Choo-Choo shouted.

"I'm here," I said, while examining the dead pirate.

"QUEEN said you went offline for three minutes! We thought they got you."

"They…almost did. My primary power cell suffered damage. I learned what they're doing here. The amplicite they're gathering amplifies the characteristics of whatever material you mix it with."

I analyzed the pirate's composition. He had amplicite in his body armor, which was incorporated into the coating that blocks heat signatures. I also detected it in their sound absorption materials.

"That's not good," Choo-Choo replied.

"Death Head will augment his pirates and their ships if we don't stop them. Halgar, do you know how to blow this place up?"

"*Blow* it up!?" He exclaimed.

"Can't risk them getting this stuff off-world. We don't have a choice."

"The company is not gonna like this. Hmmm, I guess you could overload the reactor by raising the output and disabling the cooling, and the safeties. That would blow this whole place sky high, but what about the miners?"

"I'll rescue them first."

Sirens blared and warned of an intruder. I turned around, confused who could've done that.

"Oh no! No-no-no no! Stop! Stop! Stop!" I said, feeling a sense of panic.

Who could've tripped the alarm!? Did someone else see or hear me!? I heard a low groan from my right. Then I realized my massive mistake. I didn't check if the other pirate was dead. How could I have been so stupid!?

"You won't make it off this platform alive, little android," he taunted as his body twitched and thrashed.

His systems shut down as he finished his threat. I heard heavy metallic booming footsteps. This was not good! I needed to get to that security station ASAP. With each passing second, my fear grew.

7.

I was running like hell through the narrow corridors. That pirate's threat felt like a statement of fact, as I barely avoided being cut to pieces by a sentry gun emerging from the ceiling. It tore up the corridor around it as it tried to track me. Sharp panel fragments and sparks filled the surrounding air. I considered blasting the energy turret, but that would make my plan harder to pull off than it already was, somehow.

That was not the worst of it. Scouting drones pursued me like enraged hornets. Shooting down many while running didn't stop more from coming to cut me off. Their lasers stung and caused minor damage, but their numbers were many. As I rounded a corner, I spotted a pirate with an enormous gun. I tossed my spear into his chest and ran towards him, firing several shots at him until I could get my spear. Good thing I don't breathe because I didn't have a moment to as the door behind me opened and more pirates flooded the hall.

"Get her!" They shouted.

A stray laser cut into my shoulder and lit my already beyond ruined jacket ablaze. Warnings flashed as several lasers hit me in the back. Luckily, they struck nothing vital. A pirate with a giant cannon appeared as I entered the next hall. The moment he saw me, he opened fire.

I dropped to the floor as the bright white high energy column melted everything behind me. Somehow, it didn't vaporize me.

"*Blasts!* I missed!" He growled while wrestling with the overheating weapon.

"Patches, how in the *blazes* did you *miss!?*" Iron Claw snarled, using the station's speakers.

As smoke billowed from the particle beam cannon, I made a break for it. I encountered more pirates who blocked my way, so I smashed through a wall and a door to evade them.

The particle beam cannon unleashed a relentless wave of destruction through the hallway behind me, melting anything it touched. Despite how fast I ran, the white beam of death drew closer and closer. My damaged leg slowed me down. I couldn't outrun this. I saw a temperature warning that grew brighter and brighter with each passing second. Even brushing against its heat would destroy my body. Not even Choo-Choo could fix me. As it deleted the ends of my jacket, I braced for a quick dismantling. The light faded, and I heard a loud, alarming beep.

"There's something wrong with it!" I heard Patches shout over frustrated banging.

The melted circular wound in the walls allowed me to see him hitting the giant weapon's side.

"Yeah, cuz you overheated it *again*, ya bloody twat!" Iron Claw hissed, his anger reverberating throughout the war-torn corridor.

"There was something in my eye!"

"It's called a scope, fucking use it! Hurry up, the little bitch is getting away!"

I ran for it and called Choo.

"Is the ship ready!?" I asked.

"I'll need at least thirty minutes to get her back in the air!"

"I don't think I have thirty minutes!"

I sprinted to the elevator, desperate to escape, but they had already locked it down. I aimed my cannon at the doors and blasted them open. With no time to waste, I hurled myself into the elevator and savagely used my spear to tear through the ceiling as the pirates caught up. Vaulting through the newly created opening, I landed on the roof before they liquefied me with the particle beam.

"Oh, come on already! Can *one* of you scurvy dogs kill this little runt already!?" Iron Claw snarled through the PA system. "She's heading for the security station. Lock it down lads and bring me her fucking head!"

I heard them piling into what remained of the elevator. Spinning around, I shot the brakes, sending them into the dark shaft. I should've said, "going down?" or maybe, "have a nice trip" would've been a cooler line? Missed opportunity. The climb was uneventful, but my injured shoulder prolonged it. Eventually, I made it to the right floor. I checked the power readings on my arm cannon.

I should've brought an extra energy cell.

I only had enough for three full-power shots and ten low-power ones. I switched to the cutter and sliced open the door. The pirates were waiting for me and greeted me with a barrage of energy weapon fire.

Thankfully, the doors protected me from most of their attacks. Unfortunately, the force dislodged me from the door and sent me plummeting. Panicking, I flailed and grabbed onto a protrusion from the wall. As I dangled there halfway spun around on the wall and looking down the dark elevator shaft, I questioned my career choice.

After a brief climb, I returned to the broken doors. Four heavily armed individuals stood on the other side. Fighting them head-on in my condition would be suicidal. I required an alternative passage. Switching to scanning mode, I spotted something. Swinging around the nearby beam, I kicked in the panel.

I slid into the duct and crawled through. It would place me near the security station, but this duct was used to vent the hot air the mining laser generated. If I were organic, I would be dead right now.

When I came to the exit, I expected an immediate shootout, but no one was in the dirty gray hall. I climbed out and proceeded down the corridor. I looked at my extra crispy and torn-up jacket and grimaced at it.

Continuing down the hall, I stopped halfway through. I had

to smile a bit as I aimed for the ceiling. I fired the cannon and jumped through the hole I had made. I surprised the pirates as I launched myself into the air with my spear in hand.

I skewered a pirate with thunderous force, catching them off guard. The others scrambled for their weapons, but I was faster, unleashing a hail of cannon fire that ripped through them like paper targets. Another charged with a cybernetic claw, but he was too slow. I ducked and sent a fierce punch into his stomach that caused him to double over, coughing up his lunch.

Unfortunately, he vomited on me. Gross. When he fell to his knees, I kicked him in the face to knock him out. The remaining two lunged with energy blades. I took them down with low-powered shots and ran to the station. I had little time. The ones behind the door attempted to enter but had to slice through blast doors first.

"*Unbelievable*! You are all a bunch of rank amateurs!" Iron Claw seethed.

I took control of the defenses and targeted the pirates. I also unlocked the doors for the hangars and told the miners to make it to the hangars using the PA system. I saw how many pirates were on the station. No one protected the miners; they focused on me. Good. I shut off the exterior defenses and gave QUEEN control.

"Good job Meeka!" QUEEN exclaimed as a hologram of her face appeared on the console. "Go. I'll escort the miners to safety."

I nodded and dived through the glass. I didn't stick the landing and crashed headfirst into a weapons rack, causing a loud cacophony of metal slamming against metal. As I rose, I felt QUEEN judging me. I'm sure clumsiness is not what she was hoping for when designing my line of combat androids. My foot bumped into something heavy. I looked down and saw a pidae tal spike rifle with a large cylindrical magazine lying there. It would help me conserve the cannon's energy for now. Upon hearing them break into the security room, I grabbed that and a belt of grenades.

QUEEN fried the console and had already embedded code into the system; she had control over all their defenses. I shot at the pirates and winged one of them in the shoulder before QUEEN unlocked the door.

I needed to keep their attention while heading for the reactor core. As they tried to box me in, I chucked a grenade down one corridor. The grenade didn't just explode. It was a gravitational implosion. I watched the glowing white light pull everything around it toward its epicenter. Gravity grew stronger until all vanished with a blinding flash. Reinforcements quickly followed. I retreated and vaulted over the railing, and landed several floors down.

I struck several pirates with the superheated stakes from my rifle and kept moving.

"I am going to *enjoy* ripping off your pretty little head!" Iron Claw threatened over the speakers.

In my condition, I wasn't keen on facing him. As I tried to distract the pirates, QUEEN told me about a group of pinned-down miners in one of the processing areas near the reactor. I mapped out the shortest route, which involved plowing through several walls. I engaged the pirates and handled them with another gravity imploder before landing in front of the miners.

"Are you part of the rescue team?" One of them, with white fur and red eyes, asked.

"I am the rescue team." I realized they weren't armed, and the nearest hangar was two levels up. "Come on, I'll get you to the hangar."

The white-furred one pointed at the spike rifle. "I'll be taking that."

I paused and turned to him. "Do you know how to use it?"

He lunged for me, snatching the gun from my grip before I knew what was happening. I hastily spun around to find him pointing it at two pirates, and with a single, deadly swift movement, he fired two shots into their chests, killing both of them.

Yeah, he knew how to use it.

I handed him the extra magazine, no questions asked. I activated my arm cannon and followed him down the hall, monitoring the other five miners. Except for some pirates that the white pidae tal dealt with, the path to the hangar was uneventful. Several of the miners thanked me for helping them. The white one lingered behind.

"You aren't coming with us?"

I shook my head. "I have to overload the reactor."

His red eyes widened. "You're going to *what!?*"

"Got to stop them from getting the amplicite off-world!"

"Well, good luck with that. Thank you for freeing us."

I smiled. "It's what I do."

I ran in the opposite direction, hoping the other miners would escape.

"Three of the six shuttles have escaped the platform and are heading into space," QUEEN told me as I reached the open doors and entered the reactor. "Once you overload it, you will have ten minutes before it meltdowns and explodes."

"Will everyone else be out of the blast radius?"

"Yes...oh dear."

"What?" I asked.

"Iron Claw, he's at the reactor. He's waiting for you!"

8.

I readied my spear as the reactor doors opened in stages. The first opened diagonally, then the others opened normally. I faced a long, dark corridor with flashing purple lights at the far side. I saw nothing in the passage, even when switching vision modes. Moving down the hall, I entered the reactor chamber.

I saw him.

His black cloak and hat hid his skeletal, spiky mechanical body. His glowing emerald eyes lit up at the sight of me.

"So, you're the one interfering with my plans." He boomed.

"Your reign of terror is over, Iron Claw!"

He laughed. "You come straight out of a Saturday morning cartoon!"

Then he ignited his curved energy sword in his left hand and raised his right arm, which ended in a vicious serrated hook.

"Shame I have to kill you, waste of a pretty face."

"I'm not into psychopaths."

He closed the distance between us in a flash, his blade glinting maliciously. I thrust my spear into his way, just avoiding an instant death. With the flickering energy of our weapons, I saw his beard of thorny metal chains.

He swung again, almost knocking me down. I hopped out of range of his next slash as it carved a scar into the reflective panels making up the ground. With a hiss, he charged again and sliced the bulky computer terminals surrounding me. I had no time to react. All I could do was stab with my spear to fend him off. He skilfully caught my weapon with his hook arm and tossed it aside.

"How disappointing!"

I dropped my spear and pulled back. His blade sliced part of my jacket as I narrowly avoided the strike. I activated my arm cannon and fired. He ducked at the last second and again advanced. My shot disintegrated his hat and exposed his head full of razor-sharp metallic dreads.

His slash cut into my already injured stomach, and I saw a warning about the damage. I failed to dodge his hook. He embedded it into the wound in my stomach and lifted me up. I buried both feet into his face, getting him to release me.

The moment my feet touched down, I raised the cannon and fired. With a deafening crack, I threw Iron Claw back as a shower of sparks gushed from his shoulder. I readied another shot. His hook transformed. A green flash erupted from his arm while I fired my cannon. I watched my left arm swell as the remaining energy in the cannon overloaded and detonated. The explosion blasted me off my feet and sent me hurtling through the air towards the central console while my shot sent Iron Claw through a wall.

System errors flashed, and I looked at my left arm.

Where my left arm used to be.

Everything below the shoulder was gone, leaving scorched and sparking cables where my forearm should've been. Geysers of pressurized fluids exploded from the wound as I forced myself to rise. I scanned for Iron Claw, but he was gone. I checked where he crashed. My attack sent him through a wall and plummeting into a maintenance shaft. He wouldn't linger there, and I could scarcely repel him with two arms, let alone one. I accessed the terminal, deactivated the safeties, and pushed the reactor beyond its limits. A warning blared, stating I had twenty minutes before a complete meltdown. I then damaged the terminal and all the manual controls, so no one could stop it.

"Choo! The reactor's going to blow! Meet me at landing pad twelve!" I heard shooting from the other end. "*Choo!*?" I shouted while running down the corridor.

As I ran, I did what I could to mitigate the damage from Iron

Claw's cannon. I was losing vital fluids to help regulate cooling and power certain systems. I closed the internal valves I could and began the painful process of climbing a nearby ladder with only one arm.

...

As I approached the hangar, the lack of pirates surprised me. They must've all fled when they heard about the impending meltdown. Checking the timer in the corner of my vision, I had ten minutes left. I received a temperature warning, and my body froze for a moment. I couldn't adequately vent heat from my core systems and would need external cooling soon or risk more damage.

I forced myself up the steps; I couldn't think about this now. When I reached the circular central platform, I saw the other landing pads branching off it at the top of the mushroom cap. Some pidae tal still strived to escape.

"Choo!? Where are you!?" I asked as more warnings flashed in my vision.

I heard a painful grunt through the communicator. "The pirates! They've found us! We can't take off yet!" Her voice sounded strange, and her breaths felt labored.

"Choo!? Are you okay?"

"No, I'm hit. But I'll live. We'll be there."

Her voice told me she was trying to convince herself more than me.

"Don't be reckless."

I heard a light chuckle and more gunfire before the call ended. I hoped they would make it as I focused on the escaping pidae tal. While most were already on the last box-shaped shuttle, two stragglers limped towards the vessel. I saw bruises across their bodies, clearly inflicted by Iron Claw's men.

The station rocked, and explosions soon followed. A wave of them ripped apart the platform, knocking the two miners to the ground and creating a hole beneath them. They screamed in terror and clawed desperately at the floor as the hole widened. They would not make it. I ran as fast as I could. As they slipped into nothingness, I leaped over the edge with my arm outstretched. My fingers just managed to grasp one of them. The second one had no chance. I panicked: without my left arm, I couldn't save him. But then he miraculously caught onto the dangling foot of his friend, saving himself from certain death.

"Hold on!" I exclaimed while pulling them up and away from the collapsing section.

The two pidae tal took full breaths and tottered to their feet. One of them pointed at me.

No, he wasn't.

I felt Iron Claw's hook cut my face as I turned. I rolled across the crumbling platform, stopping against the guardrail.

Iron Claw lumbered forward, his voice slurring menacingly as he raised his blade. One side of his lower jaw had dropped off. His hook arm transformed into a massive cannon resembling a flintlock pistol.

"Time to send you to the bloody scrapheap!" He shouted, training the weapon on me.

Before I could react, something slammed into his shoulder and rattled his aim. The shot soared to my left. I ran towards him and ignited my spear. Another projectile from a pidae tal spike gun collided with his chest and knocked him back. I thrust the spear forward with all my might, aiming for his vitals. But he was too quick and swatted it away, sending me flying backward through the air until I crashed against the unforgiving ground.

I rose and tried to slash. Iron Claw's foot collided with my face and knocked me off my feet. While I skidded across the ground, he turned his ire onto the escape shuttle. The glob of bright green collided with the ship, and the explosion of blue fire rocked the entire platform. I hurled myself to the ground as huge chunks of debris filled the air like a hailstorm, engulfing the rooftop in a furious storm of destruction. Shards of shrapnel ripped through metal and resin like tiny missiles.

They had no chance of surviving that.

I tightened my grip on my spear and rushed Iron Claw while he dodged some debris. He spotted me at the last second and raised the gun to protect himself. I rammed my spear into his arm, causing the cannon to misfire. I tore my weapon free, ripping out chunks of his mechanical arm with it.

Iron Claw rolled to his feet and snarled. "I'll *rip* out your optics!"

"You're going to *pay* for all the people you've killed!"

To my surprise, his arm returned to hook mode. Again, he charged me with relentless fury. Even with the spear, my reach meant nothing, and he easily swatted it away and continued to hammer me with slashes. With each passing second, I felt the pressure mounting, knowing I could not withstand his attacks for much longer. The few hits I landed with my spear only did surface-level damage and didn't slow him down. Panic set in as I knew I faced certain defeat.

The reactor's imminent explosion drew closer, and the *MSLF-Stratis* was nowhere in sight. I feared the worst for Choo and Halgar. As we fought, another chain of explosions went off somewhere nearby, making the entire platform shake and knocking us both off balance.

My body was failing me. I could feel the wear and tear of the battle on my cooling systems, making every movement slower. But I still fought on. He came at me with his sword, and while I blocked his strike, I jumped back to create some space between us.

"Run out of steam!?" He shouted while rushing in to stab me.

I smacked the sword away and lunged. I aimed for Iron Claw's stomach. He twisted at the last second, and the energy blade only sliced his side. He crashed into me and put his blade against my neck, scalding the exterior plating. I stopped the blade from cutting me further by catching his arm and pushing back slightly.

"How much did the company pay you to save these stupid moles!?" He pushed the blade closer to my neck.

"No one paid me! I came to stop you myself." I hissed while

trying to get the blade away from my throat.

Iron Claw forcefully inserted the hook where my ribcage would be and then ripped it out. He was dangerously close to my secondary power cell. He tore out pieces of my coolant systems. Alerts and warnings inundated my vision, demanding I rectify the issues before it was too late. I wasn't sure if I could stay operational for much longer as damage from overheating was unavoidable.

"You're either brave or stupid!" He growled as he pushed the blade closer to my neck.

A searing bolt of electric blue light struck his face, incinerating it. His body flew backward like a spiraling rag doll as the blast hurled him away from me, leaving an ever-growing fog of dust and smoke in its wake. I looked up to see the *MSLF-Stratis* looming behind me. QUEEN's face projected from the prow.

"Keep your hands *off* my daughter!" QUEEN growled.

The ship turned, showing its side and opening the landing ramp. I tried to stand, but I felt my systems shutting down. Then I felt two hands grip me; I looked up to see Choo-Choo as one of them and Halgar as the other.

"Come on, you dork!" Halgar shouted while they pulled me on board.

I looked back at Iron Claw. Smoke wafted off him as he clumsily crawled to his feet. The plasma blast devoured half his face. He shambled forward, knocking his eye out of its socket. Sparks flashed off the loose and damaged wiring. He looked at me with his still intact eye.

"This ain't over!" He proclaimed before diving off the exploding platform.

My systems entered the emergency shutdown as I felt the ship pulling away from the station.

9.

My systems came back online, and my optics reactivated. I lay inside the pod on my ship. I looked up at the ceiling, and the device's sides were open. Someone had opened my chest cavity and connected long tubes to my damaged body sections. Switching on my auditory sensors, I realized music was playing, a sappy pop song sung in Nimetran. I also heard the sounds of machinery, the hiss of a plasma welder, and someone humming along with the song.

"Ah, good you've rebooted," QUEEN said, appearing as a hologram on the circular table beside me. "I was worried Choo wouldn't be able to fix you with what we have on board."

"You *doubted* me?" Choo said, spinning around. A welding mask covered her head, and she carried a compact plasma torch.

I checked my system clock. One-hundred and sixty-eight hours had passed since I had gone offline.

"How bad is it?" I asked, knowing I could've just run a system check.

The mask fragmented and retracted into a housing at the base of her neck. Choo smiled at me and wiped the sweat off her brow. "They fried your nuclear power cell."

I ran a quick check and did not detect it. "You removed it!?"

Choo smiled apprehensively. "Yeah, the damage to your cooling system was causing it to become unstable. It was either that or a nuclear explosion. So I removed it."

As she spoke, I noticed she wasn't wearing any protective gear. "Wait! Did you remove my fuel cell without wearing protection!?"

Choo howled with laughter. "*Hell* no! We moved you to the hangar. I was using a remote control drone to get it out. Then we jettisoned it into space before it went off. The explosion was prettier than any fireworks show I've ever seen."

"Oh," I said, relaxing somewhat.

"I'm just glad your auxiliary power cell is still good. QUEEN gave me blueprints to make a new cell, but I don't have the radioactive isotope. I got a feeling that won't come cheap."

"No, unfortunately, it is not. It is quite rare outside of our home system," QUEEN replied.

Choo removed the rest of her welding suit, and I saw the dried blood on her shirt and pants.

"Choo!? What happened to you!?"

She looked down and then at me. "One pirate tossed a grenade. Some shrapnel hit me. Cut me pretty bad." She sat down in the chair near her workstation and grunted.

"What happened?"

"Seven pirates attacked us. Even with the drones, we barely saw them coming. Halgar and I took cover behind crates and fought back, but then more approached from the opposite direction. I got hit by that grenade and thought I was a goner. Then Halgar dragged me inside and told me to fix the bloody ship," she laughed. "Crazy little bastard, he held them off while I got this baby back online. We barely made it in time to save you."

The way she talked about him, it sounded like they had somehow become friends in the time I was away.

"Are you sure you're okay?"

Choo smiled. "Yeah, I'll live. Don't worry. They've already treated me."

"What about my radiator and cooling systems?"

"That I've almost fixed." She then stepped to her side and showed me the black and gray arm on the table. "As for your arm, you're lucky I made an extra one in my spare time."

I smiled. "Wouldn't be the first time you've lent me a hand."

Choo chuckled and rolled her eyes. "That was terrible."

"You laughed."

She shook her head. "Hold still."

I watched her align the new arm with the cleaned-up socket and snap it into place. She then connected a device to the circular ports on the shoulder. She made sure the artificial nervous system of the arm connected to the rest of me. A menu told me the nerves were attempting to integrate and install the required drivers. It finished the installation a few seconds later.

"Try touching all your fingers to your thumb." She said. I complied, and it worked. "I couldn't recreate your arm cannon due to lack of time and materials, but this one should do."

I nodded and sat up. "What happened while I was deactivated?"

"Well, you saved most of the miners. We escorted them out of the minefield and to the nearest pidae tal mining station. We're actually there now. They're helping patch up the ship as thanks for saving their employees. They also gave us some cash."

"Really?"

"Yeah. They were...really generous about that. They even got me some alloys and parts needed to fix you, but they weren't happy with the mining platform blowing up."

Choo then checked my radiator again and gave me a thumbs-up before disconnecting the coolant cables. I closed up my torso, grabbed a T-shirt and put it on, hiding most of Choo's handiwork on my chest and stomach. In the mirror, I saw Choo's fixes to my damaged face.

"What about Iron Claw?"

Choo shook her head. "He escaped before the mining platform went off. They probably took a lot of amplicite with them."

I could only imagine what a dastardly fiend like Death Head would do with the amplicite. I knew it wouldn't be good for anyone. At least I cut off their supply for now. I reviewed the files of my battle with Iron Claw. By my calculations, even if I fought him at one hundred percent capacity, my odds of succeeding were less than twenty percent. If not for Niyarla and QUEEN's interference, I would've died. I needed to get stronger if I were to stop people like him. I finished mulling over the details when a knock sounded, and Choo called for the person to enter. It surprised me to see the red pidae tal in a dull brown body suit. He had bandages on his face, arms, and a small hole in his left ear.

"Halgar!?" I said.

His eyes widened a bit. "Wow, Choo, you fixed her up."

"It's not perfect, but it'll have to do for now," Choo answered while standing and pointing to QUEEN's hologram, "I had help."

Halgar nodded. "We're almost done fixing your ship, and we refueled you free of charge."

"Thanks." I said.

"Least I can do. Without you, we wouldn't have made it off that rock."

"Oh, it was nothing," I said, adjusting my messy hair.

Halgar laughed. "No, that was definitely something. In the EdgeWorlds, people don't save others without payment first."

I smiled, recalling a line from a movie I liked. "Saving people is what I do."

"Yeah, you're back to normal, sitting here quoting Maximum Valiant."

"She is a dork," Choo laughed.

"I am *not*!" I insisted.

"You do certainly fit the description of one," QUEEN muttered.

"No, I don't!"

All three of them laughed at me. I pouted and crossed my arms and glared at them. After their laughter stopped, Halgar told me the company execs wanted to speak to me. I followed him out and into the airlock. With a mechanical hiss, the doors opened, leading to a small cubic hallway with low ceilings and almost no lighting.

"Sorry, these stations don't deal with other species often. Watch your head."

That was an understatement. The ceiling was so low I needed to crouch to follow, and even then I could barely clear it. I dinged my head on the ceiling more times than I care to admit as I followed the small red mole.

"Welcome to Kauric Station, the second largest station in the Talvran Mining Company," Halgar spoke.

I noticed the panels on the walls went from drab grays and browns to vibrant colors and symbols advertising products and brands whenever we got near them. The most prevalent was an energy drink marketed towards the miners made by the Talvran Mining Company.

"So you and Choo made nice?"

He laughed. "Yeah. Don't tell her I told you this, but she kinda reminds me of my wife."

"Wait, you have a *wife*?!" I asked, finding that fact surprising.

"You got something to say, robo dork?"

"N-no, and I'm not a dork."

Halgar shook his head. "Whatever you say."

"Your wife is like Choo?"

"Kinda. She was an engineering student moonlighting as a bartender when I met her. Got too rowdy at the bar one night and she punched me in the face. Went back the next night and apologized, she laughed about the whole thing and gave me a drink on the house, been together ever since."

QUEEN was right, organics are strange.

"Did she make that rifle you had?" I asked recalling the name written on the side: Minaru.

Halgar smiled, his face beaming with pride. "She sure did. Runs better than any spike gun I've ever seen."

As we continued through the corridors, I spotted the crew's rooms. They were small, darkened rooms designed for functionality over aesthetics. That changed as we reached an elevator and ascended to the highest level. These corridors did not bombard us with ads as we traveled through. The boxy shapes making up the hall were also more refined as well and had fewer sharp edges. As I peered into the rooms, they were far more ornate and less minimalistic, with fancy, intricate art on the walls. I saw a large metal gate with a complex symbol on it at the end of the hall. Two pidae tal were guarding the gate. Both carried large spike guns that looked like they could shred me in seconds if necessary.

"Director Volnar is beyond this door. He wanted to thank you. I'll be outside," Halgar grinned. "Don't be too much of a dork around him."

I scowled at him. "I'll try not to be."

The room I entered contrasted with the rest of the station. The far side had a big tinted window and was more oval in shape. I could hardly see the barren world beyond. An enormous desk with intricate silver and blue metal reliefs adorned it. A large machine sitting on the side of it dispensed a hot, solid black liquid with a powerful aroma. Various screens also littered the desk, and through the reflections from the window, I saw they were all stocks and expense reports. Another room lay to the left of the large window with its doors shut.

Standing by the desk was a female pidae tal wearing a more complicated, colorful body suit. She wasn't adapted to other worlds yet, as she wore thick shades obscuring most of her face. She touched her ear and said something and then smiled at me.

"Director Volnar will be right with you."

She wasn't kidding. A larger pidae tal with a pronounced gut emerged from the left door. He wore an even more regal body suit with large red pads on the shoulders and bright red accents. Instead of walking, he lounged in a giant oval-shaped floating chair with thick cushioning enveloping him.

"Greetings," he said, while adjusting his shades. "I'm told we have you to thank for rescuing our people."

I nodded. "I detected a distress signal on the planet, and I moved in to help."

He positioned his chair, so it floated behind the desk, then used a tractor beam built into the chair to pull the mug to him.

"We were actually letting one of our military contracts handle it, but thanks to you, we saved some money there. We will need it. That mining platform was a major investment, and this entire operation was a gold mine for us. Why did you have to blow it up?"

"They were sending your amplicite to Death Head's armada. He will use it to amplify his ships. I couldn't risk them sending more of it to him and his men, and I couldn't take the entire platform alone."

Volnar sipped his drink and then sat it on the coaster. "Our stock prices took a dive after the news broke. Your little stunt did more damage than the initial takeover."

I shook my head and remembered a line from a show with a similar argument. "You can recover stocks, but not lives."

"We can also replace workers. However, some people you rescued are valuable to us, and replacing them would be a nightmarish ordeal. So you have my thanks for saving most of them. I hate recruiting specialists."

I couldn't tell if he was complimenting me or complaining half the time. "Uh...thanks?"

"You have a few screws loose to do that by yourself and with no promise of payment," he laughed.

"Money is not a big motivator for me."

He shrugged. "I suppose that's true. You are an android, after all. Would save on the food budget. Anyway, we have finished fixing your fancy ship and we are almost done refueling your subspace drive," he said. "We also transferred you some of the money we would've spent on that contract."

"Meeka, might I suggest you ask if they can get the isotope for your power cell or if they know where we might find it," QUEEN suggested in my ear.

I asked Director Volnar about it, but he scratched his head. "Hmm, I don't think we have any holdings of that stuff. GigaMart doesn't stock such a rare isotope, but Koyoran Industries might be able to assist? They specialize in reactors and radioactive materials. If they have it, it will not be cheap."

I winced at that thought. "I'll have to check. Thank you for fixing our ship and helping with my repairs."

"Don't sweat it. It's the least we can do. If you ever need a security contract, contact us. We're always hiring."

That was a consideration, especially if the isotope would be a nightmare to get.

"You should upgrade your cyber security when you have a sec. I hacked your platform's security with ease."

Director Volnar paused. "Huh, we'll have to upgrade that too."

"Also, Halgar deserves a raise. He helped get me inside and saved my mechanic's life."

He nodded. "I'll make sure he gets a nice bonus and a free upgrade to his benefits."

I thanked him again and returned to my ship. Sitting in the pilot's seat, I surveyed the spherical readout of the system and nearby ones, contemplating where to go.

"So...what's next?" Choo asked, leaning over the side of the chair.

"Hmm, I guess we'll have to find the isotope." I then looked at QUEEN as she appeared beside the controls as a hologram. "Anyone else needing help nearby?"

"A colony ship five systems away is reporting a stage three molzek infestation and is requesting help from the nearby worlds."

"A molzek infestation!? Those are nasty," Choo said while grimacing. "We had a small outbreak in our hydroponics deck. They killed a dozen people and did thousands in damages before pest control wiped them out."

I grimaced at that. "Is there anything else?"

QUEEN displayed a thousand other calls for help in this sector alone. Then I saw something else that caught my attention. There was a firefight in Maegar city, but we were too far to respond quickly.

"The EdgeWorlds are always busy," Choo complained, crossing her arms.

I filtered everything by proximity to us. It was the molzek infestation. "A hero's work is never done," I said while punching in the coordinates.

THE STORY TIMELINE

The stories arranged in their chronological order.

- THE CALLISTO INCIDENT
- MUTANT AUDIT | MINER RESCUE ON VERDI IX
- DR. BG'S SATURDAY NIGHT FEVER

ABOUT

This is the first volume in a planned series of short stories involving Edgy and others in the EdgeWorlds. I hope you enjoyed it and come back when the next volume releases. For updates, recent stories, and more, you can follow my social media below and my website:

Minds: www.minds.com/the_edgy_penguin/

Twitter: twitter.com/JeffPenguin1

Website: https://shawnfrostauthor.com/

Thank you for reading. You can also check out my novel RENEGADES VOLUME 1. RISE also on Amazon and keep an eye out for its upcoming sequel, RENEGADES VOLUME 2. BLACKOUT:

COPYRIGHT

BOOKS BY THIS AUTHOR

Renegades Volume 1: Rise

Giant robots, cyborg ninjas, super villains, deadly terrorists, and evil mega corporations, the Renegades will face it all to save their world in their debut novel, RENEGADES VOLUME 1: RISE

Sixty years ago, humanity fled their dying home planet and accidentally arrived on a parallel Earth inhabited by bipedal intelligent humanoid animals called terrans. At first, the two sides coexisted, but as resentment grew, war broke out. This war went on for ten years, and afterward, they achieved a stable peace.

Now, a dangerous terrorist organization called Scythe, led by a ruthless mad man, threatens the balance of the world and seeks to eradicate all terrans. The only thing standing in his way is a misfit band of unlikely heroes called the Renegades. A teenage girl trained from birth to be a soldier, a teenage delinquent, a mysterious blue creature with unimaginable powers, two kid super-geniuses, and an ex-pro boxer with cybernetic arms unite to stop him. Going up against impossible odds and facing untold dangers, these unlikely heroes must work together if they are to stop Scythe and their leader's sinister plot.

Renegades Volume 2: Blackout

The Renegades Return

Following a lead on their sworn enemy, Ivan and his organization, the Renegades head to Japan. There they find themselves in the crosshairs of a dangerous gang of mercenaries and uncover a massive, sinister conspiracy with connections to members of their own team.

With the fate of an entire island hanging in the balance and enemies everywhere the Renegades are pushed to their limits in the electrifying sequel to RENEGADES VOLUME 1: RISE.

Includes 2 bonus short stories, OPERATION SHROUD, and AKANE'S HUNT!

Made in United States
Troutdale, OR
11/02/2024

24348105R00163